Grub Street Abroad

Grub Street Abroad

*Aspects of the French
Cosmopolitan Press from
the Age of Louis XIV
to the French Revolution*

LYELL LECTURES, 1989-1990

ELIZABETH L. EISENSTEIN

CLARENDON PRESS · OXFORD

1992

Oxford University Press, Walton Street, Oxford OX2 6DP
Oxford New York Toronto
Delhi Bombay Calcutta Madras Karachi
Petaling Jaya Singapore Hong Kong Tokyo
Nairobi Dar es Salaam Cape Town
Melbourne Auckland
and associated companies in
Berlin Ibadan

Oxford is a trade mark of Oxford University Press

Published in the United States
by Oxford University Press, New York

British Library Cataloguing in Publication Data
Data available

Library of Congress Cataloging in Publication Data
Eisenstein, Elizabeth L.
Grub Street abroad : aspects of the French cosmopolitan press from
the age of Louis XIV to the French Revolution / Elizabeth L. Eisenstein.
— (Lyell lectures; 1989-1990)
Includes index.
1. French periodicals—Publishing—Foreign countries—
History—18th century. 2. French imprints—Publishing—Foreign
countries—History—18th century. 3. Book industries and trade—
France—History—18th century. 4. Books and reading—France—
History—18th century. 5. Journalism—France—History—18th
century. 6. France—Intellectual life—18th century. I. Title.
II. Series.
Z305.E38 1992 381'.45002'0944—dc20 92-5669
ISBN 0-19-812259-4

Typeset by Downdell Ltd, Oxford
Printed and bound in
Great Britain by Bookcraft Ltd
Midsomer Norton, Bath

Acknowledgements

I owe thanks to David Vaisey, Bodley's Librarian, and to the other electors of the James P. R. Lyell Readership in Bibliography for inviting me to give the lectures which form the basis of this book. I am also grateful to Julian Roberts, Deputy Librarian and Keeper of Printed Books at the Bodleian, who helped arrange for my spending Trinity Term, 1990, as a Visiting Fellow at Wolfson College. Giles Barber of the Taylor Institution supplied invaluable data in his several publications and, as the author of 'Pendred Abroad: A View of the Late Eighteenth-Century Book Trade in Europe', in *Studies in the Book Trade in Honour of Graham Pollard* (Oxf. Bibliogr. Soc. Publications, 18; Oxford, 1975), inadvertently inspired my choice of title. Finally, I am indebted to Jack R. Censer for his useful critique of my first draft.

Contents

List of Illustrations

(*between pp. 88–89*)

I acknowledge gratefully permission to reproduce photographs from the University Library of Leiden for Figs. 1 and 14 (both procured with the help of Christiane Berkvens-Stevelinck); the Library of Congress for Figs. 2, 3, 5, 6, 12, and 13; Houghton Library (Harvard University) for Fig. 4; the Warburg Institute, London, for Figs. 8 and 9; the Folger Shakespeare Library, Washington, DC, for Fig. 10; the History of Art Library, Oxford University, for Fig. 11. Fig. 7 is reproduced from A. Barnes, *Jean Le Clerc et la République des Lettres* (Paris: Droz, 1938).

1
Perspectives on Extraterritorial Publishing

THE eighteenth-century French-language press has already given rise to a large literature. For the most part this literature has focused on developments within France. Francophone enclaves which existed beyond the fringes of the great realm, have, quite understandably, been assigned a subordinate marginal position. What follows entails a shift of focus; the periphery will be placed at the centre of the stage. By adopting this strategy, I hope to draw attention to the importance of certain institutions which had flourished for hundreds of years outside French frontiers. During the three centuries when written communications hinged on the operations of the wooden hand press, the most energetic centres of the cosmopolitan book trade were to be found outside the borders of well-consolidated dynastic states. The eighteenth-century francophone press was unexceptional in this regard. Indeed foreign firms contributed rather more than did domestic ones to sustaining the literary culture of the French Enlightenment. Although French had replaced Latin as the chief literary language of the cosmopolitan Republic of Letters, the firms which had at one time served Erasmus still had much in common with those which served Voltaire.

The importance of peripheral location for publishers aiming at far-flung markets was first made clear to me some years ago, when I was working on *The Printing Press as an Agent of Change*. Portions of that book touched on the expansion of a cosmopolitan Republic of Letters, under the aegis of certain master printers and merchant publishers who prospered despite obstacles imposed by religious and dynastic warfare.[1] In addition to collaborating with powerful state officials and church authorities, these men also functioned as independent entrepreneurs. Operating outside the borders of large well-consolidated realms, protected

[1] Elizabeth L. Eisenstein, *The Printing Press as an Agent of Change* (2 vols. Cambridge, 1979), i. 443–8.

by local rulers of small quasi-independent principalities and city states; they acted, in turn, as protectors and patrons of men of letters and learning. The duplication of scholarly texts brought foreign translators, editors, and proof-readers into their shops. They profited from sales of books listed on the Index, contributed to the publishing ventures of dissidents and free thinkers and, in some instances, joined heterodox sects themselves. In sum, they supplied organs of publicity and covert support to a European 'third force' which was unaffiliated with any one major church or dynastic state.

For specific illustration, I singled out certain printing firms, such as that of Vesalius's publisher, Oporinus in mid-sixteenth-century Basel. This firm provided protection for Sebastian Castellio when he was sought for extradition by Calvin in Geneva. It housed almost all the leading lights of the so-called 'Radical Reformation' and provided a sanctuary for Marian exiles. I also paused over the multifarious activities of Christopher Plantin of Antwerp, who served both Philip of Spain and William I of Orange while adhering to a heterodox sect. Elsewhere there was mention of seventeenth-century Dutch firms, such as that of the Elseviers, who rendered services to Galileo and other virtuosi. But my treatment stopped short of that interval in the 1680s which saw the exodus of Huguenots from France, the replacement of Latin by French as the lingua franca of the Republic of Letters, and the inauguration of a periodical press aimed at a cosmopolitan French reading public.

It is this stopping point which forms the point of departure for this book. By extending coverage to encompass the interval between the 1680s and the 1780s, I have several purposes in mind. First of all I hope to bring out, more clearly than is done in most accounts, how eighteenth-century developments were related to earlier trends. There is one suggestive heading in *L'Apparition du livre*: 'From the Renaissance printer to the philosophe-publisher'[2] which hints at a relationship. But in the three decades which have elapsed since the pioneering work of Febvre and Martin first appeared, divisions between Renaissance studies and eighteenth-century ones have persisted; many of the continuities which characterized European book history in the age of the hand press remain to be disclosed.

[2] Lucien Febvre and Henri-Jean Martin, *L'Apparition du livre* (Paris, 1958), 217.

More emphasis is needed, in my view, on the continuous existence of a decentralized and cosmopolitan communications network which served Huguenot refugees and Enlightenment philosophes alike. Firms extending far-flung trade routes from small principalities and free cities did more than merely survive down to the French Revolution; they provided essential support for influential enclaves of French expatriates and for many Parisian writers as well. It has long been acknowledged that the works of the most celebrated eighteenth-century French authors were 'read throughout Europe in editions printed outside France'.[3] But the implications of this well-known phenomenon are seldom spelt out. Whatever sort of social context is supplied for French intellectual life, it is almost always framed by the boundaries of the Bourbon realm. When contextualizing the French Enlightenment, however, conditions in Versailles and Paris need to be supplemented by the situation in Cosmopolis where some French men of letters felt more at home.

I am going to use the term 'Cosmopolis', one of several false place-names employed by early printers,[4] to designate the indeterminate, decentralized zone occupied by the dispersed citizens of the francophone Republic of Letters. The dispersal of French readers and writers throughout eighteenth-century Europe has been described in several studies.[5] All play variations on the theme of cultural imperialism, however. Influences are seen to emanate from the twin centres of Versailles and Paris and then to radiate outward beyond the borders of France. Here I will consider the extraterritorial firms, and the enclaves formed around them, not as a means of diffusing messages emanating from within France, but rather as comprising an independent field of operations; an independent field which posed a persistent challenge to the claims of cultural hegemony made by the French crown.[6] Cosmopolis thus stands for a relatively autonomous

---

[3] Ibid. 298.

[4] See e.g. Pierre Frédéric Arpe, *Apologia pro Julio Caesare Vanino Neapolitano* (Cosmopolis: Typus Philaletheis, 1712).

[5] The standard work is still Louis Réau, *L'Europe française au siècle des lumières* (Paris, 1938). See also refs. in Ch. 2 below.

[6] There is one 19th-cent. study of French literature which adopts this viewpoint without, however, dealing with the role of extraterritorial firms: Pierre André Sayous, *Le Dix-Huitième Siècle à l'étranger* (Paris, 1861).

discursive community with its own distinctive values and traditions.[7]

At one point, in his discussion of the popularization of Newtonian science, Herbert Butterfield reflects on 'the curious fact' that France gained the intellectual leadership of Europe through the prestige of an imposing group of writers associated with the court at Versailles and then used this leadership to disseminate a different type of culture altogether.[8] But the different type of culture was disseminated less by writers gathered around Versailles than by scattered enclaves of French expatriates who worked for firms abroad. During the age of Louis XIV, the extraterritorial French press conveyed to Parisians 'a vision of Europe and a conception of the main issues of the day which were often at odds with those of the absolutist monarchy'.[9] As Butterfield himself puts it, there was a transnational 'humming activity', entailing the 'publication in Holland, of journals written in French, communicating English ideas'.[10]

After the 1680s, it seems fair to say that the intellectual leadership of Europe was being exerted not so much by France as by French-language publications that were, more than once, prohibited from entering the Bourbon realm. To understand how the views of Newton and Locke became central to European thought we need to abandon the habit of thinking only about national boundaries and central cities and acknowledge the coexistence of a more indeterminate cosmopolitan zone. Lionel Gossman recently remarked that Pierre Bayle assumed a central position in European intellectual life although he was a marginal figure in every sense of that word. The paradoxical centrality of the marginal, Gossman went on to observe, seems to be characteristic of the 'culture of modernity'.[11] The existence of energetic publishing centres on the geographic margins of Europe's most powerful and well-consolidated realm may help to account for

---

[7] After this was written I learnt that Stephen Toulmin had selected the term as the title of a new book, *Cosmopolis* (New York, 1990), and was using it, idiosyncratically, to designate a particular philosophical position, associated with Cartesianism. My meaning should not be confused with his.

[8] Herbert Butterfield, *The Origins of Modern Science 1300–1800* (New York, 1951), 132.

[9] H.-J. Martin, *Livre, pouvoirs et société à Paris au XVIIe siècle (1598–1701)* (2 vols. Geneva, 1969).   [10] *Origins of Modern Science*, 140–41.

[11] Lionel Gossman, 'Marginal Writing', in Denis Hollier (ed.), *A New History of French Literature* (Cambridge, Mass., 1989), 379.

this paradoxical characteristic; at least it did much to shape the French Enlightenment during its formative years.

Let me note in passing that the expansion of a decentralized transnational network also needs more consideration from social theorists concerned with the changing structure of a so-called public sphere. Jürgen Habermas, who first drew attention to the emergence of a neutral space dedicated to rational criticism, seems to have envisaged the new arena as being contained within each separate dynastic state.[12] But the emergent public sphere also had extraterritorial aspects which need to be explored. Although such an exploration would be especially appropriate on the eve of a reorganization of the European community, Habermas's theories will only receive passing mention here.

What follows will be concerned with less theoretical and more historically specific issues. It will deal with the activities of certain *émigré* editors and publicists, with the review journals they issued and the views they expressed. The reliance of Parisian writers on extraterritorial firms will also be discussed. Special attention will be paid to those exceptional publisher-booksellers who edited texts and wrote books of their own. Such figures as Jean Frédéric Bernard, Prosper Marchand, Élie Luzac, and Pierre Rousseau will be singled out in order to demonstrate that the 'Business of Enlightenment' (to borrow from Robert Darnton) and the 'Mind of the Enlightenment' (to borrow from Ernst Cassirer)[13] were not always as distant from each other as recent studies suggest.

At present the merchants who ran their firms for profit are placed in one category; the philosophes who wrote in order 'to change the common way of understanding' are placed in another category. Between the two there seems to be no common ground. Connections between publishing history and intellectual history have thus fallen into disrepair. A single set of lectures cannot

---

[12] Jürgen Habermas, *Strukturwandel der Offentlichkeit* (Darmstadt, 1962) has recently been tr. into English by Thomas Burger: *The Structural Transformation of the Public Sphere: An Inquiry into a Category of Bourgeois Society* (Cambridge, Mass., 1989). Its use by some French historians is reviewed by Benjamin Nathans, 'Habermas's "Public Sphere" in the Era of the French Revolution', *French Historical Studies*, 16 (Spring 1990), 620-45.

[13] Robert Darnton, *The Business of Enlightenment: A Publishing History of the Encyclopédie 1775-1800* (Cambridge, Mass., 1979); Ernst Cassirer, 'The Mind of the Enlightenment', *The Philosophy of the Enlightenment* (Princeton, NJ, 1951), tr. F. Koelln and J. Pettegrove, ch. 1.

restore all connective tissue from its enfeebled state; but perhaps it can make a start at reversing current trends.

Now let us look a little more closely at our point of departure in the 1680s. There can be no doubt that the European intellectual community underwent significant changes in the 1680s. The Huguenot exodus introduced the new word 'refugee' into seventeenth-century vocabularies and infused the Republic of Letters with a fresh supply of energetic cultural intermediaries. The intellectual ramifications of this diaspora have been described in many works—most memorably, I think, by Paul Hazard in his *Crise de la conscience européenne*.[14] Gathered in enclaves in the Netherlands, Swiss cantons, German principalities, and in the vicinity of London as well, these French-speaking expatriates came as close as any group in early modern Europe to serving as prototypes of the free-floating intellectual.

The experience of exile went together with that of forced secularization. Trained as pastors but barred from their pulpits, the new *émigrés* turned to the printed word to address scattered congregations from afar. 'Although their cupboards were often bare,' wrote Rosalie Colie, 'they established intellectual journalism as a respectable profession for highly trained men who in an earlier era would have automatically made the pulpit their chief organ.'[15] A more prosaic account is given by Uta Janssens-Knorsch: 'the newswriter's job was a refugee job par excellence. It required no special qualifications except a certain amount of intelligence; no investments, no tools, no establishment, no license . . .'.[16]

Nevertheless, investments and tools did have to be supplied. Old acquaintances might be renewed by joining local French-speaking congregations; new jobs could be obtained only by gaining access to the men who ran established firms. 'In the

---

[14] Paul Hazard, *La Crise de la conscience européenne (1680-1715)* (3 vols. Paris, 1935). See also G. C. Gibbs, 'Some Intellectual and Political Influences of the Huguenot Emigrés in the United Provinces c.1680-1730', *Bijdragen en Mededelingen Betreffende de Geschiedenis der Nederlanden*, 90 (1975), 255-87.

[15] Rosalie Colie, 'John Locke in the Republic of Letters', in T. S. Bromley and E. H. Kossmann (eds.), *Britain and the Netherlands* (London, 1960), 118. It should be noted that Pierre Bayle was not a pastor but he was exceptional in this respect.

[16] 'French Refugees as Literary Agents', *Refugees and Emigrants in the Dutch Republic and England* (Papers of the Sir Thomas Browne Institute; Leiden, 1986), 59-63: p. 60. This point is slightly overstated. Some command of Latin as well as French was required (as is noted by Gibbs, 'Intellectual and Political Influences', 273).

United Provinces were publishers working for the international trade ... possessing the capital, the enterprise and the connexions for numerous and important ventures.'[17] The exiled preachers and teachers who pursued new careers as the editors and correspondents of cosmopolitan periodicals have been described by Graham Gibbs as 'the designers, directors and switchboard operators of a new intellectual communications system'.[18] But the Huguenots did not themselves set up a far-flung communications network; rather they found such a system already in place. They found publishers such as Reinier Leers in Rotterdam, heir to a publishing firm established by his parents, with his brother Arnold in Leiden and his connections with Hamburg, Berlin, Leipzig, Geneva, Paris, London, Cambridge, Edinburgh, and the countries of Southern Europe. Leers published the work of Pierre Jurieu, supported Pierre Bayle, married the widow of an Arminian pastor, kept on good terms with Abbé Bignon and furnished the royal librarian in Paris with hard-to-obtain foreign works.[19] In a recent brief account of Leers's operations, Henri-Jean Martin described the publisher as belonging to the 'little world of the book'.[20] Elsewhere other publishing and bookselling dynasties, such as the Huguetans and the Desbordes, are described as inhabiting 'a small closed world'.[21] Granted that a distinctive occupational culture was entailed, such phrases are somewhat misleading. The world known to Leers and his competitors was neither small nor closed.

The phrase 'little world of the book' is also liable to mislead us by focusing attention solely on the book and thus encouraging forgetfulness about the many other kinds of printed materials: brochures, pamphlets, almanacs, and other miscellaneous publications which almost always constituted a significant portion of the output of a given firm. The need to look beyond the book

[17] E. S. De Beer, 'The Huguenots and the Enlightenment', *Proceedings of the Huguenot Society of London*, 21 (1967), 179-95: p. 189.

[18] G. C. Gibbs, 'Huguenot Contributions to the Intellectual Life of England', in J. A. H. Bots and G. H. M. Posthumus Meyjes (eds.), *La Révocation de l'Édit de Nantes et les provinces-unies* (Leiden, 1986), 181-94: p. 184.

[19] Otto S. Lankhorst, *Reinier Leers (1654-1714) Uitgever & Boekverkoper te Rotterdam* (Amsterdam, 1983). See also Martin, *Livre à Paris*, ii. 748-53.

[20] H.-J. Martin, 'Reinier Leers', in Martin and Roger Chartier (eds.), *Histoire de l'édition française*, ii. *Le Livre triomphant 1660-1830* (Paris, 1984), 318. Ch. 5 of Febvre and Martin, *L'Apparition* (see n. 2) was entitled 'The Little World of the Book'.

[21] Febvre and Martin, *L'Apparition*, 217.

when considering communications networks is especially important for the interval to be covered here; an interval which was marked by the appearance of a cosmopolitan periodical press.

Mention of periodicals brings up another purpose of the lectures gathered in this book: to bridge the relatively wide gap that currently separates book history from journalism history. In their introduction to an essay collection on 'press and politics' in eighteenth-century France, two American editors complain that French book historians have neglected periodicals. Their own essays, however, exclude discussion of books.[22] It is foolish, as well as futile, to complain about specialization which is, after all an inevitable concomitant of an expanding knowledge industry. Schools of library science and schools of journalism do not prepare students for similar careers. Obviously custodians have to separate different kinds of reading matter, devise special catalogues for serials, and store newspapers in special places. After the eighteenth century, books and newspapers do seem to move apart; even though such hybrid forms as the *roman fleuve* or serial novel (not to mention the London *Times Literary Supplement*) remind us that significant connections remained.

But during the years considered here, as Jean Sgard has noted, it is anachronistic to consider 'the book and the journal as distinctly different cultural objects'. Both were issued from the same presses and bound into units of 8, 16, or 24 pages. Continuous pagination linked all the issues of a journal for a given year. The year's issues were usually reassembled into a volume, given a title-page and an index.[23] Of course, Sgard was writing about French-language journals and his remarks are less per-

[22] Jack Censer and Jeremy Popkin, 'Historians and the Press', in Censer and Popkin (eds.), *Press and Politics in Pre-Revolutionary France* (Berkeley, Calif., 1987), 6-7. Actually French historians are more likely to stretch the term 'livre' to encompass the journal than are Anglo-American historians who specialize in the 'book'. As noted by Raymond Birn, '*Livre et société* after Ten Years: Formation of a Discipline', *Studies on Voltaire and the Eighteenth Century* (hereafter, *Studies on Voltaire*), 151-5 (1976), 287-312: p. 293, the 2 vols. which launched 'livre et société' studies contain essays on periodicals as well as on books. See e.g. Jean Ehrard and Jacques Roger, 'Deux périodiques français du 18ᵉ siècle', in François Furet (ed.), *Livre et société dans la France du XVIIIᵉ siècle* (2 vols. Paris, 1965), i. 33-61. The misleading statistics contained in this essay (concerning reviews of foreign books by the *Journal des sçavans*) are criticized by Franco Venturi, *Utopia and Reform in the Enlightenment* (Cambridge, 1971), 15. The large number of book reviews in early periodicals is another reason for not separating the history of books from that of journals.

[23] Jean Sgard, 'La Multiplication des périodiques', in Martin and Chartier, *Histoire*, ii. 198-206: p. 198.

tinent to the English scene. The francophone press was much slower than the English one to undergo a decisive shift to a distinctive format for the newspaper. Even after 1789, most of the best known revolutionary papers were issued in an octavo format and could be placed together with books on the same library shelves.[24]

To forestall misunderstanding, I am not suggesting that periodical publication was an unimportant innovation. The output of dated products at regular intervals affected the pace of work in printing shops,[25] required special arrangements to be made with distributors and subscribers, and had many distinctive social and cultural effects. In a fascinating essay on the revolutionary newspaper *Les Révolutions de Paris*, Pierre Rétat has suggested that Parisian perception of events was restructured when an irregular series of occasional reports was changed into a regularly issued daily newspaper—an occurrence which transpired the day after the storming of the Bastille. The daily reports of events, which were collected into a volume at the end of the year, gave readers the new experience of living through an unfolding narrative which commenced on 14 July 1789.[26]

The cosmopolitan journals with which this book is concerned were issued with less frequency in less dramatic circumstances.[27] As regularly-dated printed products, however, they did create a new kind of continuing relationship for readers[28] and generated

---

[24] Jeremy Popkin, *Revolutionary News: The Press in France 1789-1799* (Durham, NC, 1990), 97-100.

[25] The greater discipline and tighter scheduling entailed in newspaper printing as compared with book printing during the 18th cent. is stressed by J. Popkin, *News and Politics in the Age of Revolution: Jean Luzac's Gazette de Leyde* (Ithaca, NY, 1989), 101-3.

[26] Pierre Rétat, 'Forme et discours d'un journal révolutionnaire', in Claude Labrousse and P. Rétat (eds.), *L'Instrument périodique* (Lyons, 1985), 139-78. An earlier example of occasional bulletins being transformed into a continuous series (albeit weekly, not daily) is offered by the Jansenist *Nouvelles ecclésiastiques* which was turned into a weekly journal on 23 Feb. 1728. The remarkable secret Parisian organization which made it possible for some 9,000 copies of this journal to be printed and distributed every week right down to 1789 and beyond is discussed by Françoise Bontoux, 'Paris Janséniste au XVIIIᵉ siècle: Les Nouvelles ecclésiastiques', *Mémoires de la Fédération des sociétés historiques et archéologiques de Paris et de l'Île de France*, 7 (1955), 205-20. (I owe thanks to Dale Van Kley for this ref.)

[27] The increase in bimonthlies and weeklies as against monthlies between 1734 and 1761 is charted by C. Labrosse, 'Fonctions culturelles du périodique littéraire', in Labrosse and Rétat (eds.), *L'Instrument périodique*, 11-136: pp. 74-8.

[28] This point is stressed by Anthony Smith, *The Newspaper: An International History* (London, 1979), 9.

new expectations. Contemporaries recognized that their appearance was of some historical significance. 'Our century might be described as the century of the journal' wrote a correspondent to Abbé Bignon in 1708.[29] In his early history of journalism (posthumously published in 1734) Denis François Camusat described the new genre as 'one of the happiest inventions produced by the French in the age of Louis XIV' and linked it with the superiority of the moderns over the ancients.[30] Subscribers to periodicals were in the new position of receiving a continuous, indefinitely extended, constantly updated series and this may well have contributed to a different sense of temporal flow than that experienced by previous literate groups.[31] It seems likely that anxiety about keeping up to date and fear of falling behind were intensified as periodical literature proliferated. In 1665, the *Journal des sçavans* explained its decision to run as a weekly rather than as a monthly: in the latter case, news would have grown stale and 'it is tiresome to read a whole volume full of things that have lost their novelty'.[32] But the tedium of stale news was a very old topos.

Keeping up to date in the eighteenth century still meant being resigned to prolonged delays in transportation and considerable irregularity in output. The *Journal des sçavans*, in its early years, scarcely lived up to its promise. With only four issues in 1669, one in 1670, and three in 1671, it could not even be described as a monthly. In 1673 no issues were published at all.[33] Because of

---

[29] Cited by Françoise Waquet, 'De la lettre érudite au périodique savant', *Dix-Septième Siècle*, 35 (1983), 347-59: p. 347. In 1715, a German observer, C. G. Hoffman, expressed almost the same view: 'We are living in the century of the journalists.' Cited by Joachim Whaley, 'The Protestant Enlightenment in Germany', in R. Porter and M. Teich (eds.), *The Enlightenment in National Context* (Cambridge, 1981), 106-17: p. 109.

[30] Denis François Camusat, *Histoire critique des journaux* (2 vols. Amsterdam, 1734), i. 1. Camusat died in Amsterdam in 1732 and his work was completed as well as publ. by Jean Frédéric Bernard. Bernard who also authored some 'Persian Letters' before Montesquieu as well as a multi-vol. survey of the world's religions is discussed below: pp. 96-7, 102-3.

[31] See suggestive remarks by David Kronick, *A History of Scientific and Technical Periodicals: The Origins and Development of the Scientific and Technical Press 1665-1790* (2nd edn. New York, 1976), 30.

[32] Cited by Sherman Barnes, 'The Editing of Early Learned Journals', *Osiris*, 1 (1936), 156-72: p. 171.

[33] Betty T. Morgan, *Histoire du Journal des sçavans depuis 1665 jusqu'en 1701* (Paris, 1928), 137, after giving these figures comments on the remarkable patience exhibited by subscribers. See also Waquet, 'De la lettre érudite', 357. (Waquet's study is confined to

the privileged monopoly assigned to this journal, competing French periodicals found it useful to disguise themselves as 'ouvrages particuliers' which were collected into volumes before being sold,[34] thereby making the line between journal and book especially difficult to draw.

Granted the significance of periodicity, there is still much to be gained by acknowledging the indeterminacy of diverse eighteenth-century printed materials: the book published in parts, the pamphlet series which is almost indistinguishable from the journal, the unbound book which is placed in the same crate as the journal, the journals which, having been collected and bound, are indistinguishable from books.[35]

Acknowledgement of indeterminacy is also helpful when dealing with the definitional problems posed by the varied names given to diverse periodicals and to their contributors.[36] Inconclusive verdicts have been rendered in recent years over how to distinguish the *journal* from the *feuille* and the *gazette* from both; over where to put the *Nouvelles* as against the *Courier* and over whether the *journaliste* or *gazetier* was most held in contempt. In a seminal article, Myriam Yardeni underlined the serious, scholarly connotations that were at first associated with the term 'journal'. (That such connotations have never left us is shown by numerous contemporary organs such as the *Journal of Chemical Physics* or the *Journal of the History of Ideas*.) She points to the learned discussion contained in late seventeenth-century journals on such topics as jurisprudence, Bible translation, Cartesian philosophy, and scientific experiments. She notes that the term *journaliste* was applied to editors such as Bayle or Le Clerc, who were not to be confused with the more vulgar *nouvelliste* or

Italian developments; the dismal picture of irregular output may reflect special circumstances there.)

34 Raymond Birn, 'Le Journal des Savants sous l'Ancien Régime', *Journal des savants* (1965), 15–35: p. 30.

35 Because of their book-like format, foreign periodicals and gazettes could be intermingled with banned books of all kinds in clandestine shipments. See e.g. description of works delivered to Paris booksellers by the wife of an army surgeon posted at Tournai in 1703–4. R. Birn, 'De Liège à Paris: La Route du livre à l'aube du siècle', in R. Mortier and H. Hasquin (eds.), *Le Livre à Liège et à Bruxelles au XVIIIᵉ siècle* (Études sur le XVIIIᵉ siècle, 14; Brussels, 1987), 11–36: p. 18.

36 Some idea of the problems involved is suggested by the almost 70 pp. Otto Groth devoted to defining the 'newspaper' in his typically German monumental work: *Die Zeitung* (4 vols. Mannheim, 1928).

gazetier. Such editors were also often described as 'auteurs' and were acknowledged to be powerful figures in the world of books.[37]

But Yardeni also notes that there were intellectual *gazetiers* as well as more vulgar ones. Collections of materials drawn from *Gazettes* and *Mercures* formed the basis for new historical narratives resulting in serious studies of contemporary history. The contributions made by *Gazettes* and *Mercures* to a new and 'cumulative science of actuality' is also underlined by Pierre Rétat in a way that seems to blur the customary division between weekly news reports and learned journals.[38]

Whatever distinctions may be drawn at present by historians, moreover, they were not always observed by contemporaries. Sometimes the *journal* was associated with a critical sifting of news and serious investigation, in contrast to the uncritical rumour mongering of the *gazette*,[39] but sometimes the two terms were used interchangeably and both were scornfully associated with Aretino's *métier*, that is, with the dispensing of gossip and scandal. Diderot's article in *L'Encyclopédie* treats one term under the heading of the other. Of the four meanings assigned to *Journal*, the third, 'an account of daily events in Europe', refers the reader to *Gazette*; the fourth mentions learned literary reviews with the acid comment that they were designed for readers who were too busy or too lazy to read whole books.[40] Writing for journals was 'a sad and servile trade' in Diderot's view.[41] Although *journalisme* was introduced as a term only at

[37] Myriam Yardeni, 'Journalisme et histoire contemporaine à l'époque de Bayle', *History and Theory*, 12 (1973), 208–29. See esp. p. 209 for a clear demarcation between *journalistes* on the one hand and *nouvellists* and *gazetiers* on the other.

[38] P. Rétat, 'Les Gazettes: De l'événement à l'histoire', *Études sur la presse du XVIIIᵉ siècle* (Lyons, 1978), 23–38. Louis Eugène Hatin's pioneering work, *Les Gazettes de Hollande et la presse clandestine aux XVIIᵉ et XVIIIᵉ siècles* (Paris, 1865), offered a tripartite scheme *gazettes*, *revues*, *receuils* and separated the literary *receuils* of Bayle, Le Clerc, et al., from the political *gazettes*. Sgard, 'Multiplication des périodiques', tries out a two-category scheme: opposing literary *bibliothèques* to political *mercures*. But this does not allow for literary *mercures* such as the *Mercure savant*. All such schemes leave numerous other terms (e.g. *journal*) in limbo.

[39] This contrast was emphatically stressed by Pancoucke who owned numerous journals and sought to dignify the genre. Suzanne Tucoo-Chala, *Charles-Joseph Pancoucke et la librairie française 1736–1798* (Paris, 1977), 197–8.

[40] 'Journal', *L'Encyclopédie ou Dictionnaire raisonné* (Neuchâtel, 1765), viii. 897.

[41] Cited from a letter, along with scornful comments about journals and journalists made by Montesquieu, Voltaire, Rousseau, and others, by Paul Benhamou, 'The Review in Desfontaines' *Nouvelliste du Parnasse*', in L. E. Brown and P. Craddock (eds.), *Studies in Eighteenth Century Culture: 19* (East Lansing, Mich., 1989), 367–81.

the end of the century,[42] the new *métier* gave rise to ambivalent attitudes even before it had been assigned a special name.[43] (Such ambivalence persists down to the present. A recent commentator writing in the *New York Times Book Review* felt it necessary to assert that there was 'nothing shameful about journalism as a venue for letters'.)[44] As is often the case, ambivalence goes together with uncertainty over terminology. A conference held in Utrecht in 1973 demonstrated that different contemporaries used the diverse terms *journaliste, gazetier, nouvelliste,* etc., in different ways and, in some instances, notably that of Voltaire, used them interchangeably.[45] Given this situation, it seems advisable to sidestep definitional argument.

One final complication deserves attention: namely the persistence of hand-copied materials alongside printed ones.[46] Practices affecting the eighteenth-century journal were reminiscent of those which affected the fifteenth-century book. The early printer who was intent on duplicating the manuscript book was a contemporary of the late scribe who returned the compliment by copying from printed editions.[47] Similarly, the editors of eighteenth-century printed journals, who duplicated items taken from hand-copied newsletters, were contemporaries of the so-called 'nouvellistes-à-la-main' who sometimes transferred material from printed journals into their manuscript newsletters.[48]

---

42 According to Morgan, *Journal des sçavans,* 18 n. 2, 'journalisme' first appeared at the end of 1789. She suggests reserving the term 'journal' for *mercures* and *revues* and using 'gazette' for daily papers (p. 19).

43 Ambivalent reactions to journalism were noted by Georges Weill, *Le Journal: Origines, évolution et rôle de la presse périodique* (Paris, 1934), 99. The difference between French and German approaches to the same topic can be seen by comparing Weill's 1-vol. work with Groth's 4-vol. one.

44 Karl Meyer, *New York Times Book Review* (18 Mar. 1990).

45 Marianne Couperus (ed.), *L'Étude des périodiques anciens: Colloque d'Utrecht* (Paris, 1973). See esp. section on 'la terminologie appliquée', 59–63.

46 See 'Confins du périodique, gazette à la main, correspondances littéraires, in P. Rétat (ed.), *Le Journalisme d'ancien régime* (Lyons, 1982), 93–132.

47 This practice continued into the 18th cent. That MS copies were made from the printed edn. of Dumarsais's *Le Philosophe* is noted by Herbert Dieckmann, *Le Philosophe: Texts and Interpretation* (St Louis, 1948), 8–9. On 15th-cent. practices see Curt Buhler, *The Fifteenth Century Book* (Philadelphia, 1960), 34–9; Cora Lutz, *Essays on Manuscripts and Rare Books* (Hamden, Conn., 1975), 129–39.

48 On 18th-cent. practices, see Françoise Weill, 'Les Gazettes manuscrits avant 1750', in Rétat (ed.), *Journalisme d'ancien régime*, 93–100; François Moureau, 'La Plume et le plomb: La Communication manuscrite au XVIIIe siècle', in Jochen Schlobach (ed.), *Correspondances littéraires inédites* (Paris, 1987), 21–30; F. Moureau, 'Les *Mémoires secrets* de Bauchamont, le *Courier du Bas-Rhin* et les *bulletinistes* Parisiens', in Jean Varloot and Paula Jensen (eds), *L'Année 1768 à travers la presse traité par ordinateur* (Paris, 1981),

There were also the semi-private, semi-public hand-copied *Correspondences* conducted for princes by publicists such as Grimm and Métra and the numerous clandestine manuscripts, listed by Ira Wade, which received printed publicity and were ultimately issued in printed form.[49] The importance of such hand-copied materials down to the end of the *ancien régime* is undeniable. Nevertheless our primary concern in this book is with the production and distribution of printed materials. The main point is that the term 'press' in the subtitle is intended to cover both books and journals; both will be included in the following discussion.[50]

Coupling books with journals makes it easier to see how the new cosmopolitan periodicals were related to earlier trends. For the most part, they were spin-offs from the book business. Publisher-booksellers had long been accustomed to supervising a special kind of periodical publication; semi-annual catalogues had been issued for over a century in conjunction with international bookfairs. The new cosmopolitan journals represented variations on this long-lived theme. As will be discussed in Chapter 2, the publishers usually owned the journal titles, chose the editors (some even served as their own editors), and provided the books to be reviewed. The new intellectual authority conferred on 'auteurs'-cum-editors such as Pierre Bayle or Jean Le Clerc did not diminish the important role played by their publishers. On the contrary, with the launching of the new periodicals, additional prerogatives and powers were acquired.[51] Publishers need to be considered along with the editors as the

58–80. The interdependence of correspondent and journalist during the 18th cent. is noted by Christiane Berkvens-Stevelinck, 'La Reception des journaux dans la correspondance de Prosper Marchand', in H. Bots (ed.), *La Diffusion et la lecture des journaux de langue française sous l'ancien régime* (Amsterdam, 1988), 129–39: p. 130.

[49] Ira Wade, *The Clandestine Organization and Diffusion of Philosophical Ideas in France from 1700 to 1750* (Princeton, NJ, 1938). The printed publicity given such MSS as 'Le Militaire philosophe' and the 'Traité des trois imposteurs' and their issue in printed edns. are discussed below, pp. 92–3, 107.

[50] Although the 4-vol. work, Claude Bellenger et al. (eds.), *Histoire générale de la presse française* (Paris, 1969), deals exclusively with journalism, the term 'presse' is assigned four distinct meanings in Robert's French dictionary: (1) the wooden hand press; (2) whatever is printed regardless of format as in 'freedom of the press'; (3) all periodicals; (4) newspaper journalism as in 'convene the press'.

[51] This is demonstrated, most convincingly, by Otto S. Lankhorst 'Le Rôle des libraire-imprimeurs néerlandais dans l'édition des journaux littéraires de langue française', in Bots (ed.), *La Diffusion*, 1–9.

'designers, directors or switchboard operators'. (If we employed the favourite term of media analysts, we would place them among the 'gatekeepers'.) Acting in time-honoured fashion as sponsors of expatriate literati, they supplied former teachers and preachers with new pulpits and lecterns. After the generation of the diaspora died out, they did much to empower French literati during the age of Enlightenment.

Unlike the privileged publishers of Paris, the extraterritorial publishers operated relatively freely as independent entrepreneurs; relatively, in the sense that local authorities, who tolerated publications intended for export, were still sensitive to pressures from representatives of great powers, and also in the sense that the penetration of the largest French markets, whether by obtaining a tacit permission or by using clandestine channels, required fairly elaborate manœuvres.[52] But merchant publishers were old hands at such manœuvres. To be sure, the regular entry of foreign periodicals required the making of new arrangements;[53] for the most part, however, established strategies continued to pay off.

After all, extraterritorial francophone printing was scarcely a new phenomenon in the late seventeenth century. As Gustave Cohen and others have pointed out, the paths taken by the Huguenot refugees who settled in the Netherlands owed much to precedents set by French writers in Descartes's day.[54] Still earlier precedents had been set in sixteenth-century Switzerland.[55] French books had been the first articles for export produced in Calvin's Geneva. In the 1530s, Neuchâtel had

---

[52] Although an immense amount of new research has appeared on the topic, the best brief introduction to the penetration of French markets by books from abroad remains Jean Paul Belin, *Le Commerce des livres prohibés à Paris de 1750 à 1789* (Paris, 1913). A clear outline of procedures entailed in obtaining tacit permission is given by R. A. Leigh, 'Rousseau, His Publishers and the *Contrat Social*', *Bulletin of the John Rylands University Library*, 66 (1984), 204-27: p. 208.

[53] The repeated but unavailing protests of French journal publishers concerning the admission of foreign gazettes and the eventual establishment in Paris of a newsagency to handle them is discussed by Hatin, *Les Gazettes de Hollande*, 45.

[54] Gustave Cohen, *Écrivains français en Hollande dans la première moitié du XVIIᵉ siècle* (Paris, 1920), *passim*.

[55] A synthesis of many studies on 16th-cent. francophone publication outside French borders is offered by Francis Higman, 'Le Domaine français, 1520-1562', in Jean François Gilmont (ed.), *La Réforme et le livre: L'Europe de l'imprimé (1517-1570)* (Paris, 1990), 105-54.

sheltered the pastor and printer who were responsible for the 'affaire des placards' in the reign of François I er.[56]

But the sixteenth-century placards were aimed at specific targets within the Valois realm. The extraterritorial publications with which we will be concerned were aimed not only at French readers within the Bourbon realm or at Huguenot refugees outside the realm, but also at French-reading Russians, Prussians, Poles, Swedes, Spaniards, Italians, and many others. That one should think not just of 'journaux français' but rather of 'gazettes internationales' was noted long ago by Eugène Hatin,[57] and was reiterated more recently by Jerzy Lojek who specializes in the francophone Polish press. Lojek notes, as an example of the remarkable reach of one journal, that current issues of the *Gazette de Leyde* were obtained in 1788 from a Jewish pedlar by an officer stationed in a remote area in Moldavia which lacked any postal service.[58] (Both Hatin and Lojek use the term 'international' which was coined by Jeremy Bentham very late in the century; for most purposes the term 'cosmopolitan' seems less anachronistic.) 'We write rather more for other nations than for the French', asserted the journalist Jean-Baptiste de la Varenne in his journal of the 1730s: *Le Glaneur*. To back up this assertion he published letters to the editor from Italian, Swiss, and German correspondents as well as French ones.[59] (It is possible, even probable, that he composed most of these letters himself.) His insistence that he had a cosmopolitan public in mind may have been partly designed to keep potential French censors at bay (a project in which he failed). Nevertheless it was not unusual for an eighteenth-century French author to count on having a far-flung public.

The replacement of Latin by French as the lingua franca of the Republic of Letters, as well as the cosmopolitan character of the eighteenth-century francophone press, is discussed in Chapter 2.

[56] G. Berthoud, *Antoine Marcourt* (Travaux d'humanisme et Renaissance, 129; Geneva, 1973), 157-222. Louis Desgraves, 'Le 450ᵉ Anniversaire de l'imprimerie neuchâteloise', *Revue française d'histoire du livre*, 53 (Apr.-June 1984), 401 ff.

[57] Hatin, *Les Gazettes de Hollande*, 5.

[58] J. Lojek, 'Gazettes internationales de langue française dans la seconde moitié du XVIIIème siècle', in P. Deyon (ed.), *Modèles et moyens de la réflexion politique au XVIIIe siècle*, i. *Moyens de diffusion* (Actes du colloque organisé par l'Université lilloise; Lille, 1973), 369-81.

[59] Cited by M. Couperus, *Un périodique français en Hollande: Le Glaneur historique 1731-1733* (The Hague, 1971), 28.

Here let me just note that when a prize competition was held in 1783 for the best essay on why French had become *the* universal language, it was sponsored not by the court of Versailles but by that of Berlin.[60] Production as well as consumption had a cosmopolitan aspect. In the Netherlands during the eighteenth century, francophone publications were turned out by English, German, and Dutch publishers as well as by French ones.[61]

One often reads about Pierre Bayle of Rotterdam, as one does about Erasmus of Rotterdam, and indeed the city celebrates both as local culture-heroes.[62] Neither are entirely suited to the role of native son but Bayle seems to be especially miscast. Along with many of his fellow expatriates he belonged to a French-speaking congregation; although he lived for twenty-five years in the United Provinces, he never learnt to speak Dutch.[63]

A deafness to local dialects came naturally to citizens who formed a 'state within all other states'. Pierre Desmaiseaux, the London-based editor of Bayle's works, described the position of such free-floating cosmopolites: 'Those who cultivate letters, arts and sciences form a state within all other states, a Republic where each member lives in perfect freedom and recognizes no other laws than those he prescribes for himself'.[64] Such perfect freedom of course was to be found only in utopian fantasies. Desmaiseaux's description harked back to Rabelais's imaginary *Abbaye de Thélème*. In the real world, as he knew perfectly well, men of letters worked under numerous constraints. When he was himself reviewing a translation of the Bible for the *Nouvelles de la république des lettres*, Desmaiseaux noted that problems were posed for the translator by the crude ancient text and commented that the authors of scripture were incapable of polishing their

---

[60] On this prize competition and on French as the cosmopolitan language for the expression of universal ideas, see vol. i. of Albert Sorel's multi-vol. work (1st publ. in 1885) *Europe and the French Revolution: The Political Traditions of the Old Regime*, tr. and ed. by A. Cobban and J. W. Hunt (New York, 1971), 146-7. How the French language assimilated foreign terms during this cosmopolitan phase is discussed by G. von Proschwitz, 'Le Cosmopolitanisme lexical au XVIIIe siècle', in R. Lathullière, *Langue, Littérature du XVIIe et du XVIIIe siècle: Mélanges offerts à Frédéric Deloffre* (Paris, 1990), 721-31.

[61] C. Berkvens-Stevelinck, 'L'Édition française en Hollande', in Martin and Chartier, ii. *Histoire*, 316-26: p. 319.

[62] Plans to erect a statue of Bayle next to that of Erasmus are noted by P. Rétat, *Le Dictionnaire de Bayle et la lutte philosophique au XVIIIe siècle* (Paris, 1971), 78.

[63] Elisabeth Labrousse, *Pierre Bayle* (2 vols. The Hague, 1963-4), i. 168.

[64] Cited by Rétat, *Le Dictionnaire de Bayle*, 66.

style. The comment was deleted by the journal editor who explained that 'it will not do in Holland to speak so disrespectfully of sacred writers'.[65]

Nevertheless, freedom for writers, together with the free enterprise of publishers, flourished better under some political arrangements than under others. Among important continuities linking earlier trends with later ones was the survival of medieval particularism. In the eighteenth century as in the sixteenth, many loosely federated small states allowed more scope for operations than did a few large well-consolidated ones. Writing about the state of journalism in the 1760s, the Abbé Bianchi observed that Venice and Holland had been early leaders in the field. In his own day, he noted that free cities or imperial cities were still more favourable 'to this commerce' than were the monarchies. 'Cologne, Frankfurt and Hambourg are more favorable than Spain, Portugal, France, Sweden or Denmark where it seems to be the rule that each state has only one law and only one gazette.'[66]

As noted above, this 'commerce' included books as well as journals and energetic centres were located as far south as the papal state of Avignon. One should bear in mind that, although the following discussion is mainly illustrated by examples drawn from the Dutch Netherlands, the same points are pertinent to other locales. As the Abbé suggested, a vital role was played by many of the free cities, principalities, and bishoprics which comprised some 330 political units within the old Holy Roman Empire. On the other hand it would be a mistake to underestimate the continued vitality of 'Holland' by likening its fate to that of Venice. The loosely federated states of the United Provinces continued to provide a favourable environment for far-flung operations until after 1789.

Contrary to common opinion, the Dutch authorities did not believe in a free press. The number of books banned within the United Provinces actually increased in the course of the eighteenth century.[67] But, as one might expect, the *de facto* situation

[65] Joseph Almagor, *Pierre Des Maizeaux (1673–1745): Journalist and English Correspondent for Franco-Dutch Periodicals 1700–1720* (Amsterdam, 1989), 27. A facsimile of the corrected piece is shown on p. 24.

[66] Cited by Hatin, *Les Gazettes de Hollande*, 49.

[67] Simon Schama, 'The Enlightenment in the Netherlands', *Enlightenment in Context*, 54–71: pp. 60–1. On forbidden books, Schama cites the standard monograph by W. P. C.

differed from the *de jure* one. At various times and in various provinces, action was taken against printers, publishers, and booksellers.[68] But rarely did all the provinces act in concert and rarely could any measure be rigorously enforced. There was no easy way to crack down on printers who could always pick up their press and join a relative or friend in another town. The same point applies to journal publishers and editors. A case in point is offered by the fate of Jean Baptiste de la Varenne and his journal, *Le Glaneur historique*. In 1733, when the Dutch estates, acting in response to the protests of the French ambassador, banned *Le Glaneur*; de la Varenne simply left the Hague, took up residence in Amsterdam, and launched a new journal under a new title: *Secrétaire du public*. Along with many of his contemporaries, he viewed censorship as being helpful to authors by raising the price of books and arousing the curiosity of the public.[69] Moreover, the Dutch authorities (and this holds true for many Swiss and German towns as well), when they did try to crack down, were more likely to censor works aimed at a local populace than at a foreign one.[70] French-language publications were generally assumed by Dutch authorities to be for export. With regard to such publications, pressure from French diplomats was usually ignored;[71] so too were complaints from Dutch Calvinist synods. As Buijnsters notes, Calvinism never did become a state religion in the United Netherlands. Enterprising publishers benefited from the friction between Dutch secular and religious authorities.[72] Inevitably, there were exceptions. LaMettrie and his publisher, Élie Luzac, ran into trouble in the 1740s. Later, the protests of Genevan pastors over

Knuttel, *Verboden Boeken in de Republiek der Vereenigden Nederlanden* (The Hague, 1914), while noting that many of the banned books listed by Knuttel were in Dutch, not French.

[68] Jeroom Vercruysse, 'Marc-Michel Rey et le livre philosophique', *Literatur Geschichte als geschichtlicher Auftrag: In memoriam Werner Kraus* (Berlin, 1978), 149-57: pp. 153-4, gives examples of crackdowns by the authorities in 1745, 1748, and 1773.

[69] Couperus, *Un périodique français*, 30, 57, 210.

[70] G. Weill, *Le Journal*, 57.

[71] J. Vercruysse, 'La Réception politique des journaux de Hollande, une lecture diplomatique', in Bots (ed.), *La Diffusion*, 39-47, points to the numerous complaints and negligible action.

[72] P. J. Buijnsters, 'Les Lumières hollandaises', *Studies on Voltaire*, 87 (1972), 197-215: p. 203.

d'Alembert's *Encyclopédie* article resonated in Holland and moved the Dutch authorities to take action.[73] The Genevan protests may serve to remind us that heterodox authors and free-wheeling publishers often found Calvinist states just as inhospitable as Catholic ones. French-speaking refugees who took up residence in the United Provinces in the 1680s did not all come from Louis XIV's France. Jean Le Clerc, Pierre Bayle's chief rival as leading citizen of the Republic of Letters, sought refuge in Amsterdam not from Catholic France but from Calvinist Geneva. A clash with Calvinist authorities in Lausanne also led Le Clerc's cousin, Jacques Bernard, to move to the Hague in 1687.[74] When writing about the quarrels between Jansenists and Jesuits, Le Clerc referred approvingly to a 'third party' ('troisième parti') which belonged to neither side. He himself eventually joined the Dutch Arminian Church and his writings would link the age of Erasmus with that of John Locke.[75] He was conscious of connections with an earlier third force and boasted of his grandfather's aid to the Genevan branch of the Estienne firm. Robert Chouet, the influential teacher of both Bayle and Le Clerc who taught at the Saumur Academy, was more closely connected with the Estiennes. His father had bought the firm in 1620.[76]

Actual linkage between generations however was probably less important than the sense of participating in a common enterprise which harked back to the golden days of Froben and the Estiennes. Exiles and *émigrés* were especially likely to value shared institutional memories. Publisher-booksellers in all regions were fond of evoking the self-congratulatory rhetoric of

---

[73] These actions are discussed by Yves Dubosq, *Le Livre français et son commerce en Hollande de 1750 à 1780* (Amsterdam, 1925), 44–54. Dubosq's account is not always reliable (e.g. he confuses Élie Luzac with his cousin Jean); his comment (p. 9) that Dutch censorship was just as vigilant and firm as French censorship between 1750 and 1780 is misleading, in my view.

[74] Annie Barnes, *Jean Le Clerc et la république des lettres* (Paris, 1938), 58–68, 122–3. Jacques Bernard was Le Clerc's successor as editor of the *Bibliothèque universelle* for two years 1691–3, then served as Pierre Bayle's successor as editor of the *Nouvelles de la république des lettres*. The publisher of the latter journal, Henry Desbordes, also fell foul of Calvinists as well as Catholics before taking up residence in Holland.

[75] On Le Clerc's activities see Ch. 2 below, pp. 56–64. He is portrayed as a spiritual descendant of Erasmus by Hugh Trevor-Roper, 'The Religious Origins of the Enlightenment', *The Crisis of the Seventeenth Century* (1st edn. 1956; New York, 1968), 193–237.

[76] Barnes, *Jean Le Clerc*, 38.

early printers as a means of legitimizing their trade.[77] In *The Tatler* of April 1710, Addison poked fun at the topos with the figure of 'Tom Folio' who 'esteems Aldus and Elsevier more than Virgil and Horace'.[78] There was also a mythology centred on Gutenberg as a Promethean culture hero. Such themes were richly orchestrated in the 1740s which saw the commemoration of the 300th anniversary of the invention. They would reach a climax in the demand to pantheonize Gutenberg during the French Revolution. Commemorations of Gutenberg and his successors will be taken up later on.[79] More pertinent at this point is the simultaneous elaboration of a counter-mythology around the figure of the publisher-bookseller as cultural villain, as a tight-fisted, calculating profiteer. Of course, this topos was also long-lived. Every age saw ambivalent reactions to a divine art which was also a commercial *métier*.

Mention of a 'commercial *métier*' reminds me to give fair warning that the business end of extraterritorial publishing will not receive its due in these pages. As my subtitle indicates, this account does not provide complete coverage but deals rather with selected aspects of the cosmopolitan francophone press. I will not pause over all the omitted topics (such as the franco-phone book trade in Canada, the West Indies, and elsewhere around the world). But money-making is too important to any publishing venture for it to be dismissed without comment. Let us take it as given that obtaining credit and showing profits were essential for any firm to keep afloat. The extraterritorial pub-lishers operated in much the same way as did other early mer-chant capitalists, with the significant exception that their products impinged directly on European intellectual life. It is with this significant exception that this book is concerned.[80]

---

[77] See e.g. Pancoucke's reference to the 'beaux jours où les Etiennes honoraient la typographie' in a letter to Voltaire, written when the future press lord was still a provincial publisher, heir to his father's firm in Lille. Cited by Tucoo-Chala, *Pancoucke*, 105.

[78] *The Tatler*, 158 (Thursday, 13 Apr. 1710). The passage continues: 'If you talk of Herodotus, he breaks out into a panegyric upon Harry Stephens' (i.e. Henri Estienne or Stephanus). [79] See below, Chs. 3 and 5.

[80] This disclaimer is partly provoked by John Feather, 'The Commerce of Letters', *Eighteenth Century Studies: The Printed Word in the Eighteenth Century—A Special Issue*, ed. R. Birn, 17 (Summer 1984), 405-25: p. 406. After noting that I have 'strangely ignored the world of commerce', Feather goes on to assert that there is only one way to pursue book history—a doubtful proposition, in my view.

My concern here, as elsewhere, is not with publishing history *per se* but with its relevance to a selected set of issues associated with intellectual and cultural change. Many years ago, Lucien Febvre suggested that more ought to be done to connect the 'geography of the book' with the movement of ideas. He pointed out the way—not only in his outline for *L'Apparition du livre* but also in his numerous earlier studies of sixteenth-century cultural history.[81] Literature, philosophy, and religion loomed large in Febvre's work and still do in current treatments of the French Renaissance.[82] But they have been devalued as topics worth exploring in recent Book and Society studies dealing with eighteenth-century France.

During the last few decades, such studies have proliferated. Much of this large literature is illuminating and entails fruitful collaboration with specialists in a diversity of fields. As the coupling of book with society suggests, there have been especially lively interchanges with social historians. But there seems to be a pronounced disinclination to make contact with the history of ideas. It should be noted that until recently the French had no phrase that corresponded precisely to our 'intellectual history' or 'history of ideas' and usually employed 'literary history' to cover such topics.[83] That the pioneering two-volume work, edited by François Furet, underwent a title change from 'Literature and Society' to 'Book and Society' is suggestive:[84] coupling book with society has led to the uncoupling of book from literature and/or from the history of ideas. Given the natural affinity of intellectuals for books (and hence, one might think, of intellectual history for the history of books), this is a somewhat paradoxical as well as unfortunate state of affairs.

[81] See e.g. the remarkable passage on hearsay and the advent of printing in *Le Problème de l'incroyance au XVIᵉ siècle: La Religion de Rabelais* (Paris, 1942), 418-87. See also Wallace Kirsop, 'Literary History and Book Trade History', *Australian Journal of French Studies*, 16 (1979), 488-535.

[82] See e.g. collection of essays: Pierre Aquilon, Henri-Jean Martin, and F. Dupuigrenet Desrousilles (eds.), *Le Livre dans l'Europe de la Renaissance: Actes du XXVIIIᵉ Colloque international d'études humanistes de Tours* (Histoire du livre; Paris, 1988), esp. concluding essay by Michael Screech, 'Histoire des idées et histoire du livre', 553-62.

[83] R. Chartier, 'Intellectual History or Sociocultural History? The French Trajectories', tr. J. Kaplan, in D. La Capra and S. Kaplan (eds.), *Modern European Intellectual History: Reappraisals and New Perspectives* (Ithaca, NY, 1982), 13-46.

[84] Lionel Gossman, book review, *American Historical Review*, 88 (1983), 404.

To be sure, our most eminent American book historian, Robert Darnton, has championed the cause of 'broadening intellectual history'. He calls for a mixed genre, 'the social history of ideas', to obtain a fresh assessment of the Enlightenment.[85] The phrase 'social history of ideas' was initially employed by Peter Gay who sought to supplement Ernst Cassirer's history-of-philosophy approach by supplying a more historically grounded 'life and times' treatment of the philosophes.[86] But, according to Darnton, Gay's approach still contains too little social history and too many 'rarefied' ideas, resulting in an 'overly highbrow, overly metaphysical view of eighteenth century intellectual life'.[87] This objection seems somewhat unfair, given the movement with which Gay was concerned. Surely anyone who attempts to consider the intellectual life of such figures as David Hume or Immanuel Kant will find it difficult to steer clear of 'high brow' or metaphysical topics. To describe the Enlightenment while excluding such topics would be a perverse exercise, aimed at lobotomizing a movement which hinged, after all, on the life of the mind. But it does seem fair to say that Gay's work falls short of supplying the Enlightenment with an adequate context. To cite but one example: an article titled 'The Enlightenment as a Communication Universe' does little more than describe the movement as urban and cosmopolitan and offers no discussion of the modes of communication the philosophes employed.[88]

[85] R. Darnton, *The Literary Underground of the Old Regime* (Cambridge, Mass., 1982), p. viii.

[86] Peter Gay, 'The Social History of Ideas; Ernst Cassirer and After', in Kurt H. Wolff and Barrington Moore, jun. (eds.), *The Critical Spirit: Essays in Honor of Herbert Marcuse* (Boston, Mass., 1967), 106-20. Gay's original use of the term is often overlooked and Darnton's reworking of it taken as canonical. See e.g. review article by J. Censer, 'Revitalizing the Intellectual History of the French Revolution', *Journal of the History of Ideas*, 50 (1989), 652-66: p. 653.

[87] Dissatisfaction with Gay's treatment was first expressed in 1971 by R. Darnton, 'In Search of the Enlightenment: Recent Attempts to Create a Social History of Ideas', *Journal of Modern History*, 43 (Mar. 1971), 113-33; now repr. in Darnton's latest essay collection: *The Kiss of Lamourette: Reflections on Cultural History* (New York, 1990), ch. 11, with the comment (p. 376) that the article still seems valid in retrospect despite objections posed by D. La Capra: 'Is Everyone a Mentalité Case?' *History and Theory*, 23 (1984), 296-311. The phrase about the 'overly highbrow, overly metaphysical view' comes from another of Darnton's 1971 articles, repr. in *Literary Underground*, 2.

[88] P. Gay, 'The Enlightenment as a Communication Universe', in H. D. Lasswell, D. Lerner, and H. Speier (eds.), *Propaganda and Communication in World History* (3 vols. Honolulu, 1979), ii, ch. 3, 84-106.

Professor Darnton, on the other hand, certainly has much to tell us about how they brought the good news from Neuchâtel to Paris. He provides a 'thick description' of rag-picking, type-setting, packaging, mailing, and marketing; he pores over some 50,000 items of commercial correspondence to track down over-the-border and under-the-cloak transactions. In a series of fascinating essays on the 'low life of literature' he unearths police records of smut pedlars and spies and injects fresh life into the old theme of the blocked mobility of an urban intelligentsia. But however large its contributions to the social history of literati, the *Literary Underground* does stop short of dealing with ideas. Exhibiting considerable disdain for the 'endless reshuffling of great books', its author does less to broaden than to devalue the work of intellectual historians.[89]

The same point applies to the major prize-winning study of the 'business of Enlightenment'.[90] In common with several other titles used in Book and Society studies, such as 'profits of ideas' and 'commerce of letters',[91] the first term (business, profits, commerce) weighs heavily; the second (Enlightenment, ideas, letters) gets short shrift. Business looms especially large in this instance, partly because the study begins after all the intellectual work of writing, editing, and illustrating the *Encyclopédie* was finished. Although the preface invites us to follow the 'life cycle of the supreme work of the Enlightenment'; the work starts with the publishing of reprints, that is, with the cycle's last phase. The story of the first edition having been told many times, the author explains, it is only the tale of later editions that will be told.[92]

This story seems to consist largely of negotiations between publishers over the division of spoils. 'The Enlightenment existed first in the speculations of philosophes then in the speculations of publishers.'[93] As the play on words suggests, mind and money have been uncoupled; how the financial speculations of the publishers relate to thoughts of the philosophes or to the 'existence of the Enlightenment' remains unclear. Nor is the

[89] *Literary Underground*, 167. For a trenchant critique of the anti-intellectual views expressed in this collection of essays, see La Capra, 'Is Everyone a Mentalité Case?'

[90] Darnton, *Business of Enlightenment*.

[91] R. Birn, 'The Profits of Ideas: *Privilèges en librairie* in Eighteenth-Century France', *Eighteenth Century Studies*, 6 (1971), 131–68; Feather, 'Commerce of Letters'.

[92] Darnton, *Business of Enlightenment*, 5.   [93] Ibid. 3.

issue clarified by detailed accounts of the activities of booksellers and the routes followed by pedlars. A special chapter on the subculture of printing workers, which depicts a dirty, noisy, obstreperous bunch, harshly treated by their employers, takes us further afield. No less disappointing is the failure to provide a well-rounded view of the Neuchâtel publishers whose pecuniary speculations are described in such fine-grained detail. As Aram Vartanian notes in an otherwise favourable review, 'copious quotations yield only disappointing greedy prose'.[94]

Perhaps prolonged exposure to thousands of items of commercial correspondence helps to explain the author's insistence that the publishers of the *Société Typographique de Neuchâtel* (the STN), Frédéric Samuel Ostervald and his son-in-law Jean Élie Bertrand, 'were out to make money rather than to spread les lumières'.[95] Repeated insistence on this point seems odd because there was no need for such men to choose between one course or the other. In regions such as Neuchâtel the two aims could be easily combined, providing double satisfaction to the partners of a given firm. Yet the point *is* insistently repeated[96] and it is the only point made about the views held by the publishers. One is left to infer that money-making so obsessed them that they thought of nothing else. In fact, they must have thought occasionally about the articles they wrote, the students they taught, the authors who visited them, the journal they edited, not to mention the books and journals they consulted.

For the STN was run by men who were also occupied with intellectual and academic pursuits. Frédéric Samuel Ostervald (1713-95) was the son of the principal pastor of Neuchâtel.[97] He

---

[94] A. Vartanian, 'The Annales School and the Enlightenment', *Studies in Eighteenth Century Culture*, 13, ed. O. M. Brack (1984), 233-47.

[95] Darnton, *Business of Enlightenment*, 40.

[96] 'They did not go into publishing for ideological reasons. Above all, they wanted to make money' (about Ostervald and an associate Bosset) in Darnton, 'Sounding the Literary Market in Prerevolutionary France', in *Eighteenth Century Studies*, 17, ed. Birn, 477-92: p. 478. In 'Le Livre prohibé aux frontières: Neuchâtel', in Martin and Chartier, *Histoire*, ii. 342-62, this thesis is extended: not only the STN but 'all other typographical societies' were 'far from being committed' and 'sought only to make money', 359. Darnton emphatically reasserts the same points in his recent study, written in French: *Édition et sédition: L'Univers de la littérature clandestine au XVIIIe siècle* (Paris, 1991), 140.

[97] Jean Frédéric Ostervald (1663-1747) was one of three of the most influential pastors in Switzerland. See Graham Gargett, 'Voltaire and Protestantism', *Studies in Voltaire*, 188 (1980), 147. He had edited the *Mercure suisse* and had authored a celebrated tr. of the Bible: *La Bible avec les réflexions d'Osterwald* (Amsterdam: Jean Frédéric Bernard, 1724).

was an author and savant, as had been his father before him. He contributed to *L'Encyclopédie* and helped to turn out the *Journal helvétique* (formerly the *Mercure suisse*). In August 1751, this journal had published the prospectus of the first volume of *L'Encyclopédie*—a prospectus that was imbued with Enlightenment ideology.[98] In later years it ran reviews of works by Jacques Pierre Brissot, Louis Sébastien Mercier, and Restif de la Bretonne, thereby publicizing authors who were published by the STN.[99] Ostervald's son-in-law, Jean Élie Bertrand (1737-79), who served as the journal's editor-in-chief until his premature death, was trained as a pastor, served as a professor of *belles-lettres* and rector of the local college. In 1770, the two men aroused local disapproval for publishing the *Système de la nature*. Ostervald was forced to resign his elective office of 'banneret' and his son-in-law was unfrocked by the local company of pastors. The publication of such a 'frightful' book led Albrecht von Haller, the Bernese physician and naturalist, to lash out at the cupidity and avarice of Ostervald and Bertrand. How could they poison the public, Haller wrote to a friend, just for the sake of money?[100] But not all the letters which were written about this episode regarded the action of the publishers in the same light. Voltaire, for example, wrote to Frederick the Great (nominal overlord of Neuchâtel) on behalf of the head of the STN. 'This man is very conciliatory and very wise and at the same time possessed of an intrepid philosophy capable of rendering service to reason and to yourself and

---

[98] Charly Guyot, *Le Rayonnement de l'Encyclopédie en Suisse Française* (Neuchâtel, 1955), 17-18, 191-2. Guyot underscores the fallacy of singling out commercial motives as the only reason for STN edns. of the *Encyclopédie* (p. 7). His numerous publications on the STN reflect the civic pride of a native son who taught at the Univ. of Neuchâtel. His treatment of Quandet de Lachenal based on his study of some 187 letters is in striking contrast to Darnton's. Compare Guyot, 'Un correspondant parisien de la Société Typographique de Neuchâtel: Quandet de Lachenal', *Musée neuchâtelois* (1936), 1-20, with Darnton's treatment of the same correspondent: 'Sounding the Literary Market', 479-83. Although Darnton cites Quandet's declaration of sympathy for the philosophes, 'I admire them and do everything I can to make their works appreciated and to assure their sale' (p. 482), he goes on to deny that the correspondent ever meant what he said. His insistent denial of any but base motives may be partly a reaction to Guyot's more sympathetic treatment; but it is hard to tell since he rarely mentions and never discusses his predecessor's work.

[99] Jean-Daniel Candaux, 'Les Gazettes helvétiques', in Couperus (ed.), *L'Étude des périodiques*, 126-71; Michel Schlup, 'Diffusion et lecture du *Journal helvétique* 1769-1782', in Bots (ed.), *La Diffusion*, 59-73; C. Guyot, *La Vie intellectuelle et religieuse en Suisse française à la fin du XVIIIᵉ siècle: Henri David Chaillet 1751-1823* (*Mémoires de l'Univ. de Neuchâtel*, 21), ch. 7.   [100] Guyot, *Le Rayonnement*, 129.

equally devoted to both.'[101] Of course it would be foolish to take the words of either von Haller or Voltaire at face value. Ostervald was a complicated man and almost as deceptive and tricky as was Voltaire himself.[102] His complex personality comes across in a description by a later editor of the *Journal helvétique*, who wrote to a friend that the publisher was 'vile, self-serving, tricky, duplicitous, contemptible . . . but not hateful and he has a sort of "bonhommie" which covers a multitude of sins. I repeat: he's not a simple man and furthermore he's not simply a business man.'[103]

To the printing workers he may have appeared in the guise of a harsh employer; to men of letters he was known to be a generous host. His correspondence was not only concerned with profit and loss. A letter from Roland de la Platière (the future Girondin minister) expressed the hopes of a provincial bureaucrat who wanted to get elected to the Berlin Academy;[104] Simon Nicholas Henri Linguet wrote to him just after leaving Brussels and taking up residence in London that he had hesitated between going to 'this island' and visiting 'your mountains'.[105] The forty-odd letters that he received from one of his former students at the Neuchâtel *collège* have been used by Professor Darnton to analyse how one reader responded to Rousseau.[106] These letters show that the publisher did more than supply products ordered from a client; he acted as a personal intermediary between author and

[101] C. Guyot, 'Imprimeurs et pasteurs neuchâtelois: L'Affaire du *Système de la Nature*', *Musée neuchâtelois* (1946), 74-81, 108-16; Voltaire's letter is cited on p. 112.

[102] His dealings with Mercier, recorded in his correspondence, were remarkably Byzantine. At first he turned down Mercier's request to have his work published by the STN with the falsehood that the STN didn't run its own publishing business but only printed on demand for other publishers; then, when Mercier was taken up by his Neuchâtel rival and former associate Samuel Fauche, Ostervald engaged in all sorts of secret manœuvres to lure Mercier away from Fauche and succeeded in becoming Mercier's publisher in the end. See C. Guyot, *De Rousseau à Mirabeau: Pèlerins de Môtiers et prophètes de 89* (Neuchâtel, 1936), 83-92.

[103] 'Le Bas-Normand est vil, interésée, tracassier, double, méprisable . . . mais point haissable et chez lui il a une sorte de bonhommie qui couvre une multitude de péchés. Je repéte: pas un homme simple. En plus, pas simplement un homme d'affaires'. Letter from Chaillet, cited by Guyot, *De Rousseau à Mirabeau*, 84.

[104] Letter of 6 Sept. 1781 cited by Daniel Roche, *Le Siècle des lumières en province* (2 vols. Paris, 1978), ii. 121.

[105] Darlene Gay Levy, *The Ideas and Careers of Simon Nicolas-Henri Linguet* (Urbana, Ill., 1980), 212.

[106] R. Darnton, 'Readers Respond to Rousseau', *The Great Cat Massacre and Other Episodes in French Cultural History* (New York, 1984), 215-57. A similar correspondence between another extraterritorial publisher (Marc Michel Rey) and a client who was also an ardent Rousseauist (F. H. Jacobi) is discussed below, Ch. 4.

reader. He elicited letters which combined book orders with effusive intimate outpourings. Ranson was figuratively 'responding' to his reading of Rousseau by quite literally responding to letters from Ostervald. The latter served his client as a surrogate for the celebrated author whom he knew.

This correspondence shows that Ostervald was warmly regarded by his former pupil. Other evidence shows that he was also known to writers as a generous host. As Chapter 5 will suggest, the STN entertained representatives of both the high Enlightenment and the low. The establishment was praised in lyrical terms by Jacques Pierre Brissot who wrote that the spirit of liberty had transported her workshop to the remote sanctuary of Neuchâtel which was ringed by mountains and hence beyond the reach of the Inquisition.[107] Jacques Mallet du Pan, the celebrated Swiss journalist, first turned to Ostervald 'as one philosophe to another' for help and hospitality in 1772. Thereafter he repeatedly sought his aid and advice, kept in constant touch by correspondence and found in him a second father.[108]

As is often the case with publishing firms in the age of the hand press, the STN seems historically significant not because it fulfilled the one and only function of 'booty capitalism' but because it combined many different functions and co-ordinated activities of diverse kinds.[109] Since the publishers were both men of letters and businessmen, they are miscast when assigned one or the other single role. When such cultural intermediaries are presented in a one-dimensional role, we forgo a chance of

[107] J. P. Brissot, *Mémoires 1754–1793*, ed. C. L. Perroud (2 vols. Paris, n.d.), i. 284. Brissot's description owed something to his reading of Abbé Prévost and perhaps something also to self-promotion by the STN. In 1769 when the firm was formed, it printed 200 circulars publicizing its fortunate location in a 'free country'. See Jacques Rychner, 'Alltag einer Druckerei im zeitalter der Aufklärung', in Giles Barber and Bernhard Fabian (eds.), *Buch und Buchhandel im achtzehnten Jahrhundert* (Proceedings of the 5th Wolfenbutteler Symposium; Hamburg, 1981), 53–81: p. 78 n. 2.

[108] Frances Acomb, *Mallet du Pan (1749–1800): A Career in Political Journalism* (Durham, NC, 1973), 28–35. Acomb's impression of Ostervald, based on his correspondence, is of a man who was 'benevolent, obliging yet shrewd'. During Mallet's stay in Neuchâtel (1772–3) he was closely associated, both professionally and personally, with Ostervald, Bertrand, and the latter's family. (Mme Bertrand, O.'s daughter, helped with the firm and later ran a school for girls in Mannheim.) Mallet contributed to the STN's *Journal helvétique*; after Bertrand's death in 1779, he offered to take over as editor (pp. 35, 125).

[109] Michel Schlup, 'La Lecture et ses institutions dans la principauté de Neuchâtel au tournant des lumières', *Revue français d'histoire du livre*, 56 (1987), 463–500, stresses the 'intellectual stimulation' (p. 465) provided by the publishers.

broadening intellectual history by disclosing connections between letters and learning, marketing and merchandise.

By focusing research exclusively on business correspondence,
we also run the danger of reinforcing a stereotype which goes
back at least to Erasmus's complaints about Aldus Manutius's
avaricious father-in-law. From the days of Erasmus, down to the
present, there is scarcely any writer who has not at one time or
another expressed detestation of the cold-blooded, calculating,
profit-seeking publisher who wrings the last penny from starving
writers while hastily marketing inferior goods. But at least
Erasmus's complaints about the father-in-law were balanced by
appreciation of the services rendered to learning by Aldus himself.
And the best balanced biography of Aldus makes room for the
diverse aspects of the firm: 'a now almost incredible mixture of
the sweat shop, the boarding house and the research institute'.[110]
In the *Business of Enlightenment*, the sweat shop and the business
office seem to have pre-empted other concerns.

Such a presentation not only reinforces the stereotype of the
publisher as Mr Moneybags; it also contributes to a golden-age
mythology which places the era of the scholar printers at a
distance from the eighteenth century, when an iron age of
commercialism presumably dawned. Certainly there is ample
evidence that such a golden-age theory was held by eighteenth-
century literati. Disgust with sharp dealing and unmitigated
greed was expressed on all sides. In Great Britain especially there
was a swelling chorus of complaints about a subjugation of
literature to commerce which was associated with the new
ascendancy of booksellers.[111]

But the continent was not far behind. Malesherbes wrote about
the distance between the heroic age of Plantin and the Estiennes,
when publishers were scholars, and his own age, when they had

---

[110] Martin Lowry, *The World of Aldus Manutius: Business and Scholarship in
Renaissance Venice* (Ithaca, NY, 1979), 94.

[111] Ian Watt, *The Rise of the Novel* (Berkeley, Calif., 1967), 52-5, offers pertinent
citations. A case-study of a publisher-bookseller who was stigmatized as a literary
middleman, 'whose only interest in literature could be measured in guineas' (p. 3), is
offered by Gerald Tyson, 'Joseph Johnson, an Eighteenth Century Bookseller', *Studies
in Bibliography*, 28 (1975), 1-16. Tyson's book-length biography, *Joseph Johnson:
A Liberal Publisher* (Iowa City, Ia., 1979), describes Johnson's services to an influential
circle of dissenters, exiles, and radicals (Joseph Priestley, Mary Wollstonecraft, Joel
Barlow, Henry Fuseli) and shows the shop functioning both as a cultural centre and a
business office.

become purely mercenary.[112] Of all those who engage in commerce, wrote Pierre Bayle in 1689, no group is so universally despised for bad faith as the publishers.[113] Prosper Marchand found the cutthroat competition so disgusting, his executor tells us, that after leaving France for the Netherlands and gaining an entry in the local guild, he gave up printing and publishing altogether.[114] Yet the record also shows that when Bayle was forced out of his teaching post he relied almost entirely (even more than had Erasmus) on the patronage and hospitality of a publisher-bookseller. Marchand also lived out his life as a house guest of the much maligned species.

Furthermore, horror stories about greed and knavery were not uncommon in earlier eras. 'He sets more store by his own good than by the general good, is more concerned for gold than for honor and thinks of nothing but profit.'[115] This complaint was directed at the pioneering atlas publisher, W. J. Blaeu, in the so-called 'golden age' of Dutch publishing. The Elseviers, often described as the last representatives of the golden age, not only received fawning dedications as friends of learning, immortals, and demi-gods; they were also accused of harsh dealings with old acquaintances and even of letting the widow of an associate starve.[116] As with all golden ages, even the era of Aldus contains disillusioning evidence when viewed close up. There is much to suggest, furthermore, that the cultural and intellectual functions of publisher-booksellers were enhanced and not diminished as the centuries wore on. I have already alluded to the output of new review journals. A proliferation of reading societies went together with subscriptions to periodicals, the maintenance of bookshop libraries, and regular gatherings of literary coteries in back rooms.[117]

---

[112] Cited by Belin, *Le Commerce des livres prohibés*, 72.

[113] Lankhorst, 'Le Rôle', in Bots (ed.), *La Diffusion*, 9.

[114] Prosper Marchand, *Dictionnaire historique ou mémoires critiques et littéraires* . . . (2 vols. The Hague, 1758), i. 2. The passage comes from the 'Avertissement de l'éditeur', a sketch of Marchand's life by Jean Nicolas Sébastien Allamand.

[115] Comment of Vossius about W. J. Blaeu in David W. Davies, *The World of the Elseviers 1580-1712* (The Hague, 1954), 139.   [116] Ibid. 67.

[117] Tyson's article describes how Joseph Johnson carried on the old tradition of using his shop as a gathering place and refuge for writers. Fuseli, exiled from Zurich, was housed above the bookshop and given work as a translator. Joel Barlow belonged to a second generation of Americans who used the place as a hospitality centre. Ostervald's STN establishment served similar functions. See Michel Schlup's two articles on reading societies in Neuchâtel: 'Diffusion et lecture', 'La Lecture et ses institutions'.

There is a special reason to be wary of reinforcing old stereotypes when dealing with our topic today. Ill will between author and publisher was compounded by the xenophobic reactions of French expatriates to the foreigners among whom they lived. As a dominant force in extraterritorial publishing, the Dutch in particular provoked unfavourable comment. English patriots during the Dutch wars had already stigmatized their enemies as 'dull accountants and avaricious merchants'.[118] The anti-Dutch stereotype dovetailed neatly with the anti-commercial motif. 'The Dutch are cold and avaricious. Here avarice is considered a virtue', complained Jean Le Clerc.[119]

Gutenberg's successors had provoked ambivalent reactions; they were idealized as cultural heroes and stigmatized as mercenary villains. Much the same was true of the Dutch Republic. Eulogies of a free state which offered refuge for seekers after truth alternated with contemptuous dismissal of a nation of herring merchants who trafficked in imperishable truths as in dead fish.[120] 'The love of gain was as natural to them as water to a goose.'[121] The mythical Amsterdam publisher who did not know how to read but made millions from Frenchmen who knew how to write was immortalized by Voltaire, who also had nasty things to say about the Swiss.[122] When it came to the love of gain, Voltaire knew whereof he wrote.[123]

It is fairly unusual to find an early modern author asserting, as did Samuel Johnson, that money-making was his main concern. ('No man but a blockhead ever wrote except for money.') Whereas men of letters usually denied that they had any mercenary motives, printers and publishers in early modern Europe often found it useful to insist that what was good for business

---

[118] Charles A. Knight, 'The Images of Nations in Eighteenth Century Satire', *Eighteenth Century Studies*, 22 (Summer 1989), 495.

[119] Cited by Barnes, *Jean Le Clerc*, 96.

[120] Schama, 'Enlightenment in the Netherlands', 61, underscores this ambivalence.

[121] Davies, *Elseviers*, 140.

[122] Voltaire's contemptuous remarks about the Dutch are cited by Jacques Marx, 'Élie Luzac et la pensée éclairée', *Documentatieblad Werkgroep 18e Eeuwe (Frans-Nederlandse Betrekkingen)* (Symposium held at the Maison Descartes, Sept. 1970), 74–105: p. 74. See also J. Vercruysse, 'Voltaire et la Hollande', *Studies on Voltaire*, 46 (1966). On Voltaire and the Swiss see Gargett, 'Voltaire and Protestantism', 106.

[123] Voltaire's mean and stingy side is not depicted by his more admiring biographers such as Peter Gay. For a devastating description of his effort to evade a small payment due a landlord for services rendered, see C. A. Sainte-Beuve, 'Voltaire et le Président de Brosses', *Causeries du lundi* (15 vols. Paris, 1050–62), vii. 103–20.

(and hence for the prosperity of a given town) was the only thing on their minds. The Amsterdam publisher, Élie Luzac, thus countered objections to his publishing LaMettrie's *L'Homme machine* by arguing that he was only doing what any good business man would do; acting in the same way as the wine merchant who saw no reason to withhold from a drunkard what could always be purchased somewhere else.[124] Avoidance of an overt profession of faith was useful to any merchant publisher whose trade cut across religious and dynastic frontiers; it is not surprising that one finds few traces of ideological commitment in a given publisher's archives. But that does not mean that the extraterritorial publisher was committed to nothing but making money.[125]

Perhaps enough has been said to suggest why there is need for a more balanced presentation of extraterritorial publishing than that offered in recent eighteenth-century Book and Society studies. To bring such studies into closer contact with the history of ideas it is also necessary to resist the current fashion for devaluing 'high' culture and for discounting the activities of what we might call the 'uncommon' reader—the reader of (and potential contributor to) learned journals and literary reviews. This brings me to the recent studies of French print culture issued by Roger Chartier and members of his seminar.[126] Elaborating on a theme first sounded many years ago by Natalie Davis in her seminal essay 'Printing and the People',[127] Chartier seeks to 'revoke or cast doubt on the canonical separation between the popular and the learned'.[128] In his view, divisions between élite and popular, learned and vulgar, literate and non-literate sectors have been much too sharply drawn by historians of early modern

[124] Marx, 'Élie Luzac', 76.

[125] 'The committed publisher never appears in the archives.' 'Far from acting on the basis of commitment, the STN and the other typographical societies sought only to make money.' Darnton, in Martin and Chartier, *Histoire*, ii. 351. On Élie Luzac's advocacy of religious toleration and his political pamphleteering, see Ch. 4.

[126] To sample this school, see R. Chartier, *The Cultural Uses of Print in Early Modern France*, tr. Lydia Cochrane (Princeton, NJ, 1987); *Cultural History: Between Practices and Representation*, tr. Lydia Cochrane (Ithaca, NY, 1988). Also two books ed. Chartier containing contributions by editor: *Pratiques de la lecture* (Paris, 1985); *The Culture of Print*, tr. L. Cochrane (Princeton, NJ, 1989). The latter work appeared in a French edn. two years earlier under a different title: *Les Usages de l'imprimé* (Paris, 1987).

[127] Natalie Z. Davis, 'Printing and the People', *Society and Culture in Sixteenth Century France* (Palo Alto, Calif., 1975), 189–227.

[128] *Cultural History*, 102.

Europe. So-called élite culture drew heavily on so-called 'popular' materials (Rabelais owed much to the market-place; the Perrault brothers to twice-told folk-tales). 'Popular culture' consisted of a complex of practices on the part of an urban public composed of diverse social sectors. Most members of this public were neither fully literate nor entirely illiterate but belonged somewhere in between. Printed materials were not passively received but were actively appropriated and put to use in accordance with differing needs.

There is much to be said in favour of this approach. It provides a much-needed corrective to many French studies which depict the printing-press as nothing but a tool for social control, a tool employed by Church and State to impress certain views upon a malleable populace. Chartier argues persuasively against the view which holds that printed messages can be 'impressed' upon the public mind just as print itself is impressed upon a blank page. He is surely correct to insist that readers rework the materials to hand and that media are more malleable than most conventional accounts suggest. He poses a valid objection to the overuse of quantitative analysis by 'sociological reductionists' who consider 'words, ideas, thoughts and representations' as mere objects to be counted. He offers a valuable criticism of the 'tyrannical preeminence of the social dimension' which equates all cultural differentiation with class division.[129] He provides an incisive analysis of what is wrong with the construct of 'popular culture'.[130] In addition he has elicited from members of his seminar, and written on his own, a series of richly documented and vividly delineated case histories.

Yet however helpful his many contributions to Book and Society studies, Chartier's approach still keeps book history from making contact with the history of ideas. Indeed, the 'cultural uses of print'—to cite from the English translation of the title of one work—seem to be defined so as to exclude its intellectual uses. Although Chartier maintains that his approach does not 'lead away from intellectual history',[131] he does explicitly exclude from his studies those fully literate, often bilingual, groups who found printed materials most useful and made most use of them. (Rabelais drew on the market-place; he also drew on the Latin

[129] Ibid. 34.   [130] See esp., introduction to *Cultural Uses of Print*.
[131] *Cultural History*, 30-1.

learning of schoolmen, friars, and physicians.) There is nothing about the uses that were made of Latin, Greek, and Hebrew editions or about the usefulness of maps, charts, tables, and diagrams or about the numerous 'how-to' and 'teach-yourself' guides that ushered in the centuries of the autodidact. There is no room for the cumulative aspects of print culture which led men of letters and learning to feel that they were poised on the cutting edge of the knowledge industry and which helps to account for their increasing disdain for the 'credulous' masses.[132] Among the many case histories of the appropriation of printed materials which are offered, not a single one bears on intellectual concerns.

To suggest what is missing, an anecdote illustrating an intellectual appropriation of a printed work comes to mind. It concerns Abraham de Moivre, who as an 18-year-old Huguenot exile in England in the 1680s managed to get an audience with the Duke of Devonshire. The Duke's previous visitor had been none other than Isaac Newton, who left behind a presentation copy of his *Principia*. While waiting to be admitted, de Moivre began to peruse Newton's work and recognized its usefulness to the point of tearing out several pages which he later put to good use for a course he was teaching in mathematics and navigation.[133]

Several of Chartier's essays are devoted to 'publishing strategies' and 'reading practices'.[134] They tell us much about the *Bibliothèque bleue,* that collection of cheap reprints of old tales which was peddled around the French countryside. But there is nothing about all the other *Bibliothèques (universelle et historique, ancien et moderne, impartiale, britannique, germanique, française,* etc.) that came out in the eighteenth century. The very titles of these journals indicate how a tension between universalism and nationalism was being manifested in the age of Enlightenment. The significance which was attached to the idea of a 'bibliothèque' itself is not without interest to the historian of

[132] In an essay on problems posed by the overproduction of intellectuals, there *is* a reference to 'the shattering of traditional forms of knowledge', but it is associated with the 17th-cent. scientific revolution rather than with the advent of printing (*Cultural History,* 140). It is also argued that, although the frontiers of knowledge were pushed back, 'the control of learning by a restricted minority was in no way changed'—a highly debatable proposition in my view.

[133] Gibbs, 'Huguenot Contributions', 194. Gibbs notes that the incident must have been at least partly apochryphal since it was supposed to have occurred in 1685 before the *Principia* was published. *Si non e vero . . .*

[134] *Cultural Uses of Print,* chs. 5, 6, 7, 8.

mentalités.[135] These review journals also have something to tell us about early modern publishing strategies and reading practices. Take for example a publisher's letter to a colleague explaining why the *Bibliothèque impartiale* ought to issue its first number in the month of January: 'one catches readers best in the winter, when the weather keeps them indoors'.[136] Or consider the role played by book reviews in guiding reader reception of diverse works.[137] Surely consideration of the book review belongs in any study of 'the cultural uses of print'.

The proliferation of *Bibliothèques* and other review journals is also of considerable relevance to the cultural politics of the *ancien régime*. Whereas the royal academies were designed to promote a liaison between 'pouvoir et savoir', between power and knowledge,[138] the cosmopolitan review journals worked to decouple the knowledge industry from central royal control. Their editors exhibited an intriguing ambivalence about whether they ought to serve only savants or make more of an effort to attract the public at large. As did the *Bibliothèque bleue*, these little portable libraries travelled overland within the Bourbon realm. But they also travelled, much more widely, across the continent and overseas, serving to knit together a transatlantic Republic of Letters. To the neglected topic of these 'quietly useful instruments of cosmopolitan intellectual life', our next chapter will be addressed.

[135] For a stimulating discussion of the concept of a 'Bibliothèque' within the Republic of Letters see Remy G. Saisselin, *The Literary Enterprise in Eighteenth Century France* (Detroit, 1979), 17.

[136] Janssens-Knorsch, 'French Refugees', 60-1, cites a letter of 11 Feb. 1749 from Élie Luzac the publisher to Samuel Formey, the editor of the *Bibliothèque impartiale*.

[137] Labrosse, 'Fonctions culturelles du périodique', contains a wealth of pertinent material as well as a fascinating analysis of the functions of the book review. On the latter, see also below, Ch. 2.

[138] D. Roche, *Les Républicains des lettres* (Paris, 1988), ch. 5, p. 159.

2

News from the Republic of Letters

CHAPTER 1 ended by alluding to those journals, often called 'bibliothèques', which appeared in book format and which served a dispersed readership as 'quietly useful instruments of cosmopolitan intellectual life'. Here, we will take a closer look at some of these periodicals and at the policies pursued by their publishers and editors. But before getting down to specific cases, a few general comments are in order.

The phrase 'quietly useful instruments of cosmopolitan intellectual life' has been taken from Norman Fiering's account of the 'transatlantic Republic of Letters'.[1] Fiering describes how the journals were to be found in colonial college libraries and private collections and how they were regarded as lifelines by Americans who were eager to keep up with what was happening in the distant capitals of the old world. His description struck a responsive chord in me. Many years ago, I was living, as a faculty wife with three small children, in an isolated college community. Icy roads in winter-time made it almost impossible to travel to any major city. I had access only to an inadequate college bookstore and a small library which seemed to be run solely for the benefit of students in engineering and agriculture. Had it not been for the copies of the *Times Literary Supplement* and other review journals which appeared in our mailbox, I would have felt completely isolated.

The experience described by Fiering was paradigmatic, not just for eighteenth-century American colonists and twentieth-century American housewives, but also for provincial Europeans in the age of Enlightenment. One recalls the story, told by Elisabeth Labrousse, of the young Pierre Bayle holding down a teaching job in Sedan and trying to get news from Paris about conferences being held, books that were forthcoming, the reputation of certain authors—all of which he classified under a

[1] N. Fiering, 'Notes and Documents: The Transatlantic Republic of Letters', *William and Mary Quarterly* (3rd ser.) 33 (1976), 642-60.

heading later to become celebrated; he was starved, he wrote, for 'nouvelles de la République des Lettres'.[2] His sense of desperation when his few contacts in Paris failed him was expressed in his correspondence with his older brother Jacob. The story is full of pathos. In late 1665, Jacob wrote to Pierre about a wonderful new development. A journal promising to provide regular news of books and authors was being published in Paris. Twenty years later, the provincial teacher had become an editor himself and was issuing a journal that displeased the French authorities. As an expatriate in Rotterdam, he was himself out of reach. But his brother Jacob, who had stayed in France, was thrown into prison. Pierre tried every stratagem, pulled every wire, and even wrote a panegyric for Louis XIV. When the order came for the prisoner's release, it was too late. Jacob Bayle had died in prison.[3]

Although the basic experience of French provincials, such as Bayle, and that of colonial Americans was the same, the journals which served as lifelines to the two groups were not identical. A listing of some of the titles found in American libraries— *Universal Historical Bibliotheque, The Present State of the Republic of Letters, The History of the Works of the Learned*—suggests that when crossing the ocean (or the Channel, for that matter) the Republic of Letters lost something of its francophone character. Indeed, the review journals were more polyglot than my repeated allusions to a francophone press may suggest. The English *Universal Historical Bibliotheque*, although mainly based on its French exemplar, contained some translated material drawn from the Latin *Acta Eruditorum* (Leipzig, 1682) and also from the Italian *Giornale de' letterati* (Rome, 1668). There were also review journals in German and Dutch during the 1680s.[4] Nevertheless, as the bilingual title 'Universal Historical *Bibliotheque*'

[2] E. Labrousse, 'Les Coulisses du Journal de Bayle', in Paul Dibon (ed.), *Pierre Bayle: Le Philosophe de Rotterdam* (Paris, 1959), 97–141: pp. 100–1. The *république des lettres* would figure in several other journal titles after Bayle's death. There was the *Histoire critique de la république des lettres*, ed. Samuel Masson (1712–18). Prosper Marchand's *Journal historique de la république des lettres* (1732) was followed by the Marquis d'Argens's *Mémoires secrets de la république des lettres* (1737–48). The latter title was recycled by the editors responsible for the MS newsletter brought out from Mme Doublet's salon and achieved an afterlife when that newsletter was issued in printed form. On the phrase itself, see n. 28 below.

[3] Labrousse, 'Les Coulisses', in Dibon (ed.), *Bayle*, 116.

[4] Fiering, 'Notes and Documents', 648. An appendix to Betty T. Morgan, *Histoire du Journal de sçavans depuis 1665 jusqu'en 1701* (Paris, 1928), lists numerous learned journals in other languages than French which had short runs before 1701.

indicates, the French-language journal provided the prototype for the English ones. Later on, after Addison and Steele, the French would return the compliment by issuing numerous 'babillards' and 'spectateurs',[5] but in the beginning, the French *bibliothèques* set the mode. Even after Addison and Steele moreover, the French term 'bibliothèque' remained in vogue. In the sixteenth century when Conrad Gesner issued a comprehensive bibliography it went by the Latin name *Biblioteca*. In the next century, Comenius's project for an indexical reduction of all books was part of a scheme named by combining Greek terms: *Pan sophia*. But when a plan for a universal review journal was drawn up by Samuel Johnson he used the French term and called it *The Bibliotheque*.[6]

As early as the 1650s, an advertisement for a French translation of a London journal promoting the Cromwellian cause, *Les Nouvelles ordinaires de Londres 1650–1663*, stressed the advantage of making the journal available in a language which extended to all Europeans and was understood by them all ('qui s'étend et s'entend par toute Europe').[7] One hundred years later French was acknowledged to have become the universal language by Germans, Italians, and Poles.

Several decades have passed since E. S. De Beer remarked that 'the recession of Latin as an international language and the expansion of French have not been studied sufficiently'.[8] The point still holds good. It is evident that Latin continued in use not only among Jesuits and other teaching and preaching orders but also among many non-Catholic savants and scientists. In the

[5] *Le Spectateur ou le Socrate moderne* was published in 8 vols. beginning in 1714 by the Wetstein firm in Amsterdam. Yves Dubosq, *Le Livre français et son commerce en Hollande de 1750 à 1780* (Paris, 1925). See also Georges Weill, *Le Journal* (Paris, 1934), 9; P. J. Buijnsters, 'Bibliographie des périodiques hollandais rédigés selon le modèle des Spectateurs', in M. Couperus (ed.), *L'Étude des périodiques anciens: Colloque d'Utrecht* (Paris, 1972), 111–21.

[6] Robert De Maria, jun., *Johnson's Dictionary and the Language of Learning* (Chapel Hill, NC, 1986), 187. On the acceptance of the term 'bibliothèque' by the French Academy, see Rémy Saisselin, *The Literary Enterprise in Eighteenth Century France* (Detroit, 1979), 16.

[7] Anne-Marie Chouillet and Madeleine Fabre, 'Diffusion et réception des nouvelles et ouvrages britanniques', H. Bots (ed.), *La Diffusion et la lecture des journaux de langue française sous l'ancien régime* (Amsterdam, 1988), 177–203: p. 182.

[8] E. S. De Beer, 'The Huguenots and the Enlightenment', *Proceedings of the Huguenot Society of London*, 21 (1967), 179–95: p. 180. The chief study on the topic is still Louis Réau, *L'Europe française au siècle des lumières* (Paris, 1938).

1750s, when the *Journal des sçavans* ceased to review works in Latin, it inadvertently severed contact with German scientific publication.[9] Nevertheless, the works of such seventeenth-century Latin-writing savants as Pufendorf, Grotius, and Leibniz penetrated eighteenth-century Europe in French translations. In the 1630s Dutch publishers served cosmopolitan readers by publishing roughly 85 per cent of their output in Latin and only 10 to 15 per cent in French; by the 1730s these proportions had been reversed.[10] The use of Latin for a cosmopolitan review journal, such as the *Acta Eruditorum*, proved to be the exception not the rule. Up to the time of their expulsion from France in 1763, the Jesuits continued to use Latin when instructing their French pupils; but when they issued a review journal of their own, it was called not *Acta* but *Mémoires*: *Mémoires pour servir à l'histoire des sciences et des arts* (known from the locale in which it was printed as the *Mémoires de Trévoux*).[11]

Thus, despite the continued use of Latin for much learned correspondence, it seems fair to say that French did displace Latin as the lingua franca of eighteenth-century European literati —on the continent of Europe at least. I am not sure how far this holds across the Channel or overseas. Most of the Hanoverians spoke German not French and there was no court in the thirteen colonies to set a vogue. In the 1770s, the journalist Linguet complained of the difficulty of locating printers in London who knew French.[12] But although knowledge of French may have been restricted in Great Britain, acknowledgement of its universality was not. When Horace Walpole thanked his French

---

[9] Jean Ehrard and Jacques Roger, 'Deux périodiques français du 18ᵉ siècle', in François Furet (ed.), *Livre et société dans la France du XVIIIᵉ siècle* (The Hague, 1965), 33–61: p. 39.

[10] M. Thomann, 'Les Traductions françaises de Grotius', *Dix-Septième Siècle*, 35 (1983), 471–85: p. 483.

[11] Trévoux belonged within the principality of Dombes—one of those many tiny realms that retained its medieval quasi-feudal status as a possession not of the French king but of the Duc de Maine. It thus lent itself to attracting a publishing enterprise.

[12] Jeremy Popkin, 'Un journaliste face au marché des périodiques à la fin du dix-huitième siècle', in Bots (ed.), *La Diffusion*, 12, cites Linguet's complaint in the 3rd issue of his *Annales politiques* that there was not a single French press in the entire city of London and that he had to use a printer who was ignorant of French. The complaint is puzzling in view of the numerous shady French publicists and pamphleteers who resided in London at the time, as described long ago by Paul Robiquet, *Théveneau de Morande* (Paris, 1882).

translator in 1783 he wrote: 'you made me speak the universal language'.[13]

But once we agree that francophone periodicals served as the primary organs of a cosmopolitan Republic of Letters, there is a further complication to be considered; namely the prior existence of a French-language journal which served all the others as a prototype and had a cosmopolitan readership but was not itself an extraterritorial publication. From the time of its founding in 1665, through the following century, the *Journal des sçavans* never ceased to be published in Paris by privileged printers under the auspices of the Bourbon monarchy. Additional complications stem from the fact that within a year after its first appearance, there were two *Journal des sçavans*—a counterfeit edition being published in Amsterdam under the pseudonym 'Pierre le Grand'. (This pseudonym concealed the name of none other than Daniel Elsevier.) The history of the *Journal* and of the counterfeit editions is the topic of an unfinished doctoral dissertation whose author has kindly shown me his preliminary findings.[14] His comparison between the foreign pirated versions (which continued to be turned out until the late eighteenth century) and the domestic original brings out some intriguing differences; for example, the extraterritorial publishers added catalogues advertising books they themselves had for sale. But it would be premature, and also unnecessarily distracting, to discuss a work still in progress here.

The few points that need highlighting are already adequately covered in earlier studies.[15] They make clear that the *Sçavans* was subjected to continuous government supervision—in contrast to the relatively free enterprise which characterized the extraterritorial journals. Founded in 1665 under Colbert's auspices and informally bound to the French crown by financing and patronage, the *Sçavans* did not become a fully official organ until

[13] Cited by Réau, *L'Europe française*, 20.

[14] Jean Pierre Vittu, who is completing his doctoral dissertation on the topic, has two articles in print: 'Diffusion et réception du *Journal des Savants* de 1665 à 1714', in Bots (ed.), *La Diffusion*, 167–75; 'Les Contrefaçons du *Journal des Savants*', in F. Moureau (ed.), *Les Presses grises: Le Contrefaçon du livre* (Paris, 1988), 303–31. His forthcoming article, '*Journal des Savants* 1665–1792', will appear in *Dictionnaire de la presse*, vol. i, ed. Jean Sgard. I owe him thanks for letting me see his work to date.

[15] In addition to works mentioned in nn. 4 and 9 by Betty T. Morgan, and Ehrard and Roger, see Raymond Birn, 'Le *Journal des savants* sous l'Ancien Régime', *Journal des savants* (1965), 15–35.

after 1700 (when the French book trade was reorganized by Chancellor Pontchartrain and his nephew, Abbé Bignon, was put in charge.)

Nevertheless, its editor, Denis de Sallo, ran into trouble almost as soon as the first issues appeared. He had to contend, at first, with aggrieved authors who objected to unfavourable reviews; then with the Ultramontanist party (for favouring a Gallican work that was put on the Index); finally and fatally with the Crown itself (for being too closely affiliated with Jansenists). After de Sallo was forced to retire, a more docile editor was appointed. Gallois followed a policy of avoiding controversy, refusing to review works likely to cause scandals and invariably praising the innocuous works selected for review. The next editor, De la Rocque, who took over in 1674, tried to enliven the journal by downplaying book reviews and featuring stories of monsters and freaks sent in by provincial correspondents.[16] These desperate measures were taken in vain. The journal became vulnerable to the charge of being timid, lustreless, and dull. De la Roque retired in 1687, leaving the journal without an editor for ten months. Before he retired, he noted that the strict controls to which the journal was subject made it impossible for any editor to match the competition that was beginning to come from abroad. De la Roque's competitors, safely ensconced in Holland, commiserated with his plight. Shortly before launching his own journal, Pierre Bayle wrote to Jean Le Clerc that the *Sçavans* editor had been kept on too tight a leash. He (Bayle) had been told he could have a freer hand 'in order to attract plenty of readers and ensure profits for his publisher'.[17]

Who was this publisher? Who launched the *Nouvelles de la République des lettres*, selected Pierre Bayle to be its editor, and told him he would be given a relatively free hand? He was Henry Desbordes, an expatriate who belonged to a Huguenot publishing dynasty and who exemplified that linkage with an earlier European book trade which was discussed in Chapter 1. His father and grandfather, Isaac I and Isaac II Desbordes, had served heterodox Protestant scholars in La Rochelle and Saumur as Huguenot publishers and scholar printers.[18] Henry Desbordes

---

[16] Vittu, 'Diffusion', 171.   [17] Birn, '*Journal des savants*', 25.
[18] Henri-Jean Martin, *Livre, pouvoirs et société à Paris au XVIIe siècle* (2 vols. Geneva, 1969), ii. 740–4.

has the unique distinction of presiding over the literary début of Jean Le Clerc, the journalistic début of Pierre Bayle, and of going to prison for publishing a work by Pierre Jurieu. Le Clerc, Bayle, and Jurieu became bitter enemies in exile. But they were allies when they first arrived in Holland and each in his own way was indebted to Desbordes.

His first service was performed in 1681 while he was still in Saumur. There, using the pseudonym 'Philalethianis', he published a volume of Latin theological essays taking issue with prevailing Calvinist dogma. The author, who called himself 'Liberius', was a young and unknown Genevan pastor who was visiting the Protestant Academy and whose real name was Jean Le Clerc. When the edition was threatened with seizure by censors, the copies were sent to Holland to be sold. Desbordes soon followed, after spending a term in prison for having published Pierre Jurieu's attack on Bossuet. By 1682 he was admitted to the publishers' guild in Amsterdam and took it on himself to launch a francophone review journal: the *Mercure sçavant* edited by a French physician, Nicolas de Blegny, whose previous venture as a journal editor in France had failed. In Desbordes's preface to the first issue: 'Le Libraire au Lecteur', the publisher characteristically assured the reader that even while the journal would satisfy curiosity about 'les sciences', 'la galanterie' would not be forgotten.[19] The publisher's assurances notwithstanding, the venture was a failure. De Blegny's forte was medical advice, not supplying lively reviews of new books. Undaunted, Desbordes decided to launch a new journal with a new editor. Upon the recommendation of Pierre Jurieu, he selected Pierre Bayle.[20]

The *Nouvelles de la république des lettres*, the first and perhaps most celebrated of all the cosmopolitan review journals, was thus initiated by its publisher in March 1684, as a spin-off from his other business. By and large this was the pattern which would be followed in the course of the ensuing century. Scientific data collection, political reporting, literary criticism were thus propelled by a series of new ventures which were initiated by publisher-booksellers, who were carrying on a long-term cosmopolitan

[19] Otto S. Lankhorst, 'Le Rôle des libraire-imprimeurs néerlandais dans l'édition des journaux littéraires de langue française (1684–1750)', in Bots (ed.), *La Diffusion*, 1–11: p. 2–3.

[20] Annie Barnes, *Jean Le Clerc et la république des lettres* (Paris, 1938), 59, 68, 97.

book trade.[21] The publishers owned the journal titles; they chose the editors and correspondents; in several instances they served as their own editors. 'The *Bibliothèque Angloise,* the *Journal Littéraire,* the *Bibliothèque Françoise,* the *Bibliothèque Raisonnée,* and the *Bibliothèque Impartiale* are cases in point where the bookdealer is at the same time printer and editor and has one or several authors working for him whom he pays per sheet of printed copy.'[22] And in most instances, they supplied the books that were to be reviewed.[23]

Up to a point, indeed, one might describe the journals as more elaborate versions of the book catalogues which had been issued periodically in earlier eras. Books on one's own list were featured prominently. But books were also supplied by routine exchanges with other firms. It should be remembered that, in their capacity as booksellers, the publishers sold works issued by other firms than their own. Publicity was helpful for boosting sales of a diversified stock and for the expansion of a given business. Periodicals engendered lists of subscribers and enabled publisher-booksellers to keep in regular contact with potential clients and contributors. Readers were constantly being solicited for materials to be reviewed or notices to be inserted, always provided no postal costs had to be paid—or almost always: Reinier Leers paid all the costs which were incurred by the far-flung correspondence conducted by Henri Basnage de Beauval, editor of the *Histoire des ouvrages des savans.*[24] The extent to which this journal depended on the initiative of its publisher is suggested by its fate; when Leers sold his business in 1709, the journal ended its run.

The Netherlands publishers were in the unusual position of serving as their own patrons and sponsors. Here again one notes a marked contrast with the prototypical *Journal des sçavans.* In comparison with figures such as Henry Desbordes and Reinier

---

[21] The importance of the initiative taken by the publishers was noted long ago by Sherman B. Barnes, 'The Editing of Early Learned Journals', *Osiris,* 1 (1936), 156-72: p. 166.

[22] Uta Janssens, *Matthieu Maty and the Journal britannique 1750-1755* (Amsterdam, 1975), 56.

[23] The diverse functions performed by the publishers is well illustrated by Lankhorst, 'Le Rôle'.

[24] Hans Bots and Lenie van Lieshout, *Contribution à la connaissance des réseaux d'information au début du XVIIIe siècle: Henri Basnage de Beauval et sa correspondance—lettres et index* (Amsterdam, 1984), p. iiv.

Leers, Jean Cusson who served as printer-publisher of the *Journal des sçavans* was and still is extremely obscure.[25] He had apparently become acquainted with Denis de Sallo when both men were pursuing legal careers and served as councillors to the Paris Parlement. He had inherited a small firm at the sign of St John the Baptist on the Rue Saint-Jacques; his widow and son continued to publish the *Sçavans* after his death in 1704. Whereas Desbordes selected Bayle, one gains the impression that de Sallo took the initiative with Cusson.[26] At least one authority, however, has detected signs of some influence being exerted by the publisher in the journal's editorial policy.[27]

It would be nice to know whether it was Jean Cusson or Denis de Sallo who provided the first issue with its celebrated preface: 'De l'imprimeur au lecteur'. Perhaps, as Harcourt Brown suggests, it was the outcome of a collaborative effort. Whoever it was, he (or they) produced an exceptionally influential text; one which was used for guidance by later editors and which fixed the mission of the review journal in a long-lasting mould. It began by proclaiming the intention of reporting all news of interest to the Republic of Letters with a resonating phrase: 'le dessin de faire savoir ce que se passe de nouveau dans la République des Lettres'.[28]

The preface makes clear that editorial policy would assign priority to books. It promised to take note of all important books and to offer not merely a list of titles, but also a review of contents and an appraisal of a given work's value. This marked the inauguration of the book review—an event which is only now beginning to receive the attention it deserves. Chapter 1 mentioned the unfortunate tendency to treat book history and journalism history as separate specialities. When these specialities go their separate ways, significant topics such as the book review are

25 His name is absent from text and index of Morgan's study.

26 Cusson served as printer-publisher from 1665 until he died in 1704; his widow took over until 1714. For pertinent documentation, see Jean Pierre Vittu, '*Journal des savants*' in *Dictionnaire de la presse*. On Cusson's law studies and friendship with de Sallo see Harcourt Brown, 'History and the Learned Journal', *Journal of the History of Ideas*, 33 (1972), 365–78: p. 368.

27 Brown, 'History and the Learned Journal', 368–9.

28 'L'Imprimeur au lecteur', *Le Journal des sçavans*, 'par le Sieur de Hedouville', 1 (5 Jan. 1665). On the phrase '*république des lettres*' see Françoise Waquet, 'Qu'est-ce que la république des lettres? Essai de sémantique historique', *Bibliothèque de l'École des Chartes*, 147 (1989), 473–501.

likely to fall between the cracks, to the detriment of specialists in both fields. As has been recently demonstrated by Claude Labrosse, historians concerned with reader reception need to pay more attention to the reviews which loomed so large in the early periodicals. Labrosse describes how they functioned as 'previews' and guided readers' reactions to a given book even before the full text itself had been·perused.[29]

Nor can historians of journalism afford to leave reviews of books to historians of literature while tracking down other kinds of news. For the indignant reactions of authors to unfavourable book reviews inaugurated a debate that is still current over the proper functions of reporters and journalists. Should they simply report relevant facts or should they appraise, interpret, judge? Perhaps the earliest insistence that journalists should limit themselves to factual and 'impartial' reporting came in the 1660s from disappointed authors who questioned the competence of anonymous reviewers to judge their works. The journal should confine itself to summarizing a book's contents, ran the complaint; it should pass no judgement on whether a work was good or bad. Above all, reviewers should refrain from acting as tyrants in the empire of letters.[30]

The primacy given to book reviews also aroused displeasure from a different quarter, from natural philosophers, physicians, and followers of the new sciences who expected the French journal to devote more space to instruments and experiments. 'Why the devil always books, books, books and nothing else!' complained a Florentine count.[31] Reports of new experiments, discoveries, machines, and inventions, although not emphasized enough according to some virtuosi, were explicitly set forth in the preface as part of the journal's mission. Internal evidence suggests that this mission was taken seriously. Even the small (octavo) editions of the journal which I consulted contained pull-outs of diagrams and drawings illustrating what was seen under

---

[29] Claude Labrosse, 'Fonctions culturelles du périodique littéraire', P. Rétat and C. Labrosse (eds.), *L'Instrument périodique* (Lyons, 1985), 7-136.

[30] Pertinent citations are given by Vittu, 'Diffusion', in Bots (ed.), *La Diffusion*, 167-75: p. 170. Guy Patin's anger at the treatment accorded a history of medals written by his favourite second son, Charles, and the comment concerning tyranny in the empire of letters is discussed by Morgan, *Histoire*, 79, 137.

[31] 'Che diavolo sempre libri, libri, libri e non altro.' Letter of Lorenzo Magalotti to Ottavio Falconieri, cited by Vittu, 'Diffusion', 170.

microscopes or through telescopes. There was, for example, the magnification of the eye of a flea taken from the *Micrographia*. But it appeared in the context of a review of Hooke's book. Apart from occasional brief reports and extracts from other learned journals, scientific reportage in the *Sçavans* was largely a matter of reviewing scientific books. On the whole the count was right. Unlike the *Philosophical Transactions*, 'books, books, books' dominated the journal. The trend would become even more pronounced in the extraterritorial literary reviews.[32] Much as a new debate over the proper functions of a journal was precipitated by the book review, so new divisions were opened up between scientists and literati as a result of decisions concerning appropriate allocations of space.

Another feature which was inaugurated with far-reaching consequences was the obituary column. The preface to the *Sçavans* promised to take note of the deaths of all celebrated authors and to accompany each notice with a bio-bibliographical account. This feature, which harked back to fifteenth-century practices,[33] enabled the cosmopolitan Republic of Letters to assume a self-congratulatory posture by performing the same sort of functions that were assigned to royal academies and that would be exemplified in Fontenelle's celebrated *Éloges*. It contributed to the eventual 'sacre de l'écrivain', recently described by Paul Benichou and discerned long ago by Carlyle in his essay on 'the Hero as a Man of Letters'.

Unlike Fontenelle's eulogies, which were sponsored by the Royal Academy of Sciences, the tributes delivered by the expatriate editors were detached from institutional affiliation and provided occasions for the affirmation of intellectual autonomy. When he announced the policy on eulogies to be followed by his journal, for example, Pierre Bayle was emphatic about basing selection on the single criterion of service to knowledge. We will not enquire about religious affiliation, he wrote, but only about contributions to knowledge. Monks will receive attention along

---

[32] When the Calvinist physician, Pierre Silvestre, complained to Bayle that the journals of Le Clerc et al. were too preoccupied with theology and *belles-lettres* and neglected reportage of experiments and discoveries, he mentioned the *Journal des sçavans* along with the *Philosophical Transactions* as being of more use to scientists. E. Labrousse, 'Les Coulisses', in Dibon (ed.), *Bayle*, 97–141: pp. 103–4.

[33] See discussion of Johannes Trithemius's *Liber de Scriptoribus Ecclesiasticis* and same author's *Catalogus Illustrium Virorum Germaniae* in Eisenstein, *Printing Press*, i. 94.

with everyone else: 'all Savants should regard each other as brothers. We are all equal as . . . children of Apollo'.[34] The brotherhood of intellectuals in other words, should take precedence over the sectarian quarrels which divided men of cloth. (Of course, brotherhood is not incompatible with fratricide. Brothers or not, intellectuals have generally been a quarrelsome lot and *émigré* enclaves are especially prone to feuds. Bayle's envenomed relationship with Jean Le Clerc will be noted below.)

In addition to setting aside space for the commemoration of dead authors, the preface of 1665 also promised to provide space for notes, reports, letters, and other communications from correspondents and readers. Many years ago, Harcourt Brown noted that by thus providing a paper forum for discussion, the journal produced a 'kind of revolution in the world of letters'.[35] As with all revolutions, this one had antecedents. Appeals to readers to send in pertinent comments or data go back to prefaces contained in early printed reference works. The advent of printing had encouraged the articulation of new attitudes towards 'the public' which was viewed not as a many-headed monster but as a pool of potential collaborators in a process of data collection (and also of course as a pool of potential purchasers and/or subscribers). The advent of a periodical press and the competition between rival journals greatly increased the pressure to obtain continuous reader response. 'I entreat the assistance of all those who wish well to the progress of learning and beg they will favor me with extracts of curious books, with such original pieces and accounts of new inventions and machines and any other improvements . . . as are fit to be communicated to the public. In which case I shall either mention their names or observe a religious silence as they shall desire.'[36] The last sentence, offering contributors a choice between celebrity and anonymity, pointed to two of the seemingly contradictory features of print. Personal charisma and impersonal authority were both together heightened by the same medium. (The mask of pseudonymity provided yet another alternative.) Repeated calls for help issued to the public at large, the provision of space for letters to the editor, sometimes

---

[34] Preface to *Nouvelles de la république des lettres* (March 1684): 2nd edn. Amsterdam: Henry Desbordes, 1686. [35] Brown, 'History and the Learned Journal', 377.
[36] *The Present State of the Republick of Letters* (6 vols. London: William and John Innys, 1720–30), i, Preface, p. iii] (by Andrew Reid, editor).

even the priming of the pump by writing letters under assumed names: all this did indeed constitute a 'kind of revolution in the world of letters'. To repeat a point made in Chapter 1, such features are surely worth more attention in any discussion of the structural transformation of a 'public sphere'.

Letters to the editor were open letters and in this regard they were subtly different from the hand-copied correspondence which had been the chief means of scientific and literary reporting in the seventeenth century. Semi-private correspondence acquired a more impersonal form when unknown readers were invited to serve as contributors even while remaining nameless. Perhaps it was partly to compensate for the impersonality of this new mode of association that fictitious societies and clubs were created. The first appearance of the club framework in literature was John Dunton's Athenian Society. Dunton, a London bookseller, hit on the ingenious idea of running a question-and-answer column in his *Athenian Gazette* (1691–7). Hoping to impress his readers with credentials resembling those of the Royal Society he also created an imaginary gathering of learned men which he described in flattering terms in his 'history of the Athenian Society'. He decorated the frontispiece of his *Young Student's Library*, a large compendium of translated extracts from various learned cosmopolitan reviews of the day, with an engraving showing the so-called 'Athenians' conferring with each other. The Athenian Society was a forerunner of Mr Spectator's Club. It also owed much to Dunton's close reading of the cosmopolitan literary reviews and of the prototypical *Journal des sçavans* as well.[37]

In keeping with its appeal to an undifferentiated public, the final words of the preface to the *Sçavans* proclaimed an intention to serve all men of letters, not just those who bought books but also those who could not afford them and yet wanted to have a general knowledge of them. In the letter from Jacob Bayle to his younger brother Pierre, mentioned earlier, Jacob wrote enthusi-

---

[37] Gilbert McEwen, *The Oracle of the Coffee House: John Dunton's 'Athenian Mercury'* (San Marino, Calif., 1972) and Stephen Parks, *John Dunton and the English Book Trade* (New York, 1976) offer pertinent data. McEwen holds (pp. 51–2) that Dunton's project owed much to Jean Cornand de la Crose, an early associate of Jean Le Clerc's who moved to London in 1687. He follows A. Barnes, *Jean Le Clerc*, 117, in attributing to de la Crose responsibility for founding an English version of Le Clerc's journal, *The Universal and Historical Bibliotheque*, but this attribution is wrong, according to Parks.

astically about the new journal as being especially helpful to anyone beginning to acquire a library since it offered a guide to books to be bought. It was also useful, he added, to those who could not afford many books, since one could gain a general acquaintance of them without purchasing them.[38]

This letter suggests that the review journals ought to figure more prominently in recent discussions of 'intensive' as against 'extensive' reading practices. In my view, both practices have long coexisted and it is misguided to look for a shift from one to another in any one time-frame such as the mid-eighteenth century.[39] After all, the usefulness of quickly skimming many books and, at the same time, carefully reading a few was noted in a celebrated sixteenth-century essay: 'Some books are to be tasted, others to be swallowed and some few to be chewed and digested.'[40] There is also the 'intensive reading' of Bibles among fundamentalists today to be compared with the wide-ranging reading of Renaissance literati. Furthermore, collections and anthologies, such as John Dunton's *Young Student's Library* of the 1690s or the *Book of Knowledge* known to American youngsters in this century, offer outlines and extracts, poems, and stories taken from many books, even while serving as a single book to be possessed, read, and reread from cover to cover. Such considerations also apply to the functions performed by the review journals. They certainly made it easier to get a glancing acquaintance with many books by way of abridgements, abstracts, and summaries. Encounters with diverse journals in reading-rooms and coffee-houses meant encountering divergent views of the same books and this may have helped to sharpen the critical faculties of some *cognoscenti*. At the same time, the journals also served readers with limited access to books as little portable libraries that were read and reread—read 'intensively', that is, to the point where their contents were completely absorbed. Jacob Bayle, writing to his younger brother about the new journal, seems to have memorized the printer's preface almost word for

[38] Cited in Labrousse, 'Les Coulisses', in Dibon (ed.), *Bayle*, 99.

[39] A useful summary of the so-called 'reading revolution' or 'leserevolution' discerned by Rolf Engelsing in his studies of 18th-cent. German practices is given by Roger Chartier, *The Cultural Uses of Print in Early Modern France*, tr. L. Cochrane (Princeton, NJ, 1987), 223–4.

[40] Francis Bacon, 'Of Studies', *Essayes* (1597), in S. Warhaft (ed.), *Francis Bacon: A Selection of his Works* (Toronto, 1965), 33.

word. In his own first editorial, Pierre Bayle indicated his intention to provide a full account of a few books and also a brief account of many.

Although the *Journal des sçavans* certainly served as a prototype for the later extraterritorial journals, the difficulties experienced by its editors in the 1670s and 1680s provided opportunities that the expatriate editors were quick to exploit. The contrast between the constraints imposed by royal officials and churchmen and the freedom enjoyed by those who had only their publishers to please was indeed repeated so often in editorials that it become something of a cliché.

By the later eighteenth century, the mere fact that a journal was published outside France was held in its favour. In a letter to Beaumarchais of 10 April 1778, the editor of the *Courier de l'Europe* noted that if the *Courier* were published in France and thus subjected to Paris censorship it would lose all its 'originality, vivacity and energy'.[41] There was considerable irony in this instance. Once it was under way the *Courier* received subsidies from the French foreign minister in exchange for promoting Bourbon policies from London.[42] Its publisher never acted as a mere minion of the French, however, since he also took money from the British on the sly.[43] As John Adams shrewdly noted, the *Courier* was 'the most artful paper in the world, continually accommodating between the French and English ministry'.[44] Its 'originality, energy and vivacity' probably owed less to independence from ministerial supervision than to a nervous oscillation between two rival powers. The special circumstances which affected this particular paper however are somewhat beside the point. The point is that from Bayle's era to that of Beaumarchais, it was generally believed that intellectual energy could only flow freely in francophone journals produced outside France. There is considerable evidence to suggest that this opinion was soundly

---

41 Cited by Jeremy Popkin, 'Le Paris révolutionnaire dans le système journalistique européen', in P. Rétat (ed.), *La Révolution du journal 1788-1794* (Paris, 1989), 109-16: p. 110.   42 Hatin, *Les Gazettes de Hollande*, 38.

43 Hélène Maspero-Clerc, 'Samuel Swinton, éditeur du *Courier de l'Europe* . . . et agent secret du gouvernement britannique', *Annales historiques de la révolution française*, 262 (1985), 525-31. A recent study presents relevant documents, Gunnar and Mavis von Proschwitz, 'Beaumarchais et le *Courier de l'Europe*: Documents inédits ou peu connus', *Studies in Voltaire* (1990), 273 and 274.

44 Cited by Popkin, 'Le Paris révolutionnaire', 110.

based. Avignon, for example, had a lively journal with a large circulation as long as it remained one of the papal states. When the territory was taken over by France between 1768 and 1774, and again after 1785, the paper lost its vivacity and circulation figures dropped.[45]

Pierre Bayle's celebrated preface to the first issue of the *Nouvelles de la république des lettres* (March 1684) helped to fix the invidious comparison between French controls and extra-territorial liberties in a permanent mould and seems worth paraphrasing at some length.[46] It starts out with a reference to the *Sçavans* as a prototype and goes on to underscore the advantages enjoyed by the residents of Holland over other countries. For one thing, there are more publishers here than in any other place in the world. For another, Dutch printers are so free that they can handle communications from all parts of Europe unencumbered by problems arising from having to obtain privileges. Had Milton lived in the Dutch Netherlands, he would not have needed to write Areopagitica. Our presses serve Catholic refugees as well as Protestant ones. So little do we fear the arguments of the adherents to Rome that their books are freely sold here—a far cry from the countries of the Inquisition where (according to reports) it is forbidden even for Catholics with controversial views to have their works displayed by booksellers, so fearful of argumentation are the censors. Liberty of the press ('cette honnête liberté de l'imprimerie') is so obviously advantageous to any journal serving savants it is surprising that no one has undertaken such a journal here in Holland.

We will steer a middle path between slavish flattery and stern censoriousness. We will exhibit no malice, show no prejudice either for or against any author . . . We do not claim to have any supreme authority . . . We will take on the role of a reporter rather than that of a judge. (As noted previously, it is in the guise of the book reviewer that the ideal impartial reporter makes his historical début. But the journalistic virtues of 'neutrality' and 'impartiality', previously upheld by disappointed authors reacting against unfavourable reviews in the *Sçavans*, were extended

---

[45] René Moulinas, *L'Imprimerie, la librairie et la presse à Avignon au XVIIIe siècle* (Grenoble, 1974).

[46] What follows is my translated paraphrase of the preface to *Nouvelles de la république des lettres* (March 1684).

by Bayle to encompass the extremely sensitive, value-laden arena of religious warfare.) We will offer faithful extracts of those books which oppose us as well as those which support us. (This passage contained a 'dig' at intolerant Calvinists such as Pierre Jurieu; but it was his disdain for Catholic censors that the presumably impartial editor repeatedly underscored.) Messieurs of Roman Catholic Church need not be alarmed by this journal. We will respect their sensitivities which are so acute. . . . We will be so circumspect that these *Nouvelles* will not be forbidden. (This was not a good prophecy. Entry of the journal into France was forbidden in January 1685, less than a year after its first issue.)[47] We will even indicate if a book contains anything suspicious so that Messieurs of the Congregation of the Index either in Rome or in Paris or elsewhere need not read much in order to know whether a book is contraband.

The editor of the *Nouvelles*, unlike that of the *Sçavans*, did not have to report to a crown minister and could poke fun at Catholic censors. But serving his publisher by attracting subscribers did have to be kept constantly in mind. In his account of major discontinuities between the seventeenth and eighteenth century, Herbert Butterfield singles out 'that appeal which came to a climax in Fontenelle and his successors—the appeal against the learned world of the time, against both Church and universities, to a new arbiter of human thought: the general reading public'.[48] This appeal to the 'general reading public' was manifested most consistently and powerfully in the new review journals, under pressure from the extraterritorial publishers.

As Elisabeth Labrousse points out, Bayle's venture into journalism showed a different side of the philosopher than the one that is usually depicted. Starting from Desmaiseaux's *Life of Bayle*, Bayle's biographers have portrayed him as a 'serene figure, indifferent to literary glory, enclosed in his study, detached from all prejudice'.[49] But far from being a closet philosopher remote

---

[47] Labrousse, 'Les Coulisses', in Dibon (ed.), *Bayle*, 115. See also J. A. H. Bots, 'Le Réfuge et les *Nouvelles de la république des lettres* de Pierre Bayle', in J. A. H. Bots and G. H. M. Posthumous Meyjes (eds.), *La Révocation de l'Édit de Nantes et les Provinces Unies* (International Conference at Leiden, Apr. 1985) (Amsterdam, 1986), 88.

[48] Herbert Butterfield, *The Origins of Modern Science 1300–1800* (New York, 1951), 128.

[49] Gustave Lanson, *Histoire de la littérature française* (14th edn. Paris, 1920), 637. Bayle's biographers thus followed the pattern set by Lucas's life of Spinoza according to

from the market-place, the editor of the *Nouvelles* exhibited a constant anxiety about his journal's appeal to the public.[50] Intent on making his review attractive to readers, he introduced running headlines and tables of contents, took care to translate Latin titles into French and persistently solicited letters to the editor. In June 1684, he wrote to Jean Le Clerc that he was being urged to aim his journal beyond the limited circle of savants toward the larger social milieu inhabited by Chevaliers and Ladies and all other intelligent readers, to strike a happy medium between the gossipy gazette and the scientific journal, to include reviews of light matter, and to diversify as much as possible.[51] In addition he never ceased to be anxious (just as he had been as a youth, writing to his brother from the provinces) about keeping up to date on recent and forthcoming books. Two years after the journal got going he vented his fury at the failure of publishers and booksellers to respond to his requests for review copies. He described how wrong he had been to put Holland at the centre of the European book trade and to have once held such a high opinion of Dutch publishers.[52]

Bayle's concern about keeping his readers *au courant* doubtless owed something to his recollection of his own existence as a young provincial who yearned in vain for news of books and authors. His anger was probably also fuelled by news of the Revocation, which must have been a terrible blow to one who insisted that French Protestants must never waver in their loyalty to their King. But his anxiety about being adequately supplied with material and his sense of being betrayed also owed something to the unwelcome appearance in 1686 of a new francophone cosmopolitan review journal, the *Bibliothèque universelle et historique*. This competing journal was issued by a syndicate of

Paul Vernière, *Spinoza et la pensée française avant la révolution* (2 vols. Paris, 1954), ii. 27. On Lucas, see Ch. 3 n. 76 below. How the image of Bayle depicted in Desmaiseaux's *Life* was appended to the 1730 edn. of the *Dictionnaire philosophique*, and then was sanctified by Voltaire, is described by P. Rétat, *Le Dictionnaire de Bayle et la lutte philosophique au XVIIIᵉ siècle* (Paris, 1971), 132-3.

[50] Labrousse, 'Les Coulisses', in Dibon (ed.), *Bayle*, 105, compares him to a merchant engaged in market research.

[51] Cited by H. C. Hazewinkel, 'Pierre Bayle à Rotterdam', in Dibon (ed.), *Bayle*, 20-47: pp. 28-9.

[52] 'Avertissement de l'auteur', *Nouvelles de la république des lettres* (Jan. 1686). In the June issue, a note (p. 732) indicated that the angry editor was partly mollified by having learnt that he had made the publishers feel ashamed of themselves.

Amsterdam publishers who were 'eager to cash in on the success of the *Nouvelles*'[53] and who were well supplied with books. It was to be edited by a former collaborator soon to become bitter enemy, Jean Le Clerc.

Le Clerc had been a contributor to Bayle's journal. For him to join a competing enterprise smacked of disloyalty. Indeed Le Clerc had hesitated to serve as a rival editor until after the two men had a falling out over Bayle's unfavourable reaction to a theological work by Le Clerc which, in Bayle's opinion, betrayed the influence of Spinoza. This work gained Le Clerc international notoriety as an audacious biblical critic and theologian. Against Bayle's criticism, Le Clerc offered the weak defence that he had set forth Spinozist views only in order to expose them for refutation. Bayle did not pursue the issue but remained unpersuaded. Shortly after the first issue of the new journal had appeared, Bayle wrote contemptuously to a friend about the way Le Clerc boldly publicized heretical writings and condemned everyone else's work save that of a favoured few. Ill feeling between these two leading citizens of the Republic of Letters only became more envenomed as the years passed.[54]

As noted above, advocacy of toleration on the part of the expatriate editors went hand in hand with embittered internecine warfare. A long-lived thesis set forth many years ago held that the journals edited by Bayle and Le Clerc simply served as vehicles of a concerted Protestant propaganda offensive mounted by Anglo-Dutch forces.[55] But the editors scarcely presented a united front. Not only did they reject Calvinist orthodoxies along with Catholic ones. They also rejected heterodox views which differed from their own. Bayle's quarrels with orthodox Catholics and Calvinists were in many ways less bitter than his feuds

[53] S. Barnes, 'Editing of Journals', 167.

[54] A. Barnes, *Le Clerc*, 109-15. (On the intensification of the feud between the two men after 1699, see pp. 228-37.) Barnes's treatment needs supplementing by more recent accounts. See e.g. discussion of theological and philosophical issues in Maria C. Pitassi, *Entre croire et savoir: Le Problème de la méthode critique chez Jean Le Clerc* (Leiden, 1987), 19-21. On Bayle's initial hostility to Le Clerc's journal, see H. Bots, 'Un journaliste sur les journaux de son temps: Le Cas de Pierre Bayle', *La Diffusion*, 203-11: p. 210. Bots notes Bayle's preference for the *Histoire des ouvrages des savants*, ed. by his hand-picked successor, Henri Basnage de Beauval, and published by Bayle's chief patron and publisher, Reinier Leers.

[55] Jacques Marx, 'La *Bibliothèque impartiale*: Étude de contenu', in M. Couperus (ed.), *L'Étude des périodiques* (Paris, 1972), 89-107: p. 90, refers to a key work by Abbé Joseph Dédieu, *Le Rôle politique des Protestants français* (Paris, 1921).

with Arminian and Remonstrant writers such as Le Clerc and Le Clerc's cousin Jacques Bernard.[56] Bayle's fideist leanings were fundamentally incompatible with Le Clerc's lifelong commitment to a rational theology.[57] Theological doctrines loomed especially large in the disputes between the Genevan and the Frenchman. Questions pertaining to literary property rights played a more important role after Bayle's death, in the rivalry over the disposition of his literary estate. Politics and aesthetics came to the fore in the later feud between factions siding with Voltaire against Jean Baptiste Rousseau. But all such disputes showed how intolerant of each other fellow advocates of toleration could be.

That the new standards of impartiality upheld in editorials should not be taken at face value needs to be underlined. When used as organs of feuding factions, the cosmopolitan journals carried reviews and reports that were partisan in the extreme. In some instances, the publisher, fearful of alienating readers and determined to maintain at least the appearance of fair play, found it necessary to intervene. In other cases, the publishers were themselves partisan and editors were given a free hand.[58] In so

[56] Jacques Bernard (1658-1718) on his maternal side was, like Jean Le Clerc, descended from the Gallatin family. He also studied under Chouet at the Genevan Academy and became a pastor in 1679. After leaving Lausanne for Leiden, he obtained a chair of philosophy at the university. He took over from his cousin as editor of the *Bibliothèque universelle et historique* (1691-3) and then, in a move which became the source of much later confusion, became editor of the *Nouvelles de la république des lettres* (1699-1710). (After a 6-year lapse he resumed the editorship from 1716 to 1718.) Jacques Bernard was often accused of Socinian leanings and sided with his cousin against Bayle. As an editor of the *Nouvelles*, he was Bayle's successor but only in a literal or nominal sense. Bayle's true hand-picked successor as editor, Henri Basnage de Beauval, ran a different journal, the *Histoire des ouvrages des savants* (1687-1709), published by Reinier Leers.   [57] This is brought out by Pitassi, *Croire et savoir*, 19-21.

[58] Joseph Almagor, *Pierre Des Maizeaux (1673-1745)* (Amsterdam, 1989), 79-101, provides a detailed account of how the feud over Bayle's literary estate between Pierre Desmaiseaux and Prosper Marchand (together with the latter's publishers, Fritsch and Böhm) was carried on in the following journals: *Histoire critique de la république des lettres*, ed. Samuel Masson (Utrecht, 1712-18); *Nouvelles littéraires*, ed. Henri du Sauzet (The Hague, 1715-20); and the *Journal literaire* (The Hague), which numbered Marchand on its board of editors, as discussed below. Almagor describes how the two journals associated with Masson and Marchand carried on the vendetta while du Sauzet (a publisher as well as editor) intervened to discontinue it. Other feuds, between Rousset de Missy (in the *Bibliothèque raisonnée* and *L'Épilogueur moderne*) and La Barre de Beaumarchais (*Lettres sérieuses et badines*), and between the Catholic publisher, Jean van Duren, and the Protestant one, Pierre Paupie, in the 1730s and 1740s, are noted by Jean Sgard, Discussion, in Couperus (ed.), *L'Étude des périodiques*, 106-7. See also below, Ch 3, pp. 86, 98.

far as they helped to perpetuate vendettas, the journals scarcely provided a 'neutral space' dedicated to rational criticism. As often as not, they served as the vehicles of a covert warfare between rival factions.

Le Clerc's preface to the first issue of the *Bibliothèque universelle et historique* must have wounded Bayle, for it pointed with some complacency to the advantages of the new editor's position. In the course of justifying the appearance of yet another review journal, given the work already under way in Paris, Leipzig, and Rotterdam, Le Clerc echoed Bayle's remarks on the advantages of living in a free country, but he also noted that some editors lived too far away from the centres of the book trade and so received too few books too late. He pointed to the special advantage of being in Amsterdam and of serving a syndicate of firms, 'the best equipped and most celebrated in all of Europe'. In addition, the task of covering all important works produced throughout Europe should not be left to any one editor since no single individual had command of all languages or of all topics. This statement seemed unexceptional and indeed it merely repeated a prefatory comment previously made by Bayle. But it could also be taken as a reminder that Le Clerc had developed one useful skill that Bayle lacked. Unlike the Frenchman who never did learn to read English, the Genevan had mastered it as a literary language. His journal would be celebrated for the amount of space it devoted to intellectual developments across the Channel.[59] In another passage which points to the far-flung public he had in mind, he underscored the advantages of facility with modern languages. There's no need to put your contributions in French or Latin, he wrote in his preface. If it is easier for you to write in English, Italian, or German, I can assure you of a faithful translation.[60]

Jean Le Clerc proved to have a special flair for the functions he assumed and much greater staying power than did his one-time

[59] A. Barnes, *Le Clerc*, 74. See also Hendrika J. Reesink, *L'Angleterre et la littérature anglaise dans les plus anciens périodiques français de 1684 à 1709* (Paris, 1931). Le Clerc, however, never did learn to speak English. Like Bayle, moreover, he knew no Dutch.

[60] Preface, *Bibliothèque universelle et historique de l'année MDCLXXXVI* (Amsterdam: Wolfgang, Waesberge, Boom, and Van Someren, 1686), i. Another prefatory passage anticipated the citation from *The Present State of the Republic of Letters* (at n. 36), by promising that the desire of any contributor to remain anonymous would be respected and anonymous contributions would be welcome.

friend. Bayle's journalistic career ended in 1689 when he turned his energies to writing the *Dictionnaire philosophique*. Although Le Clerc's editorial activities on his three *bibliothèques* were interrupted from time to time by other projects, taken together they spanned an interval of forty odd years.[61] These four decades of service placed him in a position of unrivalled pre-eminence within the Republic of Letters. The correspondence he received from such figures as Leibniz in Hanover and Vico in Naples testify to his immense prestige. Vico in particular was pathetically grateful for Le Clerc's acknowledgement of the value of his work and wrote that it encouraged him to complete his 'New Science'.[62]

Jean Le Clerc represented that 'third force' in Europe to which I alluded in Chapter 1 perhaps even more fully than did Bayle. As a Genevan he was not troubled, as was Bayle, by any sense of residual loyalty to a dynastic ruler. He also broke more publicly and formally than did Bayle with the orthodox Calvinist tradition in which he had been reared; by joining the Dutch Remonstrants and renouncing the *Consensus Helveticus* to which he had sworn allegiance as a young Genevan pastor. This break was not easy for Le Clerc. When forced to leave Geneva because of his heterodox views, he went first to London hoping to find a position among the Latitudinarians within the Anglican Church. It was his trip to England in search of a post, and not his later editorial work, which provided the incentive for his learning English.[63] But he failed to find any patron or post in England during 1682–3 and indeed had to rely on hand-outs sent by his Dutch mentor Philip van Limborch (via the latter's publisher, Henry Wetstein).[64] Only after his English venture failed, did he cross

---

[61] *Bibliothèque universelle et historique* (1686–93); *Bibliothèque choisie* (1703–13); *Bibliothèque ancienne et moderne* (1714–26).

[62] A. Barnes, *Le Clerc*, 209–12. That Vico regarded Le Clerc's favourable notice as partial compensation for his failure to achieve local academic success is evident from scattered references contained in *The Autobiography of Giambattista Vico*, tr. and ed. M. H. Fisch and T. G. Bergin (Ithaca, NY, 1944). See under 'Le Clerc' in index.

[63] He mastered the language by working on a tr. into Latin of John Hammond's *Annotations on the New Testament* (1653). When his heavily annotated 2-vol. tr. ultimately appeared in 1698, its critical apparatus infuriated conservative Anglicans; one of whom wrote a rebuttal vindicating Hammond 'from the Rude and Unjust Reflections made upon him by M. Le Clerc'. A. Barnes, *Le Clerc*, 141 n. 1. Le Clerc's trs. and edns. almost always put a 'spin' on the original text.

[64] A. Barnes, *Le Clerc*, 70. Van Limborch's publisher, Henry or Johann Heinrich Wetstein, who had been an apprentice of Daniel Elsevier, should not be confused with

the Channel which served as his Rubicon and break his oath to uphold the *Consensus Helveticus*. He joined van Limborch in Amsterdam and became a member of the Remonstrant congregation there. His relationship with this Dutch congregation was frequently strained, partly perhaps because he spoke no Dutch. But van Limborch, with whom he conversed in Latin, managed to intervene on his protégé's behalf, securing for his needy friend a pension and ultimately a permanent seminary post.[65]

In making this decisive break with the Genevan Church, Jean Le Clerc was, in one sense, cutting himself off from his familial 'roots' as well as the Genevan milieu in which he had been reared. His mother, née Gallatin, belonged to one of the Republic's first families. His father had served on the town councils and ultimately was made a magistrate, thus becoming one of Geneva's twenty-five governors. But, in another sense, Le Clerc was reaffirming ancestral traditions as well as the contemporary teachings of his Genevan mentors. He was linked by a dense network to the heterodox theologians of his own day and to the biblical humanists and scholar printers of earlier eras. His grandfather Nicolas, a refugee from Picardy who prospered as a Genevan merchant, had helped to finance the operations of Henri II Estienne. Jean claimed that he himself had inherited part of that famous printer's library. Closer ties to the Estiennes were manifested by Le Clerc's beloved teacher at the Genevan Academy, Jean Robert Chouet (who was also remembered affectionately by another former student, Pierre Bayle). Chouet's father was a Genevan publisher-bookseller who, with his brother, had bought the Estiennes' firm. Chouet's uncle, Louis Tronchin, was a leading light among the liberal theologians of Geneva who opposed the *Consensus Helveticus*. He served as Jean Le Clerc's teacher and mentor.[66]

During his student years, Le Clerc also managed, while travelling outside Geneva, to pick up heterodox works that he read on his own in order to keep up with new developments in Hebrew scholarship and biblical criticism. He read and was deeply

his cousin, Johann Jakob Wetstein (1693–1754), the Greek scholar who after being condemned in his native town of Basel as a Socinian, took up residence in Amsterdam, delivered a Latin eulogy at Le Clerc's funeral in 1736, and succeeded the latter as professor at the Remonstrant college in Amsterdam.

[65] A. Barnes, *Le Clerc*, 99.   [66] Ibid. 38.

impressed by Grotius's commentary on the New Testament; he also managed to obtain copies of Spinoza's *Tractatus Politico-Theologicus* and Richard Simon's *Histoire critique du Vieux Testament*.[67] But probably the most powerful influence exerted by heterodox publications came from his finding, while in Grenoble, a copy of a book written by an apostate from Calvinism whose works were unavailable in Geneva. The author was his own great-uncle Étienne de Courcelles. De Courcelles had been a Genevan pastor. His Latin edition of Descartes's *Discours sur la méthode* made that work known throughout Europe. After leaving the Genevan Church, he followed the pattern later pursued by his great-nephew, going to Amsterdam and accepting a post as professor of theology at the Dutch Remonstrant Seminary.[68]

In addition to his great-uncle, more immediate family members helped to shape Jean's career trajectory. His father, Étienne Le Clerc (named for the great-uncle), was not only engaged in Genevan civic affairs. He had started out as a physician but became absorbed in studying Greek editions of Hippocrates and abandoned medicine for classical scholarship; he held the Greek chair at the Genevan Academy before his elevation to the post of magistrate of the Republic. Jean's uncle David was a biblical scholar who held a chair of Hebrew at the same academy and taught other biblical languages (Arabic, Chaldean, Syriac) as well. Through his family, as well as his studies, Jean was thoroughly acquainted with all the controversies that swirled around polyglot versions of the Bible. His first publication in Holland was a collection of essays by his father and uncle on 'Sacred Questions', with an introduction and annotations by Jean. Published in 1684, by Wetstein, it presented the views of Le Clerc's relatives in a way that was more likely to appeal to Dutch Remonstrants than to Genevan Calvinists.[69] Its editorial

---

[67] How Le Clerc's reading of Grotius in 1677 started him on the road to Arminianism is noted by A. Barnes, *Le Clerc*, 49. See also Pitassi, *Croire et savoir*, 35-6. On Le Clerc's reactions to the biblical criticism of Spinoza and Simon, see A. Barnes, *Le Clerc*, 66-7, and Pitassi, *Croire et savoir*, 23.

[68] That his great-uncle's work acted upon Jean as a 'revelation' is underscored by A. Barnes, *Le Clerc*, 53. See also Pitassi, *Croire et savoir*, 105-6 n. 35. In an appendix (pp. 94-5) Pitassi gives a transcription (taken from a Le Clerc MS) of a tense interview held on 9 Sept. 1683 between the orthodox Calvinist professor of theology at Geneva, François Turretini, and Jean Le Clerc, who was defending himself against accusations of Arminian and Socinian leanings. There Turretini accuses Le Clerc of regarding Étienne de Courcelles as 'his God'. [69] A. Barnes, *Le Clerc*, 101-2.

apparatus was tilted in favour of certain propositions condemned by the *Consensus Helveticus*, including one on the vexed issue of the placement of Hebrew vowel points.[70]

Le Clerc's commemoration of his ancestors went together with contributions to the posthumous reputation of his own special culture heroes notably Grotius and Erasmus. The first issues of his first *Bibliothèque* opened with instalments of a long (73 pages) review essay of a new edition of the letters of Hugo Grotius, an essay which cast the Dutch Arminian in a heroic mould. It described his imprisonment by intolerant Calvinists, his dramatic escape, and his triumphant appearance in Paris where all the learned world flocked to hear him.[71] It also contained a note explaining that, in order not to tire the reader by devoting too many pages to a single book, the review was being offered in instalments with the sequel to follow in the next issue.

Unlike 'Joannes Clericus', the scholarly author of multi-volume works, 'Jean Le Clerc' the francophone journal editor was concerned about the possible restlessness of readers. The review was not explicitly aimed at getting the reading public of 1686 to flock to bookshops for a look at a collection of hitherto unpublished letters by Hugo Grotius. But it did serve the interests of the syndicate of publishers who sponsored the *Bibliothèque*; it was their edition of Grotius's letters which spearheaded the first two issues. Still, if Le Clerc was being helpful to the commercial interests of the syndicate, he was also being true to his own beliefs. His reading of Grotius's commentary on the New Testament had impressed him during his student years; his annotated edition of Grotius's *De Veritate* was produced after he

---

[70] See ibid. 102–3, for full title of *Quaestiones Sacrae* (Amsterdam: Henry Wetstein, 1684) and discussion of extensive annotations by its editor. Elsewhere (p. 58) she mentions Jean's investigation of polyglot Bibles as a 24-year-old on a visit to Saumur. There also, probably thanks to his friendship with Jacques Cappel, he read the celebrated work on vowel points by Jacques's cousin, the Hebrew scholar Louis Cappel whose publications alarmed orthodox Calvinists and led François Turretini to insist that the *Consensus* contain a clause asserting that the vowel points were dictated by the Holy Spirit. Pitassi, *Croire et savoir*, 18, 61, 153 n. 132, also discusses the issue of vowel points in connection with Le Clerc's opposition to the *Consensus Helveticus*. She points to a useful article: Richard A. Muller, 'The Debate over Vowel Points . . .', *Journal of Medieval and Renaissance Studies*, 10 (1980), 53–72. Muller notes controversy associated with Cappel's work and Brian Walton's London *Polyglotte* (1653–7). He sketches earlier 16th-cent. developments but skips over Bible printing. On disputes associated with Plantin's Antwerp *Polyglot* and the spin-off publication of Arias Montano's monograph, see my *Printing Press*, i. 332.

[71] *Bibliothèque universelle et historique*, 1 (Jan. 1686), 1–29, and 2 (Feb. 1686), 121–66.

had fully matured as a Latin scholar, some twenty years after the first issues of the *Bibliothèque universelle* had appeared. After being translated from Latin into English, this version ran through some nine editions; it was Le Clerc's Grotius that most eighteenth-century English readers knew.

Le Clerc also did much for Erasmus's posthumous fame. Even while bringing the work of the Christian humanist to the attention of both Latin and French reading publics, he downplayed Erasmus's anti-Lutheran pro-Catholic positions and stressed anticipations of the doctrines held by Remonstrants in his own day. There was his great multi-volume folio Latin edition of the collected works; there was also a French essay on the life of the Rotterdam scholar which was published in instalments in the *Bibliothèque choisie*. The reader was told how Erasmus inspired envy for his virtue and erudition and had enemies among both Catholics and Protestants while he was alive. Since his death and after the end of the religious wars, however, all those from both denominations who were reasonable and enlightened (*raisonnables et éclairées*) joined in praising his erudition, his moderation, and his love of liberty.[72]

His memorials to Erasmus and Grotius, along with his biblical criticism and theological studies, would make the name of 'Joannes Clericus' known to erudite contemporaries and to later scholars concerned with the history of learning.[73] But his chief claim to fame in the eyes of posterity would be as the French publicist, 'Jean Le Clerc', who alerted the European reading public to the work of an English physician, residing as an exile in Holland from 1683–9, named John Locke. Le Clerc did not merely publicize Locke's work; although he certainly did that. He played a major role in persuading the exiled philosopher to use the press to air his views. As Rosalie Colie put it, 'Locke had not got the publishing habit' until he encountered Limborch and Le Clerc.[74] In July 1686, Locke made his début in print at the urging of Le Clerc, who arranged for an essay on organizing commonplace

---

[72] 'Des Erasmi Opera', *Bibliothèque choisie* (Amsterdam: Wetstein, 1703), i, article IX, 379 ff.

[73] A Portrait of 'Joannes Clericus' illustrates Ch. 3 (Fig. 7). The Latin scholar depicted by Bernard Picart is in front of a bookshelf containing Le Clerc's tr. of Hammond's New Testament commentary (see n. 63 above).

[74] R. Colie, 'John Locke in the Republic of Letters', in J. S. Bromley and E. H. Kossmann (eds.), *Britain and the Netherlands* (London, 1960), 111–30: p. 123.

books to appear in the *Bibliothèque universelle*. In January 1688, the same journal offered a 90-page French translation of an extract from a work by Locke which had not yet appeared in English—a philosophical essay concerning understanding. Not until two years later was the full English version published in London and advertised by Le Clerc in his journal.[75]

Extracts from each of Locke's other treatises were carried in Le Clerc's journals thereafter.[76] (The 'Two Treatises of Government' thus received exposure in a form that is sometimes overlooked.)[77] The English philosopher was also persuaded to contribute review essays of his own.[78] There is some question as to whether or not he was the author of an important review of Newton's *Principia*.[79] The reviewer noted with approval Newton's rejection of Descartes's whirlpool theory. Acceptance of the Newtonian as against the Cartesian cosmology (a position which would be popularized by Voltaire some forty years later) was advocated by Le Clerc himself in a Latin manual composed for the course he taught at the Remonstrant Seminary, a manual he dedicated to Locke.[80] When Newton sent Locke an anti-Trinitarian treatise he had written, Locke sent it on to Le Clerc to be translated into French and published anonymously. But the secretive physicist took fright and asked that the manuscript be withdrawn from publication. Le Clerc complied.[81]

[75] Interestingly enough, the abridged version of Locke's *Essay on Human Understanding* which appeared in John Dunton's *Young Student's Library* was a retranslation into English of the *Bibliothèque*'s French abridgement. It was in this form that the essay was first known to users of the Harvard College Library in 1723. Fiering, 'Notes and Documents', 650.

[76] A full listing is given in the index compiled by H. Bots et al. (eds.), *De 'Bibliothèque Universelle et Historique,' 1686–1693* (Amsterdam, 1981), 243–4.

[77] See Oscar and Lilian Handlin, 'Who Read John Locke?' and my letter to the editor: *The American Scholar*, 58 (1989); 59 (1990), 478.

[78] According to Maurice Cranston, *John Locke* (London, 1957), 293, Locke 'wrote nearly everything that was published in the *Bibliothèque Universelle* between July 1687 and February 1688'.

[79] This review appeared in the *Bibliothèque universelle*, 8 (Mar. 1688), 436–45. According to J. L. Axtell, 'Locke's Review of Newton's *Principia*', *Notes and Records of the Royal Society of London*, 20 (1965), 152–61, it was by Locke. Colie, 'Locke and the Republic of Letters', 124, concurs. But the authoritative index given by Bots et al. (see n. 76), 249, attributes it to Fatio de Duillier. On contributions made to Le Clerc's journals by de Duillier and by Robert Boyle see also H. Bots, 'Recueil des informations dans deux périodiques hollandais . . .', in P. Rétat (ed.), *Le Journalisme d'ancien régime* (Lyons, 1982), 55–67.   [80] A. Barnes, *Le Clerc*, 143.

[81] H. W. Turnbull et al. (eds.), *The Correspondence of Isaac Newton* (7 vols. Cambridge, 1959–77), iii. 123 n. See also Frank Manuel, *A Portrait of Isaac Newton* (Cambridge, Mass., 1968), 184, 218.

Among those who helped to usher in the age of Newton, Jean Le Clerc played a relatively minor role. The opposite was true of his role as an advocate of Locke. Aided by van Limborch, he held conferences in Amsterdam on Locke's work. He arranged to have Pierre Coste translate Locke's writings into French. In the ultimate tribute, anticipating a fashion followed by the disciples of Rousseau, Le Clerc assured Locke that he was bringing up his son in accordance with the precepts of Locke's treatise on education.[82] After Locke's death in 1704, Le Clerc assembled materials for a eulogy. His 'Éloge de Locke' which ran in the *Bibliothèque choisie* of 1705[83] was published in English the following year and still provides a basis for biographies of the English philosopher. It seems fair enough to say that Jean Le Clerc did as much as any single individual could do to usher in the age of Locke.

In devoting himself to publicizing Locke's work, Le Clerc was not, for once, guided by the publishers he served. But neither were his promotional activities entirely devoid of self-interest. Le Clerc was no more than any other man of letters a free-floating intellect; indeed he was more tied down by family responsibilities than many of his kind—as a married man, father of four, and son-in-law of an impecunious Italian man of letters.[84] When he campaigned on Locke's behalf, he was not unaware of the physician's connections with Lord Shaftesbury, the Mashams, and other potential English patrons.

Especially after 1688, when Locke and other English acquaintances returned to find employment under William and Mary, he had high hopes of obtaining a post himself and dreamt of getting a chair of Greek or Hebrew at Oxford. His 1709 edition of Grotius's *De Veritate*, which linked Grotius to the Latitudinarians, was dedicated to the Archbishop of Canterbury. His persistent support of Bishop Burnet (a resident in the Hague in 1686) not only tied in with his publishers' interests but was also

---

[82] Colie, 'Locke and the Republic of Letters', 128.

[83] *Bibliothèque choisie*, vi, art. v, 342–412.

[84] Le Clerc's father-in-law was Gregorio Leti, a prolific man of letters who dedicated 6 vols. on court ceremonies to Louis XIV and then denounced the French king as a tyrant after taking up residence in Amsterdam. He was ridiculed for inserting into the preface of one of his innumerable books letters written from different parts of the world praising his works. He was always on the move and always short of money. He did, however, have helpful sons-in-law. In addition to the daughter who became Mme Le Clerc there was another who married a London publisher-bookseller named George Guiguici or Guiger who proved useful to Jean Le Clerc. A. Barnes, *Le Clerc*, 126–8.

in accord with these personal ambitions. Scarcely an issue of his journal failed to mention the author of the *History of the Reformation of the English Church* (a French edition of which was published by Wolfgang in Amsterdam). But Burnet was fearful of being contaminated by the accusation so often directed at Le Clerc of being a secret Socinian.[85] Le Clerc never did achieve his goal. He remained a citizen of Cosmopolis until he died in 1736.

By then, editorial guidance of some of the extraterritorial journals was taking a less individualistic, more collegial form.[86] The *Journal literaire* of the Hague (which was started in 1713), for example, was directed by a board of editors, who met every week for a decade or more, to read papers, discuss contributions, agree on policy. This entailed a new form of intellectual sociability; one which was not affiliated with any one church, academy, or university but which did rely on services rendered by a given publishing firm. In many ways editorial staff meetings represented an extension of the 'little world of the book'. Much as early printing shops had fostered encounters between representatives of diverse occupations, nationalities, and creeds, so too did the weekly meetings of journal editors. But as with the use of the printing shop as cultural centre, few historians or literary sociologists seem to have noted the emergence of the editorial board as a new and distinctive institution. Perhaps for this reason it lends itself to being taken as something other than itself.

The board of the *Journal literaire*, for example, has been singled out recently, by Margaret Jacob, as the 'inner circle' or 'inner core' of an association with an ulterior purpose—a shadowy subversive organization affiliated with early freemasonry and aimed at propagating pantheism, materialism, and republican-

---

[85] A. Barnes, *Le Clerc*, 161–4.

[86] The collegial form characterized editorial guidance on some, but by no means all, of the journals. Christiane Berkvens-Stevelinck, *Prosper Marchand: La Vie et l'œuvre (1678–1756)* (Leiden, 1987), 114, views the formation of the *Journal literaire*'s editorial board as marking the end of the era of Bayle, Basnage, Le Clerc, and other one-man editorial operations, and sees the 'explosion' of printed materials as necessitating collaborative ventures. But she also notes that Marchand, himself, almost single-handedly turned out an issue of the successor to the *Journal literaire* (p. 124). The era of Le Clerc's *Bibliothèque ancienne et moderne*, moreover, overlapped with that of the *Journal literaire*. Collegial and one-man operations continued to coexist during the rest of the century, so it seems wrong to envisage any straight-line trend.

ism.[87] At the very centre of this inner circle, Jacob locates the figure of Prosper Marchand, who did serve on the board of the *Journal literaire* and, almost singlehandedly, turned out its successor the *Journal historique de la république des lettres* (1732–3).

Marchand was a remarkably active and versatile cultural intermediary. He served as bibliophile and bibliographer, editor, indexer, proof-reader, author, caption writer, and journalist. In contrast to Bayle, Le Clerc, and the other expatriates discussed above, Marchand started out not as a student in a seminary but as an apprentice to a printer-publisher-bookseller on the Rue Saint-Jacques. He bridged the little world of the book known to privileged Parisian guildsmen and the more indeterminate realm inhabited by French *émigrés* in the Netherlands. He also bridged two cultural generations and participated in the transformation of Pierre Bayle from Huguenot philosopher into enlightened *philosophe*. In addition, he represented print culture in a self-reflexive mode. His history of early printing pointed the way to the later hommage paid to Gutenberg during the French Revolution. The articles he wrote in his posthumously published *Dictionnaire* also helped to pattern the history of free thought along lines which have persisted until now. We must reserve judgement concerning his position within a quasi-masonic secret society and express uncertainty as to whether there was any such secret cell at all. But it does seem clear, from his remarkably well documented public life, that he was a leading citizen of Cosmopolis. The next chapter will provide a closer look at Prosper Marchand's world.

[87] M. Jacob, *The Radical Enlightenment: Pantheists, Freemasons and Republicans* (London, 1981). See esp. ch. 6. The editorial board is described as the 'inner circle' on p. 183, as the 'inner core' on p. 185. For further discussion of Jacob's thesis, see Ch. 3, pp. 88–91 below.

3

The World of Prosper Marchand

OF the diverse aspects of cosmopolitan print culture, there is one, as yet unmentioned, which catches the eye as one looks through the Marchand archives in Leiden: namely the importance assigned to illustrative materials. Printed illustrations were especially useful for cosmopolitan communications because pictorial statements transcended the boundaries that separated diverse language zones. Artists and engravers were regarded as respected citizens of the eighteenth-century Republic of Letters.[1] 'Gravure' was placed in the company of music, painting, and sculpture in the diagram of human knowledge in the *Encyclopédie*. Illustrators contributed in important ways to shaping the 'news' that was featured in Chapter 2. Visual aids were featured prominently in reports of experiments and discoveries. As noted previously, the small (octavo) format of the learned journal was not allowed to inhibit the provision of adequately detailed pull-out reproductions of diagrams and drawings of what was seen under microscopes or through telescopes.

But of course scientific illustration scarcely exhausted the uses to which printed images were put. Reports of battles and treaties were supplemented by diagrams, drawings, and maps.[2] Pornography, as we learnt from recent bicentennial lectures on the French Revolution, was perhaps even more ubiquitous in eighteenth-century illustrations than it had been in Aretino's

---

[1] See Christiane Berkvens-Stevelinck, 'L'Édition française en Hollande', in Henri-Jean Martin and Roger Chartier (eds.), *Histoire de l'édition française*, ii. *Le Livre triomphant 1660-1830* (Paris, 1984), 316-26: p. 319. I owe thanks to Dr Berkvens-Stevelinck for guiding me through the Marchand archives in Leiden and for being an unusually helpful correspondent. Her two books, *Prosper Marchand et l'histoire du livre* (Bruges, 1978) and *Prosper Marchand: La Vie et l'œuvre (1678-1756)* (Leiden, 1987)—hereafter, Berkvens-Stevelinck, *L'Histoire du livre*, and *La Vie*—have also proved indispensable.

[2] Pierre Rétat, 'Au confins de la presse: Information graphique . . .', in Rétat (ed.), *Le Journalisme d'ancien régime* (Lyons, 1982), 151-67.

day.[3] There were also didactic and evangelizing images designed 'for the sake of simple folk', to teach children their letters or to impress the barely literate with some official message. It is rather the resort to enigmatic images designed for the sake of sophisticated readers, with which Marchand's biographers have to be concerned. Such images were aimed at initiates while holding censors at bay and often pose puzzles that have no certain solution. Special expertise is required to decode them. Accordingly I will leave it to others to take up the challenge; what follows will deal mainly with textual materials. Nevertheless, a few illustrations will also be supplied, for prints and engravings occupied too important a place in Marchand's life and work to be completely set aside.

Marchand's closest collaborator and his best friend was one of the most celebrated illustrators of the early Enlightenment, Bernard Picart (1663–1733). Picart's father had been a distinguished engraver; his own talents won him prizes early in his career and he became a protégé of the chief royal painter, Charles Lebrun. His early work in the 1690s focused on subjects that Watteau later made famous; he portrayed actors of the Théâtre-Italien in their roles as Arlequin, Columbine, Scaramouche, and the rest. His father, Étienne Picart, had long been established on the Rue Saint Jacques. Bernard's marriage to Catherine Prost in 1702 provided another link with the Parisian sub-culture of privileged publisher-booksellers.[4] His first encounters with Prosper Marchand dated from before this marriage; he had become acquainted with the newly admitted member of the Parisian company of *libraires* around 1698. The two men remained fast friends for the rest of Picart's life.

---

[3] Lectures as far apart as the Univ. of Haifa, Israel, and Georgetown Univ., Washington, DC, were invariably accompanied by pornographic slides, usually featuring Marie Antoinette in diverse poses. More often than not, the point seemed to be not to illuminate 18th-cent. attitudes but to titillate 20th-cent. audiences. Unfortunately repetition led to boredom. The most unlikely intrusion of 18th-cent. pornography into 20th-cent. learned discourse is the reproduction of the frontispiece of *Thérèse philosophe* taken from a facsimile of a 1780 edn. in the *Bulletin of the American Academy of Arts and Sciences*, 43 (Oct. 1989), 18. It appears in the context of a 'Stated Meeting Report' on 'The Forbidden Bestsellers of Prerevolutionary France' given by Robert Darnton.

[4] See biographical sketch by Odile Faliu, *Cérémonies et coutumes religieuses de tous les peuples du monde dessinées par Bernard Picart*. Preface by Emmanuel Le Roy Ladurie (Paris, 1988), 10.

After Picart's death, Marchand worked closely with Picart's pupil, Jacob van der Schley. He wrote captions for both illustrators. He also designed vignettes, title-pages, and frontispieces to be executed by the engraver; for this purpose he set down detailed instructions and sometimes provided rough sketches in his own hand. The survival of these instructions and sketches in the Marchand archives offers a rare opportunity to go behind the scenes, so to speak, and observe how the views of one individual entered into the iconography of the Enlightenment during its formative years.

His collaboration with illustrators is but one of Marchand's multifarious well-documented activities. Marchand was a saver and a pack-rat. His archives in the university library at Leiden contain an extraordinarily miscellaneous assemblage. Materials inscribed in his own hand range from assorted odd-sized scraps of fine rag paper to a 995-page manuscript catalogue listing the titles of books published in Paris between 1650 and 1705.[5] Marchand was an expert bibliographer as well as a lifelong bibliophile. One of his first jobs when admitted to the company of Paris *libraires* was to handle book auctions and catalogue private libraries. Rather like Dewey of the Dewey Decimal system, he was known among Paris bookmen as the inventor of a new system for cataloguing—a system which was used by French librarians and bibliophiles until the end of the nineteenth century. Before he died, he came up with a plan for organizing the rapidly developing field of periodical literature and indexing articles. All his life he exhibited a special concern about bringing a rapidly proliferating print culture under control. As the complete bookman he seems well suited to being featured in a Lyell Lecture series, especially since, as we shall see, he was indebted to Sir Thomas Bodley's first librarian for one of his own early works.

He was born in Saint-Germain-en-Laye in 1678,[6] the youngest of four sons of a royal musician. His mother died when he was 5

[5] All the MS materials in the archives (including annotations made in printed books) are now listed in a printed catalogue compiled by Christiane Berkvens-Stevelinck, with the help of Adele Nieuweboer, *Catalogue des manuscrits de la Collection Prosper Marchand* (Leiden, 1988). The contents of the boxes containing odd-sized scraps, sketches, etc. are described under the heading of MARCH. 28 (pp. 58–66). On Marchand's MS catalogue of books published in Paris, see also John D. Woodbridge, 'The Parisian Book Trade in the Early Enlightenment: An Update of the Prosper Marchand Project', *Studies on Voltaire*, 193 (1980), 1763–72.

[6] So Marchand would have been 76 and not 88 in 1754. The latter age is mistakenly given by Berkvens-Stevelinck, 'Prosper Marchand: Trait d'union entre auteur et editeur', *De Gulden Passer*, 56 (1978), 66–99: p. 81.

and he was sent to Guise, in Picardy, to live with his maternal grandparents. As a 12-year-old he rejoined his family in Versailles to take up studies there. He proved proficient in ancient languages and within three years was taken on as an apprentice by a Paris *libraire*. In 1698, at the age of 20, he became a full member of the privileged corporation of publishers. This meant admission into the small tightly controlled micro-society or sub-culture which monopolized the official French book trade under the supervision of royal officials. Four years later, he had set up shop on the Rue Saint-Jacques, facing the fountain of Saint-Severin under a sign he devised and his friend Bernard Picart executed (Fig. 1). The phoenix was, of course, emblematic of resurrection and rebirth. It was loaded with special significance in alchemical lore. Was it intended by Marchand to stand for a rebirth of letters after the Dark Ages or for a recovery of ancient learning destroyed in the flames of the Alexandrian library or for both these developments and something more esoteric as well? The answer is uncertain. The emblem, at least, offers useful evidence of an early collaboration between publisher and illustrator.

The location of the firm at the sign of the Phoenix reflected a continuous tradition that had been sustained for more than two centuries. The Rue Saint-Jacques had witnessed the very first commercial printing operation in France. The three German printers, who had been invited, in 1470, to set up a press by the rector and librarian at the Sorbonne, moved to that street to open up shop after their business at the college was finished.

Marchand was himself very conscious of the activities of his predecessors. Always eager to find out more about earlier printers and publishers, he enlisted friends, correspondents, and the aid of the public at large to help him track down stories and trace genealogies.[7] His efforts ultimately bore fruit in the form of a book devoted to the history of early printing. As is evident from the title page (Fig. 2), the book was published in the Hague by Pierre Paupie in 1640.[8] In this instance, Marchand was acting

---

[7] Relevant material (listed in *Catalogue*, 51-4) includes notes about Peter Schoeffer's family tree as well as that of the Estiennes. Marchand's preface to his history of printing cites Cheviller's *Origine de l'imprimerie de Paris* with a request to readers to send in any relevant corrections. Prosper Marchand, *Histoire de l'origine et des premiers progrès de l'imprimerie* (The Hague: P. Paupie, 1640), p. v.

[8] There were actually two firms involved. In addition to Paupie, there was a firm run by the widow of Marchand's friend Charles Levier (or LeVier) who had died in 1735. Mme Levier collaborated on the publication. Marchand's difficulties with Paupie over

not as a printer, publisher, or bookseller, but only as an author. In this capacity, as is so often the case, he found himself at odds with his publisher. He was especially chagrined that his book failed to appear in time for either the Leipzig or the Frankfurt fair of 1739.[9] The usual authorial impatience at delay was intensified by anxiety over beating out competitors who were rushing to press with works celebrating the 300th anniversary of Gutenberg's invention in 1440.[10] The 'jubilee year' of 1640 had already seen the issue of several commemorative publications, at least one of which, by Mallinckrot, was owned by Marchand (Figs. 3 and 4). The latter's book finally appeared in the spring of the 'jubilee year' of 1740—much too late for the impatient author who lashed out publicly at the laziness and dissipation of the printing workers who had been allowed to hold up the project.

There is a striking contrast between the actual operations which caused Marchand such anxiety and the idealized ones depicted on the top of his first page (Fig. 5).[11] Minerva has taken charge of foundry and printing shop; the motto 'Ars Artium Conservatrix' is held by putti, who are portrayed playfully doing the work which was actually done with some effort by sweaty, grimy journeymen. 'Real printing shops were dirty, loud and unruly—and so were real printers. The presses creaked and groaned. The ink balls filled with wool soaked in urine gave off a fierce stench.[12] And the men waded about in filthy paper, swilling wine and banging their composing sticks against type cases . . .'. This description by Professor Darnton seems pertinent, even though it was written to underscore the unreality not of Marchand's illustrations but of the plates in the *Encyclopédie*, 'where the printers look like wind-up dolls . . . as if they in-

publishing the second part of the book and the good services performed by Jacques Levier (the widow's son) are noted by Berkvens-Stevelinck, *La Vie*, 40-1.

[9] Berkvens-Stevelinck, *La Vie*, 42.

[10] On the date 1440, which appeared in Erhard Ratdolt's edn. of Eusebius's *Chronicon* (Venice, 1483) and was repeated by Ulrich Zel in his *Cologne Chronicle* of 1499, see Margaret B. Stillwell, *The Beginning of the World of Books 1450-1470* (New York, 1972), 93. She points out that this date still governed the international celebration of 500 years of printing held in 1940.

[11] Marchand's sketch for this illustration together with van der Schley's engraving are depicted in *Catalogue*, figs. IVa and IVb.

[12] Robert Darnton, *The Business of Enlightenment* (Cambridge, 1979), 242-3. Some allowance needs to be made for 20th-cent. fastidiousness. The stench of urine (and of manure and other 'noisome' materials) was probably less offensive in the 18th-cent. and was certainly not a special attribute of printing-shop interiors.

habited an immaculate mechanical utopia'.[13] Of course smells
and noises are not easily conveyed by printed illustrations. (The
medium of print lent itself rather to representing the silent
colourless odourless universe of the new physics.) Moreover the
Encyclopédie plates were designed not as contributions to labour
history but rather to implement a Baconian mission of disclosing
craft secrets and trade 'mysteries'. In this light, recent interpreta-
tions seem somewhat anachronistic. William Sewell, for example,
elaborates on Darnton's passage by taking the latter's 'wind-up
doll figures' to represent the 'robotic workers' of the modern
factory system. In Sewell's view, the figures are treated as 'docile
automatons'. They appear to be so isolated from each other and
so removed from their traditional artisan culture that they point
to the bleak future of capitalist exploitation.[14] (One wonders
whether the same thing could not be said about any illustration
which makes use of figures derived from pattern books.)

Whatever else might be said about the images of foundry and
printing shop contained in Marchand's book, there is little likelihood of their giving rise to thoughts about proletarianization or
indeed of their attracting the attention of labour historians. The
presence of a goddess and numerous putti evokes rather that
special genre of early modern technical literature which sought
to dignify a given mechanical trade by linking it with classical
mythology. Yet these classical allusions do not take us completely
out of the orbit of actual printing workers. Minerva was the
patron saint of journeymen typographers; her image had been
paraded in sixteenth-century streets;[15] her presence in the
engraving represents the perpetuation of a long-lived craft tradition which was coextensive with the age of the wooden hand
press.[16] Not all printers spent their days swilling wine and
banging composing sticks. Some were skilled artisans with some

[13] Ibid.

[14] William Sewell, 'Visions of Labor: Illustrations of the Mechanical Arts before, in,
and after Diderot's *Encyclopédie*', in S. L. Kaplan and C. J. Koepp (eds.), *Work in France*
(Ithaca, NY, 1986), 258–86.

[15] Natalie Z. Davis, 'Strikes and Salvation in Lyons', *Archiv für Reformationsgeschichte*,
56 (1965), 48–64.

[16] The interruption of regular business to allow journeymen typographers to enjoy
a four-day celebration of the founding of printing was still being observed in the
Netherlands down to the end of the 18th cent. Max Fajn, 'Marc-Michel Rey:
Boekhandelaar op de Bloemmark', *Proceedings of the American Philosophical Society*, 118
(1974), 260–8: p. 265.

knowledge of the history of their special craft; at least one deserved to be described as an encyclopaedist. (The *Encyclopédie* article on printing was written by the foreman of the very shop where the first edition of Diderot's work was produced.)

But it would be absurd to confine the significance of Minerva's presence to the survival of a particular craft tradition. This particular goddess was loaded, indeed overloaded, with esoteric meanings among eighteenth-century *cognoscenti*. Her repeated appearance in earlier engravings by Marchand's friend Picart has given rise to speculation concerning a special 'Minerval' brand of freemasonry.[17] In 1736, around the time Marchand was finishing his book, a medal bearing the image of Minerva together with the Enlightenment motto 'Sapere Aude' had been struck in Berlin to commemorate the founding of a francophone, quasi-masonic society which sought to propagate Christian Wolff's philosophy.[18]

Minerva appears in a loftier position in the splendid frontispiece of Marchand's book, which depicts 'The Spirit of Printing Descending from the Heavens' (Fig. 6). This engraving occupied a special niche in the New York Public Library exhibition on printing and the French Revolution. There it was accompanied by a somewhat sardonic caption: 'Under the Old Regime, the printing press was celebrated as a gift descending from the heavens which would spread enlightenment through a benighted world.'[19] The idea of printing being 'brought down from the heavens' was rooted in early tributes paid to the 'divine art'. Nevertheless Marchand's celebratory view seems to be at odds with the late twentieth-century *zeitgeist*. To our eyes, there is something disconcerting about an object that is so obviously man-made and earth-bound as a wooden hand press being brought down from on high by a goddess. More recent attempts to commemorate communications technologies, however, suggest that incongruity is difficult to avoid. In 1989 French

[17] See e.g. Picart's 1707 engraving displaying Minerva expelling ignorance (Fig. 8) which is discussed below. Also Margaret C. Jacob, *The Radical Enlightenment: Pantheists, Freemasons and Republicans* (London, 1981), 164-5; Dorothy Schlegel, 'Freemasonry and the *Encyclopédie* Reconsidered', *Studies in Voltaire*, 90 (1972), 1433-60.

[18] Franco Venturi, *Italy and the Enlightenment*, ed. S. Woolf, tr. S. Corsi (London, 1972), 34-6.

[19] Exhibition Catalogue: R. Darnton and Daniel Roche (eds.), *Revolution in Print: The Press in France 1775-1800* (Berkeley, Calif., 1989), plate 6 between pp. 104 and 105.

officials were rather at a loss about just how to celebrate the 200th anniversary of the French Revolution. They looked back to the 100th anniversary—much as Marchand looked back to 'jubilee' of 1640—and found a suitable neutral symbol in the Eiffel Tower which had been built to mark the first centenary. So it was decided to hold a series of commemorative events there. In addition to a re-enactment of Gustave Eiffel's historic first climb to the top, a series of media spectaculars were held. On 14 May 1989, a televised rock concert was produced which was intended to embody 'the spirit of communications'.

Like the spirit of communications, the spirit of printing is necessarily somewhat abstract. Historians are always uncomfortable with spirits in any case, preferring phenomena which can be placed in definite locales and take tangible forms. This brings up the question of just where Marchand's history of printing was produced and where he himself was residing when he wrote it. Marchand had left France in 1709 some thirty years before the book was published and the frontispiece designed. It may seem like mere quibbling to take issue with the New York Public Library catalogue caption which places the engraving 'under the ancien regime' and presents it in a book titled 'the press in France'. But the seemingly minor distinction between the press in France and the French press outside France is of major importance for understanding the configuration of Prosper Marchand's world.

Although he lived most of his life as a citizen of Cosmopolis, Marchand never ceased to live in a French-speaking world. Despite thirty years in the Netherlands, he never mastered Dutch well enough to use it; amusing anecdotes were told about his getting lost *en route* to friends' houses because he couldn't speak enough Dutch to ask directions of the natives.[20] As was the case with Bayle and Le Clerc (and, later on, with Marc Michel Rey), Marchand was deaf to local dialects. Dutch was treated by these French expatriates much as a Genevan might treat Savoyard.[21] There were other links with the early Huguenots. Marchand

---

[20] Berkvens-Stevelinck, *La Vie*, 168.

[21] This point is made (in connection with Bayle) by Elisabeth Labrousse, *Pierre Bayle*, i. *Du pays de foix à la cité d'Erasme* (The Hague, 1963), 168. Their ignorance of Dutch distinguished the francophone *émigrés* of the 18th cent. (from Bayle to Marc Michel Rey) from 16th-cent. publishers such as Christopher Plantin, who learnt Dutch while helping to compile a French-Dutch dictionary. See Eisenstein, *Printing Press*, i. 99-100.

served as the editor of the third edition of Bayle's *Dictionnaire* for which Picart did the frontispiece. Picart also engraved a portrait of Jean Le Clerc in his role as Latin scholar (Fig. 7).[22]

Marchand's existence on the Rue Saint-Jacques entailed continuity with one tradition, that of the privileged publisher working under official controls; his years as an expatriate linked him to a different tradition associated with a decentralized communications network and a cosmopolitan European third force. Is there perhaps some relationship between the iconography of 'the Spirit of Printing' and the outlook of the *émigré* in the Netherlands? With this question in mind let us look at the frontispiece more closely. The goddess representing the Spirit wears a crown surmounted with the five vowels. As noted in our previous discussion of Jean Le Clerc (in his guise as the Latin theologian Joannes Clericus), vowels were the topic of much learned discussion concerning the authenticity of Hebrew texts of the Pentateuch. Although Marchand was not trained in any seminary he seems to have gained some familiarity with trilingual studies: Hebrew letters are on the bottom border of the garment worn by the 'Spirit'; Greek letters decorate the drapery on her lap; the Roman alphabet is scattered over the shawl that encircles her head as a kind of nimbus. She holds a wand bearing Marchand's initials. On her left is the ubiquitous Minerva; on her right is Mercury, another heavenly body who was overloaded with significant meaning by eighteenth-century literati.

If one thinks only of his role as messenger of the gods, Mercury's presence in an engraving celebrating the invention of printing appears to be unexceptional. But, as noted above, the images designed by Marchand were not aimed at 'simple folk'; they often conveyed esoteric messages that require special expertise to decode. Mercury not only doubled as thief and trickster; he also tripled, in a manner of speaking, as 'Hermes thrice blessed', giving rise to a large literature we must pass over here. Nor are we competent to pass judgement on the continuing debate over the figure of Mercury as presented by Bonaventure Des Périers in his sixteenth-century allegory *Cymbalum Mundi*, despite its special relevance to Marchand's work. As noted

---

[22] The books in the background of this portrait contain a reference to Hammond, whose *Annotations on the New Testament* Le Clerc translated from English into Latin. See above Ch. 2.

below, Marchand published this cryptic collection of tales and contributed a much reprinted preface to it.

Before taking up this preface and other early writings by Marchand, we need to consider the bottom half of the 'Spirit of Printing'. Let us turn from the heavens towards the figures on the ground (even while noting that we still remain in the realm of mythology). Personifications of the first 'nations' to be entrusted with the 'divine art' are represented, with pride of place assigned to Germany. The portraits of Gutenberg and Fust on the medallions seem to be based on those used by Mallinkrot to commemorate the bicentennial of 1640 (Fig. 4). The two men have now become archetypes: Gutenberg, the impractical inventor who lost control of his 'brain child'; Fust, the exploitative financier who took it over and set up business with his future son-in-law, Peter Schoeffer.[23] But in Marchand's view Fust deserved full credit as a collaborator. He was in danger of being confused not with a greedy capitalist but rather with 'an imaginary personage', a 'fraudulent magician' named Faust, owing to lies circulated by monks who hated anyone associated with the invention of printing.[24]

The grouping also entails a celebrated priority dispute: 'Just as 7 Greek towns competed for Homer,' the text reads, 'so too did German and Dutch towns compete for honour of giving birth to the inventor.'[25] The placement of Laurens Coster in the role of second fiddle, however, aroused the indignation of patriotic

---

[23] Pierce Butler, *The Origin of Printing in Europe* (Chicago, 1940), 130. Peter Schoeffer is thus cast in the archetypical role of the man who marries the boss's daughter. The perpetuation of countless printing dynasties would hinge on such marriages; Plantin and his five daughters comes to mind.

[24] Prosper Marchand, *Dictionnaire historique ou mémoires critiques et littéraires concernant la vie et les œuvres de divers personnages distingués particulièrement dans la république des lettres*, ed. Jean Nicolas Sébastien Allamand (2 vols. The Hague: Pierre de Hoondt, 1758), i. 249. For background on Gutenberg medallion, see George Painter, 'The True Portrait of Johann Gutenberg', *Gutenberg Jahrbuch* (1965), 73-9. Although the medallion holding the portrait of Peter Schoeffer is blank, Marchand did collect data on the Schoeffer dynasty, as shown by his correspondence with 'sGravesande (MARCH. 24: 1, fo. 7): *Catalogue*, 51. In his *Histoire de l'imprimerie*, 21-2 n. 1, he takes Jean Le Clerc to task for not realizing that Opilio was the Latin name for Schoeffer and thus giving Fust an extra son-in-law.

[25] A note in the *Histoire de l'imprimerie*, 4 n. C, shows that Marchand objected to the long-held view that modern inventors were simply recovering the secrets originally told to Adam by God. He also noted that Chinese printing had preceded European practices and offers a long discussion of literature on this topic, including the hypothesis that a German merchant had picked up the art from visiting China (p. 16 n. J).

Dutch authors who were becoming increasingly hostile to the unassimilated French in their midst. Chronological priority, which looms so large in the dispute over Gutenberg versus Coster, is oddly ignored in the assigning of a third place to William Caxton. The establishment of the first press on English soil in 1476 came well after printers had set to work in both Italy and France. But neither the Italians nor the French celebrate their first printers the way the English, the Germans, and the Dutch do; perhaps partly because the first printers in Italy (Sweynheim and Pannartz) and also in France (Ulrich Gering and his partners) were not native sons. There is the additional factor that the celebration of printers in Catholic lands tended to be muted.

The text of Marchand's history of printing shows that this factor weighed heavily with him. Only after the Protestants elevated the press to the skies and praised it as an excellent 'gift of heaven' which led to the Reformation, he wrote, did monks attack it with all their strength and condemn it as a 'vicious infernal art'.[26] In elevating his picture of the wooden press to the skies and depicting it as a gift of heaven, Marchand was thus siding with a Protestant cause. His grouping of printers clearly sets the three Protestant powers against the two Catholic ones. His choice of figures to represent the latter seems calculated to give offence to the post-Tridentine Roman Church. Italy, to be sure, is represented by a figure wearing the triple tiara of papal Rome. But Italy holds a Venetian not a Roman printer. Aldus Manutius prospered between the 1490s and 1510s, when the independent Republic on the Adriatic was at odds with the pope and Venetian presses were free to turn out anticlerical material.

There is even more dissonance in the treatment of France. The embodiment of that country holds Robert Estienne, royal printer, Bible printer, and member of that dynasty which figured in the Genevan heritage of Jean Le Clerc. Tracing the Estiennes' genealogy was a lifelong preoccupation of Marchand's. An elaborate family tree was tipped into his posthumously published *Dictionnaire* of 1758. More than fifty years earlier, in 1700, he had produced a Latin manuscript treatise on the family which was decorated by Bernard Picart. Its dedication, 'to Jacques Estienne, Paris printer and publisher from Prosper Marchand, Paris pub-

---

[26] *Histoire de l'imprimerie*, 28 n. Q.

lisher', shows that Marchand initially perceived his own career as carrying on the long enduring guild traditions sustained on the Rue Saint-Jacques.[27] Marchand's subsequent break with Paris printing helps to explain why he chose the particular medallion held by 'France'.

As Marchand knew perfectly well, Robert Estienne was a late-comer to the world of the master printers of Paris. He worked between 1526 and 1550 and represented the third generation of a celebrated Paris printing dynasty. But although he was far from the first native son to ply his trade, he was the first member of his family to leave his native land and take up his trade on foreign soil. After his Latin editions of the Bible were condemned by the Sorbonne, he left France for Geneva where he spent his last eight years. Marchand's admiration for the scholarly Bible printer was manifested in his posthumously published *Dictionnaire*, where Robert Estienne is described as the '*premier imprimeur* not only of Paris and indeed of all of France but even of the entire world'.[28] So for Marchand, Robert Estienne had the distinction of being the 'first' French printer in that special sense that is still given to the word 'premier'. Nevertheless, his being singled out in the engraving as the paradigmatic printer of Catholic France had a paradoxical aspect since this distinction was conferred on one who had set up business in a foreign Protestant land.

It is worth underlining the fact that there is no personification of 'Geneva' to set beside that of 'France', just as there is none of 'Venice' to be juxtaposed with 'Italy'. Marchand's presentation of the history of printing conforms to a pattern which started, perhaps, with the German glorification of Gutenberg in the late fifteenth century and which prevails even now by being structured along 'national' lines. Indeed, the tendency to use the nation state as a main frame seems to have become ever more pronounced. In addition to the continuous output of histories of German printing, Italian printing, Spanish printing, Dutch printing, and the like, a new series of multi-volume projects are under way. The recently completed four-volume history of the

---

[27] MARCH. 26, *Catalogue*, 56-7, contains MS versions of a genealogical and historical treatise on the Estienne dynasty dedicated to 'Jacques Estienne, Paris printer and publisher by Prosper Marchand, Paris publisher' first composed in Latin then partly translated into French (by Gabriel Martin) both dated MDCC.

[28] Marchand, *Dictionnaire*, i 229 n 3

book in France is to be followed by even more massive collaborative works pertaining to Great Britain and the United States. Doubtless these projected works will prove immensely useful. I have myself contributed to the first volume of the *Histoire de l'édition française* and repeatedly used the second one when preparing the lectures that are published here.[29] Despite their usefulness, however, such projects do tend to conceal the important political underpinning supplied by Venice, Geneva, and numerous other quasi-autonomous principalities and city-states of early modern Europe. To return to Marchand's depiction of the spirit of printing: only the unstated dissonance between the figure of France and the medallion of the *émigré* printer she holds hints at the two different francophone communities which were entailed.

The experience of Robert Estienne had long been of special significance to the author of the history of early printing. In 1709, some thirty years before the book was published and the frontispiece designed, Marchand had left his shop on the Rue Saint-Jacques. With his good friend, Bernard Picart, he took off for the Dutch Netherlands and announced his conversion to the Reformed faith. In 1710, after joining the Walloon Church, gaining admittance to the local publisher-booksellers guild, and renting a house with the Picarts, he set up an office in the Hague. He never again returned to France.

Why did he and Picart make this drastic move? Clearly a religious conversion was entailed. Marchand was still nominally a Catholic when he arrived in the Hague and it was there that he formally renounced 'the errors, false cults and tyrannical government of the Roman Church'.[30] But his defection from the Catholic regime had been germinating for several years. That he had strong anticlerical convictions is evident from the 'explication du frontispiece' he composed in 1706 to go with Picart's engraving for an edition (published in Ratisbone in 1709) of the *Satyre Ménippée*. 'The Spirit of the Ligue', it begins, 'is represented by a monster clothed in a monk's gown symbolizing the Holy Religion emerging from the infernal abyss'.[31] The

[29] The section on 'L'Édition en Français hors de France', in Martin and Chartier, *Histoire*, ii. 304–62, contains especially pertinent articles by Berkvens-Stevelinck, Darnton, Birn, et al.   [30] Berkvens-Stevelinck, *La Vie*, 2.

[31] Ibid. 160. The handwritten 'explication' is in the archives MARCH. 28, fos. 255–7. *Catalogue*, 65. The printed edn. that I consulted at the Bodleian Library (DOUCE R

Satyre, that late sixteenth-century polemic against the Catholic Ligue, described the Parisians as being set upon by fanatic Spaniards and Neapolitans: 'We are like Christians in Turkey or Jews in Avignon. Paris is a lair of wild beasts.' Did this convey Marchand's own disgust at the quarrels between Jansenists and Jesuits over the Bull *Unigenitus* in the Paris of his own day? It is clear that he distanced himself from both groups and was fond of using sixteenth-century French texts as vehicles for expressing his views on current affairs. His eulogy when Picart died (in 1733) referred to his frequent meetings with the engraver and the latter's younger brother during Marchand's Paris years. As members of a small study group, they had discussed current debates among theologians, were unimpressed by Bossuet, sided with the Calvinists against the Jansenists, and also admired the views of heterodox Cartesians such as Malebranche.[32]

More immediate evidence is provided by the manuscripts which date back to the years Marchand spent on the Rue St. Jacques. In addition to the 'explication' of the *Satyre* frontispiece mentioned above, there is Marchand's *History of the Bible of Sixtus V,* which was drafted in Paris in 1704 (and published abroad in 1725). This work concerned an edition of the Vulgate hastily issued in 1590 under the aegis of Pope Sixtus V. The edition was accompanied by an edict claiming that this version was the only authentic one and that it superseded all prior versions. The edict was a blunder; the version was so corrupt that it had to be swiftly withdrawn from circulation—making it something of a collector's item. Its many errors were quickly pointed out and listed by Protestants. Its most assiduous critic was none other than the first librarian of the Bodleian, Thomas James. James was adept at making Catholic censors serve the ends of Protestant publicists. He kept track of all the passages that the Catholics expurgated, as well as all the titles that they banned in order to be sure English Protestants would have such reading matter available.[33] James's four-volume Latin treatise on

---

379-81), *Satyre Ménippée de la vertue du Catholicon d'Espagne* . . . (Ratisbone: 'chez les heritiers de Mathias Kerner', 1711), contained a note in ink above the frontispiece indicating knowledge of the caption's author: 'V. Marchand, Dict. I, 168.'

[32] Berkvens-Stevelinck, *La Vie,* p. 3.

[33] On Thomas James (1573?-1629) and his *Bellum Papale* (4 vols. London, 1600), see the *Dictionary of National Biography.* As a Protestant publicist, he figured in my earlier work, Eisenstein, *Printing Press,* i. 416; ii. 677 n.

Sixtus's Bible (1600) included a 40-page itemized list, beginning with Genesis and ending with the Apocalypse, of every mistake and mistranscription that the librarian had found. After studying this list, Marchand felt he could add nothing to it and simply commended it to his readers. His own contribution was characteristic. He offered notes underlining the special bibliographical features which would enable collectors to distinguish the rare Sixtus V edition from other similar versions.[34]

Although he followed James's scholarly lead, Marchand stopped short of repeating the English librarian's violent attacks on the papacy. In 1704 he still had not broken with the Catholic Church, although he was moving down the same road as had the scholarly Bible printer Robert Estienne whose annotated Latin editions had been condemned by the Sorbonne. It is not clear when the cause of the vernacular Bible translators began to engage him. In the posthumous *Dictionnaire*, Jacques Lefèvre d'Étaples is hailed as the restorer of sane theology and the true religion. Olivetan and other French translators of the Bible who were condemned by Catholic authorities also receive favourable mention. (There is even a reference to the recent translation made by a Swiss pastor named Ostervald, the father of the publisher celebrated in the *Business of the Enlightenment*.)[35]

As his writings on vernacular Bibles suggest, Marchand had evangelical as well as bibliographical and scholarly concerns. Indeed, he knew his scripture in just the way that Erasmus and Luther had urged on all good Christians. Another item in the archives is a little booklet Marchand composed, *Method for Reading the Complete New Testament in 4 months*. 'Every day,' the author writes, 'I read 2 chapters; one in the morning, the other before bedtime. By reducing 260 chapters to 244 and reading 2 per day I am done in 4 months'.[36] Benjamin Franklin could not have put it better. For all that it hints at a secular concern with not wasting time and mastering speed reading, this

[34] Berkvens-Stevelinck, *La Vie*, 30-8. On p. 38 it is noted that Marchand eliminated some of the gibes that James directed at the popes and adopted a more 'moderate' tone which is attributed to his having not yet broken with Rome.

[35] 'Fevre, Jacques le', *Dictionnaire*, i. 252. Berkvens-Stevelinck, *La Vie*, 121, notes that this article was based on a 'Comparison of several Bible translations' which Marchand had previously published in the *Bibliothèque françoise*.

[36] *Méthode pour lire commodement le Nouveau Testament entier dans l'éspace de quatre mois* (8 pp.), printed booklet: MARCH. 28, fos. 1-4, *Catalogue*, 58.

booklet also points to the sort of intensive unmediated lay Bible reading that was frowned on by Counter-Reformation Churches. Although Marchand never attended a seminary as had Bayle and Le Clerc, he did wrestle with theological arguments, was knowledgeable about biblical scholarship, encouraged Bible reading, and remained a church-goer during his life as an expatriate. To present him only as an anticlerical, a Cartesian, or a libertine is to overlook the likelihood that he also had strongly held Christian beliefs. But he certainly had no use for churchmen who condemned the new philosophy.

During his years as a Paris publisher, he served as an occasional correspondent for the *Nouvelles de la république des lettres* which was edited, from 1699 to 1710, by Jean Le Clerc's friend and relative, Jacques Bernard. (Rather unexpectedly for a cataloguer and bibliographer, Marchand had a flair for literary journalism. It would engage him more fully later on.) In 1707, the *Nouvelles* published a gossipy item, sent in by Marchand, about the previous year's stupid censorship action of the Archbishop of Paris who objected to the publication of a doctoral thesis by one Brillon de Jouy. The most objectionable part of the thesis was the title-page vignette engraved by Bernard Picart (Fig. 8). Under the caption, 'La Vérité recherchée par les philosophes', Minerva was shown throwing the figure of Ignorance, which was provided with donkey's ears, to the ground. The figure of Philosophy held Descartes's hand and guided him towards Truth. The point of the gossipy item was that the Archbishop was so horrified when an adviser told him the figure of Ignorance wearing donkey's ears was Aristotle that he condemned the thesis. Later he decided to allow publication if the vignette was expurgated.[37] This item evokes many stories about how Galileo offended Pope Urban VIII. (There is a reference to the Copernican system in the illustration and in the accompanying text.)[38]

In 1706–7, then, the Paris publisher-cum-journalist was already linking the Catholic hierarchy not just with inferior biblical scholarship but also with encouraging ignorance of

[37] *Nouvelles de la république des lettres* (Aug. 1707), 232–5. Marchand's MS version of the item is described by Berkvens-Stevelinck, *La Vie*, 106. (A typographical error on p. 107 has turned Bri*ll*on de Jouy into Bri*ss*on.)

[38] Marchand's publication of a work on the Copernican system, *La Sphère du monde* (Paris: P. Marchand, 1709), is noted by Berkvens-Stevelinck, *La Vie*, 99.

developments in mathematics, physics, and astronomy. It is clear
that he was against the Aristotelians and on the side of the new
philosophy associated with Descartes. His position on the
Cartesian as against the Newtonian world-view seems to be more
obscure. Later, he would be associated with two of the most
prominent Newtonïans in the Netherlands: 'sGravesande, co-
editor of the *Journal literaire,* and Allamand, Marchand's
eulogist and literary executor. But someone else, perhaps an
English Newtonian, was probably responsible for reworking
Picart's vignettte, after it had been detached from the condemned
thesis, into a pro-Newtonian form (Fig. 9).[39]

His caption for the *Satyre Ménippée* shows Marchand to have
been an anticlerical. His work on biblical editions reveals some of
his continuing scholarly and religious concerns. As a Paris correspondent for the *Nouvelles,* he appears on the side of the
moderns against the ancients and as an advocate of the new
philosophy against the Aristotelians. Finally there is a work
written in 1706 (and published by Marchand in Amsterdam in
1711) which points to an early affinity with libertines and free
thinkers. This is the long (43-page) preface to the *Cymbalum
Mundi,* an enigmatic allegorical sixteenth-century work and a
celebrated landmark in French prose, written by a contemporary
of Rabelais. An eighteenth-century English translation suggests
how the work was presented to a later public: '*Cymbalum Mundi*
or the *World's Little Bell* by Bonaventure des Perriers: 4 satyrical
dialogues very ancient merry and facetious from a copy printed
in 1538 by a gentleman to the bedchamber of Queen Margaret of
Navarre.' The translation goes on to summarize the contents of
the four dialogues. According to this, the first dialogue tells
about Mercury being sent by Jupiter to earth to get a book
bound. He falls in with two thieves who steal the book and learn
it is the Book of Destinies. The second dialogue pokes fun at
Chemists seeking a philosopher's stone. The third makes fun of
fortune-telling. The fourth is a dialogue between talking dogs.[40]

[39] I owe thanks to the curator of photographs of the Warburg Institute for supplying
me with the two illustrations. It was a Warburg scholar, Fritz Saxl, who first drew my
attention to the substitution of Newton for Descartes in his celebrated essay: 'Veritas
Filia Temporis', in R. Klibansky and H. J. Paton (eds.), *Philosophy and History: Essays
presented to Ernst Cassirer* (1st edn. 1936; New York, 1963), ch. 15.

[40] *Cymbalum Mundi or Satyrical Dialogues on Various Subjects by Bonaventure des
Perriers* (London: T. Sharpe for J. Newton, 1723). This version contains Marchand's
preface in translation, pp. i–xliii.

Needless to say, modern scholars are not in agreement as to how to interpret these dialogues. They disagree over what the author intended, over the identity of the historic figures whose names are disguised by ciphers, and over what was conveyed to different generations of readers. To cite only three of the many views which have been expressed: according to Lucien Febvre, the work recounts theological disputes between Luther, Calvin, Bucer, and Erasmus,[41] and gives the author's views on transubstantiation, divine pre-cognition, miracles, and other mysteries of the Christan faith.[42] According to Wolfgang Spitzer, the work is really an elaborate allegory on false fame, with dialogues pivoting around the relations between author and public.[43] Peter Nurse holds that Des Périers was arguing not merely against false fame but against any kind of worldly fame. His allegories were not about the noise made by books in the world but about the need to keep silent in the face of divine mysteries.[44]

Marchand's preface[45] seems calculated to keep the reader guessing, not only about Des Périers's intentions but also about the preface-writer's views. He notes that the author has been falsely accused of impiety and irreverence and of pretending to write about Greek gods in order to deny the existence of any Supreme Being. It was also said that Des Périers was punished for his blasphemy by ending his life as a miserable suicide. But there is no evidence that a suicide took place, Marchand argues, and it is doubtful that all atheists die miserably. Des Périers's

---

[41] According to Michael Screech, 'The Historian of French Thought and the Printed Book', paper delivered at the 37th Annual Conference, Society for French Historical Studies, Vancouver, Canada (22 Mar. 1991) Febvre wrongly identified DRARIG as Erasmus when the anagram actually stood for GIRARD (Roussel). There is general agreement that Luther, Calvin, and Bucer are the other names that are disguised by ciphers.

[42] Lucien Febvre, *Origène et Des Périers ou l'Énigme du 'Cymbalum Mundi'* (Geneva, 1942; this is a publication of a 1937 lecture). In *Le Problème de l'incroyance au XVIᵉ siècle* (Paris, 1942), 4–5, Febvre brings out those features of Des Périers's life (such as his affiliation with French translators of the Bible and the circle around Margaret of Navarre) which were likely to appeal to Marchand.

[43] Wolfgang Spitzer, 'The Meaning of Bonaventure des Périers' *Cymbalum Mundi*', *Publications of the Modern Language Association of America*, 66 (Sept. 1951), 795–819.

[44] *Cymbalum Mundi*, ed. Peter H. Nurse (Manchester, 1958), Introduction, pp. vii–xlv.

[45] See Berkvens-Stevelinck, *La Vie*, 91, on the 1706 MS of this preface by 'Felix de Commerci' (Marchand's pen name) and on the 1711 Amsterdam publication of: *Cymbalum Mundi ou quatre dialogues de Bonaventure des Périers, avec une Lettre critique dans laquelle on justifie cet ouvrage d'athéisme et impiété, par Felix de Commerci.*

book is described as detestable, pernicious, and stuffed with impiety, Marchand goes on, but almost all those who thus describe it also say that they have never seen the book and never want to see it. (At this point, the present-day reader can scarcely avoid thinking about *The Satanic Verses*.) Marchand claims he has seen the book and assures us that it contains nothing useful to atheists—unless, of course, one misconstrues the text by saying, for example, that Jupiter sending Mercury to earth stands for God sending his only son . . . etc. One finds oneself working out just such a possibility after reading the preface-writer's ostensible denial of it.

This tactic so often used by libertines and philosophes alike—of arousing suspicion in the very act of denying any cause for it—seems to have been derived from Lucian, who actually did at one point draw a parallel between Jupiter sending Mercury to the Athenians with God sending Jesus to the Jews.[46] Marchand's preface may have harked back to the ancient satirists. It looked forward to a later clandestine book trade as well. When describing Des Périers's work as a book much talked about but rarely seen, Marchand coupled it with another even more elusive and notorious work, *De Tribus Imposteribus*.[47] This work was associated with a long-enduring textual tradition that treated Jesus, Moses, and Muhammad as fraudulent conjurers; it would become the topic of an influential article in Marchand's posthumously published *Dictionnaire* (as noted below). The preface thus provides a preview of how Marchand and his coterie would use ancient texts as well as newly concocted ones, imaginary books as well as real ones, to tease readers, slip messages past censors, and (perhaps inadvertently?) provoke unceasing controversy among later scholars.

In speculating about reasons for Marchand's departure, I have focused on intellectual concerns and left aside commercial ones. This is only partly because I have failed to track down the fate of the Paris accounts of the shop at the sign of the Phoenix. It is

[46] Febvre, *Origène et Des Périers*, 60, 76, and 84. Febvre mentions two important publication dates: 1512 when *Contra Celsum* was published by the firm of Bade and Petit in Paris and 1700 when a French translation was published in Amsterdam.

[47] According to Michael Screech, Marin Mersenne had confused *Cymbalum Mundi* and *De Tribus Imposteribus* with each other. Marchand's preface (p. xxix) singles out Mersenne among those who circulated stories about Des Périers being an atheist who died a miserable death.

true that Marchand was not a shrewd businessman and that, unlike the vast majority of publisher-booksellers, he did not put business considerations first. He insisted on travelling to Holland with his large private library at considerable expense, despite urging from friends that he sell his books and pocket the proceeds. As a passionate book collector and something of a spendthrift, he died poor.[48] So it is conceivable that his Paris firm was losing money. Yet Marchand's services were in demand as an expert on estate sales and book auctions right up to his departure. Picart's skills were also in steady demand. It seems unlikely that financial pressures forced the two to leave.

Once he had left, Marchand remained in the publishing and bookselling business for only four years.[49] According to his executor and friend, Jean Nicholas Sébastien Allamand, he found conditions in the Dutch book trade not to his liking and expressed disgust with the bad faith and sharp practices he encountered. Possibly he was unprepared by his Paris experience as a privileged and protected *libraire* to cope with the sort of wheeling and dealing that characterized a relatively unregulated industry. In any event, after a year or so in the Hague, Picart and Marchand closed shop and tried their luck in Amsterdam where Marchand again was admitted to the booksellers' guild and both men joined the local Walloon Church. Picart, who had lost his first wife during his Parisian years, was remarried in 1712 to Anna Vincent, the daughter of a Huguenot paper merchant, and settled in Amsterdam. But Marchand soon abandoned his business there to take up freelance work.[50] He started by accepting an invitation to work in Rotterdam for the two publishers (Gaspard Fritsch and Michael Böhm) who had bought up Reinier Leers's stock and wanted Marchand to edit Pierre Bayle's correspondence and help with a new edition of the *Dictionnaire*.

His six years' work on Bayle's papers involved Marchand in warfare with other claimants to Bayle's estate, especially with the London-based editor Pierre Desmaiseaux but also with publishers of rival editions of the *Dictionnaire*. Ignoring the protests of local pastors, the Genevans got out a rival edition in 1715 well ahead of

[48] Berkvens-Stevelinck, *La Vie*, 8-9.
[49] See Berkvens-Stevelinck, *La Vie*, 145, for discussion of the 16 works Marchand published between 1710 and 1714.
[50] He continued to engage in buying and selling books, however. Berkvens-Stevelinck, *La Vie*, 138.

Fritsch and Böhm. (The wars over Bayle's *Dictionnaire* provide a preview of later fights over new editions of the *Encyclopédie*.) Marchand's edition was issued in 1720—an unfortunate piece of timing since it was dedicated to the French regent and had a frontispiece by Picart celebrating John Law's scheme; by 1720, the bubble had burst.[51] The prolonged feud between Marchand and Desmaiseaux over the editing of Bayle's papers was conducted largely through rival review journals and makes for lively reading even now.[52] In view of Marchand's own hostile comments about Dutch publishers, it is intriguing to see that he himself was stigmatized by Desmaiseaux for being a greedy swindler who was naturally given to trickery, as a typical 'publisher who was writing for publishers'.[53] Desmaiseaux poisoned the atmosphere when Marchand made a visit to England in 1725 in order to canvass the possibility of settling there. He soon retreated to the Hague where he had already been engaged in diverse activities—so diverse that one is at loss finding any one term to describe his many roles. (The French say *homme du livre*; 'bookman' will have to do.)

He served as editor for various publishers, as consultant and adviser to authors, and was much in demand as a 'corrector' or proof-reader. He devoted much of his time to journalism; he was on the editorial board of the *Journal literaire* (The Hague) which appeared between 1713 and 1732 and singlehandedly produced its successor the *Journal historique de la république des lettres* (1732–3).[54] He wrote reviews and articles for several *Bibliothèques* (*germanique, françoise, britannique*). In addition, he designed title-pages and frontispieces, engaged in research and

---

[51] The wars over the edns. of Bayle's *Dictionnaire* are discussed by A. J. Q. Beuchot in his edn. of Bayle's *Dictionnaire historique et critique*, ed. Beuchot (16 vols. Paris, 1820-4), i, preface. Vol. xvi, 'Préface des éditions précédents; Vie de Bayle', also has pertinent material. See also Berkvens-Stevelinck, *L'Histoire du livre*, ch. 4, and P. Rétat, *Le Dictionnaire de Bayle et la lutte philosophique au XVIIIe siècle* (Paris, 1971), 121-3.

[52] Desmaiseaux's stream of anonymous articles attacking Marchand's work as editor of Bayle's *Lettres choisies* (1714) which appeared in Samuel Masson's *Histoire critique de la république des lettres* are listed and discussed by Joseph Almagor, *Pierre Des Maizeaux (1673-1745), Journalist and English Correspondent for Franco-Dutch Periodicals 1700-1720* (Amsterdam, 1989), 79-101. The *Journal literaire* (The Hague) was the vehicle used by Marchand. Berkvens-Stevelinck, *L'Histoire du livre*, 79-133, devotes a chapter to the feud.   [53] Cited by Almagor, *Des Maizeaux*, 87.

[54] See Berkvens-Stevelinck, *L'Histoire du livre*, pp. xv-xvi, for Marchand's hand-written version of the prospectus for the successor journal. The same author, *La Vie*, 115, describes Marchand's struggle to bring out vol. 2 of the journal on his own.

writing, and acted as an antiquarian book dealer. A passionate bibliophile, he continued throughout his life to augment and refine his personal collection by selling off some items while purchasing others.

His richly documented career as a bookman is in marked contrast to his sparsely documented private life. Picart was married twice and had a younger brother who travelled with him. We cannot be sure whether Marchand ever married, whether he had any affairs with any women—or, for that matter, with any men—or whether he remained celibate. We do know, however, that he had a circle of devoted friends and that even after Picart died he never lacked for companions.

During his residence in the Hague, he belonged to a distinctive coterie; serving as the secretary of a literary society-cum-dining-and-drinking club called 'les Chevaliers de la Jubilation'. The relatively cryptic records of meetings held by these 'Knights' have given rise to a recent debate. Most authorities believe that the organization was simply a convivial wining-and-dining fraternal gathering and that its elaborate rules and minutes were intended as parodies to entertain members. (One thinks of the elaborate dinners set up by associations of journalists in late twentieth-century Washington.) But Margaret Jacob argues that more subversive activities (modelled on the rituals set forth in John Toland's *Pantheisticon* and connected with early freemasonry) were being carried on.[55] Her description of the 'Knights' has persuaded at least one reviewer of the existence of a 'radical masonic lodge' an 'early politically radical secret society of atheistic pantheists' to which Marchand belonged.[56] Yet as Jacob herself notes, the elaborate rules, regulations, and terms of address set forth in the records of the 'Chevaliers de la Jubilation' not only prefigure some aspects of eighteenth-century masonry, they are prefigured themselves by earlier convivial literary societies—in particular by 'Les Chevaliers de l'ordre de l'Union de la Joye' which had met in the Hague in the mid-seventeenth century. This earlier 'confrairie', which claimed to

[55] Jacob, *Radical Enlightenment*, 153-66, appendix, 267-79. For debate between Jacob and Berkvens-Stevelinck see *Quaerendo*, 13 (1983), 50-71, 124-48; 14 (1984), 63-76. For a vigorous refutation of Jacob's arguments see also G. C. Gibbs, 'The Radical Enlightenment', *The British Journal for the History of Science*, 17 (Mar. 1984), 67-80.

[56] James E. Force, 'The Origins of Modern Atheism', *Journal of the History of Ideas*, 50 (1989), 153-67.

follow the rule of Rabelais's *Abbaye de Thélème*, was described more than fifty years ago, by Gustave Cohen, as a 'free masonry of free thinkers'. It numbered among its members Jean De Witt and Christian and Constantin Huyghens. According to Cohen, it insisted on secrecy to avoid attracting the hostility of Calvinist synods.[57]

Jacob notes that a similar fear of arousing the hostility of members of the Walloon congregations to which they belonged helps to account for the secrecy that surrounded the 'Knights'.[58] Her argument hinges not only on interpreting the cryptic records of meetings but also on the activities of members of an 'inner circle'. As noted above, this 'inner circle' or 'inner core' consisted of members of the editorial board of the *Journal littéraire*.[59] This journal has long figured in secondary literature, not because of the novelty represented by its collegial editing but because for literary historians it represents the coming of age of a new generation, one which is regarded as more irreverent and more determined to promote the 'moderns' than were earlier Huguenots such as Bayle.[60]

From 1713 until 1722 the editorial board met every week in the Hague.[61] The very frequency of meetings points to the existence of a close-knit group; as far as I know, few precedents exist for this kind of focused collegial intellectual activity. In this regard the board deserves more consideration, not so much as a possible 'inner circle' of some other, indefinitely extended,

[57] Jacob, *Radical Enlightenment*, 157, mentions a reference to this society in Herbert Rowen's biography of *John De Witt* (Princeton, NJ, 1978). The earlier description is in Gustave Cohen, *Le Séjour de Ste-Evremond en Hollande (1666-1672)* (Paris? 1926), 51-2.

[58] Jacob, *Radical Enlightenment*, 162.   [59] See Ch. 2 n. 86.

[60] Pierre André Sayous, *Le Dix Huitième siècle à l'étranger* (Paris, 1861), 32-40; Joseph Texte, *Jean-Jacques Rousseau and the Cosmopolitan Spirit in Literature*, tr. J. W. Matthews (London, 1899), 29. The only monograph on the journal is a long outdated German doctoral dissertation by Paul Hemprich, *Le Journal littéraire de la Haye 1713-1737* (Berlin, 1915).

[61] This innovative arrangement flourished under the journal's original publisher, Thomas Johnson, but came to an end in 1722 when board members dispersed. Berkvens-Stevelinck, *La Vie*, 111. See also Elisabet Carayol, 'Thémiseul de Saint-Hyacinthe 1684-1746', *Studies in Voltaire*, 221 (1984), 33-8. After republishing some old issues, Johnson retired from business in 1727. From 1729-33 Gosse and Neaulme, having bought up Johnson's copyright, issued vols. 13-19 under different editorial guidance. In 1733 when Marchand was singlehandedly trying to issue a successor journal (see above) a Catholic publisher Van Duren took over from Gosse and Neaulme and employed La Barre de Beaumarchais as his sole editor. Marchand's dislike for this last publisher and editor is noted below.

Ex Libris PROSPERI MARCHAND,
Bibliopolæ Parifienfis , viâ
Jacobæâ , fub Phœnice.

Fig. 1. Phoenix: engraving by Bernard Picart. Prosper Marchand's
printer's mark, used when he was a Paris publisher on the rue Saint-
Jacques.

HISTOIRE

DE

L'ORIGINE

ET DES

PRÉMIERS PROGRÈS

DE

L'IMPRIMERIE.

PAR Mr. PROSPER MARCHAND.

A LA HAYE,

Chez PIERRE PAUPIE, Libraire.

M. DCC. XL.

Fig. 2. Title-page of Marchand's *Histoire de l'origine et des premiers progrès de l'imprimerie* (1740), commemorating the 300th anniversary of the invention of printing.

JUBILÆUM TYPOGRAPHORUM

LIPSIENSIUM:

Oder

Zweyhundert-Jähriges

Buchdrucker JubelFest/

Wie solches deroselben Kunst-Verwandte zu

Leipzig/ am Tage Johannis des Täuffers/ Anno Christi
1640. vnd also gleich 200. Jahr nach Erfindung dieser edlen
Kunst/mit Christlichen Ceremonien celebri-
ret vnd begangen.

Mit beygefügten vnterschiedenen Commendationibus,

Gratulationibus vnd Ehren-Schrifften/ so von Hoch-vnd Wolgradir-
ten dieser Löbl. Kunst gewogenen/hoch-vnd geneigten Herren/Pa-
tronen vnd Beförderern/zu Ehren vnd freundlichen
Gefallen eingeschicket worden.

GOtt dem allein weisen Geber vnd Erhalter al-

les Guten/zu Lob/Ehr/Preis vnd Danck; Teutscher Na-
tion, als deren Erfinderin/zu vnsterblichem Ruhm/der lieben Posteritet
aber zu Christ-eyferiger Nachfolge / vnd sonsten zu männigliches Wissen-
schafft/ Wenn / Wo/Wie / vnd durch Wen solche erfunden/vnd was für
hoher vnd wichtiger Nutz der Kirche Gottes vnd allen gläu-
bigen Christen in allen-Ständen daraus
entsprossen.

In öffentlichen Druck gegeben/vnd bey den gesampten

Buchdruckern daselbsten zu finden/

Im Jahr Christi

M. DC. XL.

Fig. 3. *Jubilaeum Typographorum*: 1640 publication of a printers' festival
held in Leipzig, commemorating the 200th anniversary of the invention of
printing.

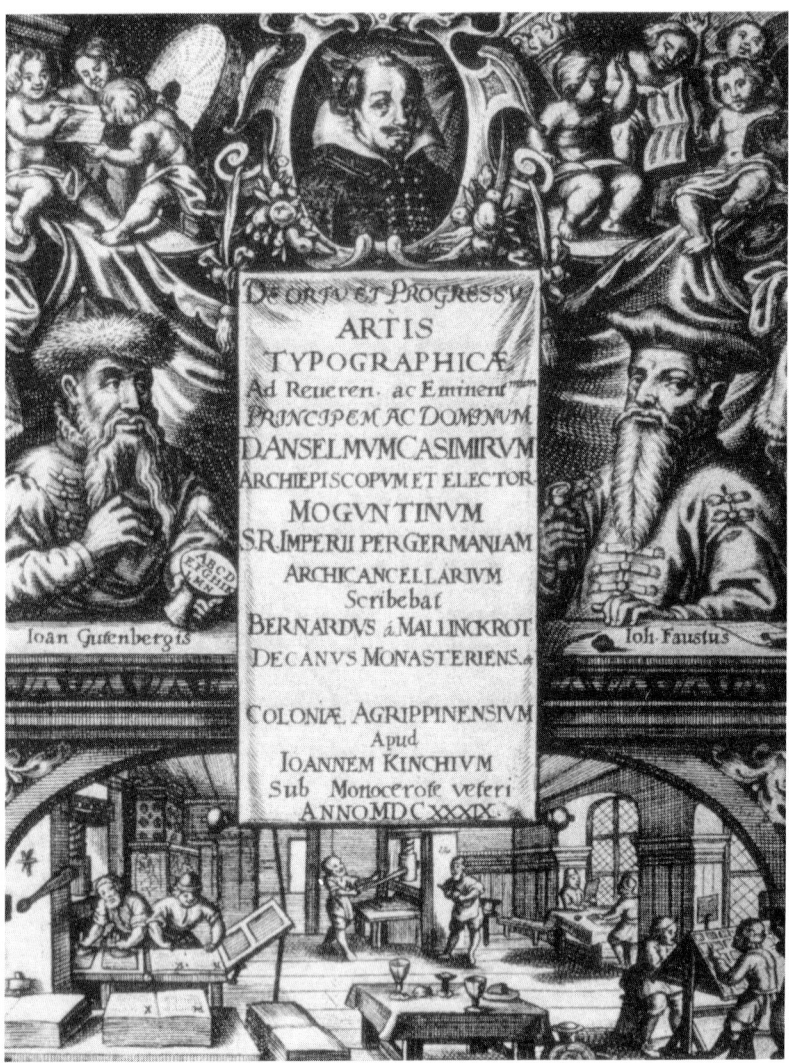

De Ortu et Progressu
ARTIS
TYPOGRAPHICÆ
Ad Reueren. ac Eminent
PRINCIPEM AC DOMINUM
D. ANSELMVM CASIMIRVM
ARCHIEPISCOPVM ET ELECTOR
MOGVNTINVM
SR. IMPERII PER GERMANIAM
ARCHICANCELLARIVM
Scribebat
BERNARDVS à MALLINCKROT
DECANVS MONASTERIENS.

COLONIÆ AGRIPPINENSIVM
Apud
IOANNEM KINCHIVM
Sub Monocerote veteri
ANNO MDCXXXIX.

Ioan Gutenbergis

Ioh. Faustus

Fig. 4. Title-page of Bernhard von Mallinckrot's *De Ortu et Progressu Artis Typographicae* (1639), also commemorating the 200th anniversary of the invention of printing, with engraved portraits of Gutenberg and 'Faustus' (Fust) above and printing-shop interior below.

La Fonderie dirigée par MINERVE, de même que l'Imprimerie.

J.V.Schley delin. et sculp. 1739.

Fig. 5. Minerva presiding over foundry and printing-shop. First page of Marchand's *Histoire de . . . l'imprimerie*, engraved by Jacob van der Schley.

L'IMPRIMERIE, descendant des Cieux, est accordée par Minerve et Mercure à l'Allemagne, qui la présente à la Hollande, l'Angleterre, l'Italie, & la France, les quatre prémières Nations chés les quelles ce bel Art fut adopté

Fig. 6. 'The Spirit of Printing Descending from the Heavens'. Frontispiece of Marchand's *Histoire de . . . l'imprimerie*, engraved by Jacob van der Schley.

JOANNES   CLERICUS.

Geneva Natus   an. 1657. 19 Mart. S.V.

Nil sine magno

Vita labore dedit   mortalibus.

Fig. 7. Joannes Clericus. Bernard Picart depicts Jean Le Clerc as a Latin-writing theologian and scholar. The volume with 'HAM' on its spine commemorates Le Clerc's translation from English into Latin of the work of an English theologian named Hammond. Le Clerc learnt English in the course of this translation.

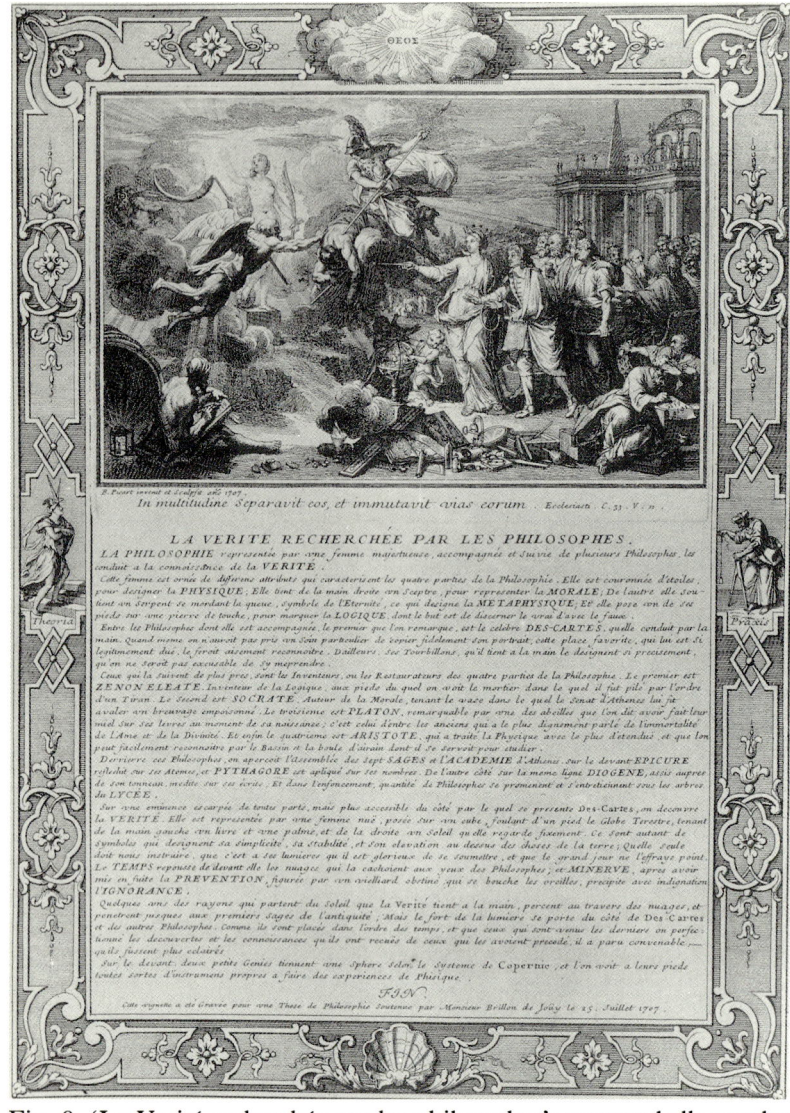

Fig. 8. 'La Verité recherchée par les philosophes': engraved allegory by Bernard Picart for Brillon de Jouy's dissertation which was defended on 15 July 1707. Philosophy, wearing a starry crown, is leading philosophers, with Descartes in front place, towards Truth. Father Time clears away the clouds which had veiled the naked personification. While Truth gazes at the sun which is held in her right hand, Minerva indignantly repels Ignorance who is shown with donkey's ears.

Fig. 9. 'Truth Sought by the Philosophers'. Fig. 8 has been reproduced with the figure of Newton substituted for that of Descartes and the caption translated into English. References to Picart and Brillon de Jouy have been deleted; the bottom line now reads: 'Printed for and sold by H. Overton and I. Hoole at the White Horse without Newgate.'

Fig. 10. Frontispiece engraved by Bernard Picart for *Journal literaire*, 9 (The Hague: Thomas Johnson, 1717), showing Picart's favourite motifs of Minerva, putti, geometrical drawings, and instruments.

TABLEAU DES PRINCIPALES RELIGIONS DU MONDE

En premier lieu on voit la RELIGION CHRETIENNE, au pied d'un grand arbre présentant la BIBLE couverte, qu'un Ministre Americain affecte de fermer d'une main et montrant de l'autre la livre en, et. ...

Fig. 11. Tableau of the principal religions of the world. Frontispiece to *Cérémonies et coutumes religieuses de tous les peuples du monde représentés en figures de Bernard Picart* (8 vols. in folio; Amsterdam: Jean Frédéric Bernard, 1723–48). The caption refers to the representations of Roman Catholic, Greek Orthodox, and Protestant churches as well as of a Jewish rabbi. It also alludes to contemporary quarrels between Jansenists and Jesuits and to the Asians and pre-Columbian American worshippers depicted in the background. The foreground is occupied, not by Moses and the Ten Commandments, but by a prophet of Islam holding a tablet inscribed with Muhammad's teachings.

Fig. 12. Interior of a Dutch synagogue. Engraving by Bernard Picart in *Cérémonies et coutumes*, i, facing p. 122. After prolonged negotiations, a friendly Portuguese Jew residing in Amsterdam enabled Picart to gain access to this synagogue.

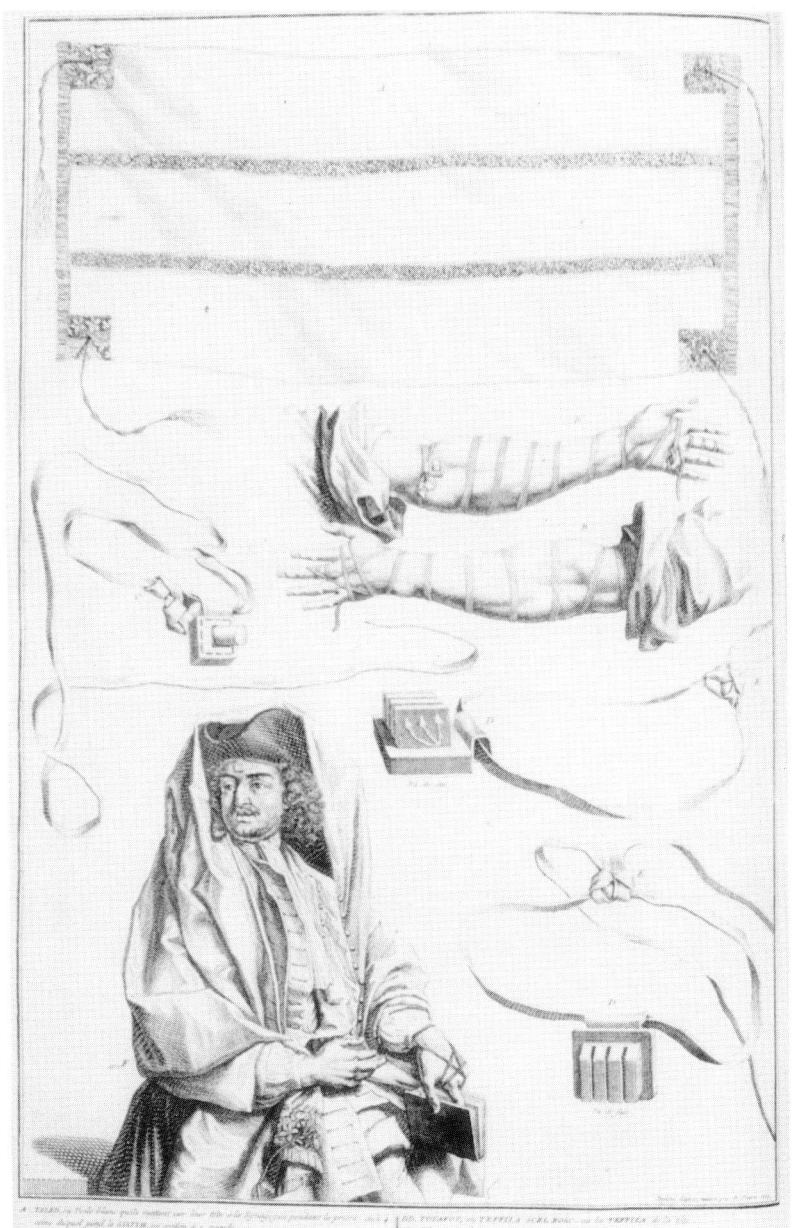

Fig. 13. Jewish ritual objects and vestments. Engraving by Bernard Picart in *Cérémonies et coutumes*, i, facing p. 126.

Isaac Onis, Aaron Monceca, et Jacob Brito, *présentent leurs*
LETTRES JUIVES
à Dom Quichotte, Sancho Panca, et Maitre Nicolas le Barbier.

Fig. 14. Frontispiece showing the Jewish travellers presenting their letters to Don Quixote, Sancho Panza, and Nicholas the Barber, engraved by Jacob van der Schley for vol. i of Jean-Baptiste de Boyer, Marquis d'Argens, *Lettres juives ou correspondance philosophique historique et critique* . . . (6 vols.; The Hague: Pierre Paupie, 1738). Marchand's sketch for this frontispiece and his instructions to the engraver are in the archives (MARCH. 28, fos. 243–6, *Catalogue*, 65) and suggest that the figures are meant to represent rival journal editors with whom Marchand was feuding.

Fig. 15. Detail from frontispiece to vol. i of *Lettres juives* (Fig. 14) showing van der Schley's portrait of Prosper Marchand above 'Alter Emendat' on right.

Fig. 16. Sketch made by Prosper Marchand for the engraver, Jacob van der Schley, to guide the design of the frontispiece (see Fig. 6) of Marchand's *Histoire de . . . l'imprimerie*. (MARCH. 28, fo. 218, *Catalogue*, 64.)

shadowy organization; but rather as a clearly delineated new kind of literary institution in its own right. In addition to Marchand, the journal editors included the Dutch mathematician and Newtonian, Willem Jacob 'sGravesande (1688–1742); the French libertine writer, Thémiseul de Saint-Hyacinthe (1684–1746); the Dutch journalist and poet, Justus van Effen (1684–1735); and the Dutch savant and civil servant, Albert Henri de Sallengre (1694–1723)—a varied group whose individual activities point away from commitment to any narrowly defined political or philosophical position. That the materials discussed in the weekly meetings included politics as well as science and literature is shown by the long review of Paul Rapin's treatise on Whigs and Tories which appeared in the 1717 issue. (Picart's frontispiece for the 1717 volume is presented in Fig. 10.) Rapin's 'whiggish' account received highly favourable notice. Other evidence shows that Marchand opposed absolutism, favoured the 'Glorious Revolution', and was enraged by supporters of James II.[62] But it is by no means certain, indeed it seems unlikely, that all the board members favoured 'republicanism', or that they should be characterized as forming a 'republican coterie'.[63]

Jacob admits that 'sGravesande was committed to the Christian faith as well as to Newtonianism; that Saint-Hyacinthe never embraced 'the pantheism or materialism found among his associates'; and that van Effen was a 'liberal Christian', a member of the Dutch Reformed Church who, in the 1730s, turned francophobic (and homophobic), expressing hostility to all French expatriate influences.[64] The 'inner circle' thus seems to lack ideological unity. The requisite 'radical' views are supplied rather by the so-called 'collaborators and associates' of the 'Knights' who did not serve on the editorial board.[65]

---

[62] See discussion of his collaboration with d'Argens, below.

[63] Jacob, *Radical Enlightenment*, 159.

[64] Jacob, *Radical Enlightenment*, 187, 190, 191. Van Effen's francophobic articles in the *Hollandische Spectator* of the 1730s are discussed by G. C. Gibbs, 'Some Intellectual and Political Influences of the Huguenot Émigrés in the United Provinces c.1680-1730', *Bijdragen en Mededelingen Betreffende de Geschiedenis der Nederlanden*, 90 (1975), 255-87: p. 271. See also P. J. Buijnsters, 'Les Lumières hollandaises', *Studies on Voltaire*, 87 (1972), 197-215: p. 205. Gibbs also alludes to the 'sodomite scandals' covered by the *Europische Mercurius* (Amsterdam, 1730) which were attributed to intrusive French influences by patriotic Dutch journalists.

[65] See e.g. Jacob's references to John Toland (*Radical Enlightenment*, 155) and to Rousset de Missy (p. 197).

In attempting to pin down adherence to particular positions, Jacob tends to look beyond the 'inner circle' towards figures, such as Rousset de Missy, who were connected with quite different journalistic enterprises.[66] She also expands the coterie to encompass almost any of the francophone publishers who happen to engage in correspondence with each other. To substantiate the assertion that the 'Knights' had 'contacts all over Europe', for example, she points to the activities of two publishers: Gaspard Fritsch and Henri du Sauzet. Fritsch, who had hired Marchand to work on Bayle's papers, did remain in contact with him. Du Sauzet, however, was always more of Marchand's enemy than his friend.[67] Whatever their connections with the 'Knights', it was in their ordinary capacity as publishers that both men extended their networks. Should one assign special significance to the fact that du Sauzet publicized books by some of the 'Knights' when he was merely promoting the works of authors on his list?[68] Why should we take the 'international character' of the networks extended by francophone publishers as pointing 'once again in a Masonic direction'?[69] Cosmopolitan

---

[66] On this Huguenot journalist-historian (1686-1762), who edited the *Mercure historique et politique*, 1724-49, see G. C. Gibbs, 'The Role of the Dutch Republic as the Intellectual Entrepôt of Europe', *Bijdragen en Mededelingen Betreffende de Geschiedenis*, 86 (1971), 323-49: pp. 343-4. Rousset de Missy's later role as editor of *L'Épilogueur moderne*, 1750-4 is treated by Dieter Gembicki, 'Le Journalisme à sensation', Rétat (ed.), *Le Journalisme*, 241-55. Gembicki takes note of Rousset's multiple ties to freemasonry as author, propagandist, and Grand Master without assigning much significance to this point (p. 252 n. 23). He emphasizes the way Marchand collaborated with Rousset on *L'Épilogueur moderne* to carry on the feud between Jean Baptiste Rousseau and Voltaire, siding with the former against the latter. Both men objected to Voltaire's tribute to the age of Louis XIV and his espousal of enlightened despotism. But their anti-Voltairian polemic also entailed attacking the poet's effort to popularize Newtonianism and to defend the cause of the moderns against the ancients in a way that seems somewhat inconsistent with Marchand's close association with Newtonians such as 'sGravesande and Allamand and his favouring the cause of the 'moderns' elsewhere. On Marchand's contributions to the journal, including his satiric verses on the struggle between Jansenists and Jesuits in the 1750s, see Berkvens-Stevelinck, *La Vie*, 119-20.

[67] Jacob, *Radical Enlightenment*, 184. Fritsch's business dealings with Henri du Sauzet (1686-1754) are elsewhere (p. 197) cited as evidence that du Sauzet provided a link between the 'Knights' and 'official Dutch Free masonry'. That du Sauzet was an enemy, not a friend, of Marchand's is noted by Berkvens-Stevelinck, *La Vie*, 156.

[68] Du Sauzet's journal, *Nouvelles littéraires contenant ce qui se passe de plus considerable dans la république des lettres* (12 vols. 1715-20), is described as publicizing books by the 'Knights': Jacob, *Radical Enlightenment*, 231. As publisher of Justus van Effen's *Bagatelle* (1718) and Henri de Sallengre's *Mémoires de littérature* (1715-18) (see Almagor, *Des Maizeaux*, 246), he was simply publicizing books on his own list.

[69] Jacob, *Radical Enlightenment*, 158.

networks were essential for extraterritorial publishers, whether they were masons or not.

The arguments I have put forth elsewhere in connection with Frances Yates on the Rosicrucian Enlightenment seem to apply with equal force to Margaret Jacob on the Radical Enlightenment.[70] It is difficult (if not impossible) to disentangle the routine, yet often clandestine, operations of a given firm from those of sworn members of a secret society or heterodox sect. It is all too easy to extend the influence of a secret society to encompass the interlocking, cosmopolitan book-trade networks that were extended across Europe. Extreme caution is needed to avoid reading allusions to inner-circle secrets in ordinary business transactions. However much caution is exerted, a generous margin for uncertainty should be left. When dealing with a bibliophile, such as Marchand, one must also allow for the attraction exerted by any 'rare' or 'curious' book. The presence of 'subversive' titles in a private library may be merely evidence of a desire to obtain a 'collector's item' and offers uncertain guidance as to the collector's views.[71] In general, it seems fair to say that Jacob's treatment makes insufficient allowance for uncertainty.

But Jacob's critics who scoff at the idea that Marchand and some of his companions were engaged in subversive activities probably also need to make more allowance for uncertainty.[72] In his preface to the *Cymbalum Mundi*, Marchand blandly asserts that there was nothing impious in Des Périers's work. It may be incautious to take such an assertion only at face value and to overlook the other possibilities at which the preface-writer seems to hint.[73] Jacob's critics have singularly little to say about the production and promotion of those clandestine texts that titillated and scandalized French readers during the eighteenth century.[74]

---

[70] Eisenstein, *Printing Press*, i. 140-1.

[71] Jacob, *Radical Enlightenment*, 226 ff., seems to overlook the bibliophile's passion for rare books when discussing titles in Marchand's private library.

[72] See references cited above, n. 54.

[73] Berkvens-Stevelinck, *L'Histoire du livre*, p. xviii, seems to miss the possibility of irony and to take the preface rather too literally.

[74] Jacob, *Radical Enlightenment*, 217-30. On the importance of these works see *inter alia*: Ira Wade, *The Clandestine Organization and Diffusion of Philosophic Ideas in France from 1700 to 1750* (Princeton, NJ, 1938); Roland Mortier (ed.), *Difficultés sur la religion . . . Texte intégral du 'Militaire Philosophe'* (Brussels, 1970), 9-39; P. Rétat (ed.), *Traité des trois imposteurs: Manuscrit clandestin du début du XVIII* siècle* (Lyons, 1973), 7-20.

Whether these texts were actually concocted, or simply doctored and circulated, and which of Marchand's friends had a hand in their manufacture, remains debatable. But it is clear that the tantalizing items placed in journals and reference works helped to sustain curiosity about them.

A good case in point is the *Traité des trois imposteurs*. This work has been described as 'the most important clandestine manuscript of the 18th century'.[75] Its printed history began with the publication of a hybrid volume consisting of (1) *La Vie*, an admiring biography of Spinoza (written around 1678 by Jean Lucas, a French journalist in Holland),[76] and (2) *L'Esprit* (composed around 1700) which contained, among other excerpts from diverse texts by diverse authors, the first French translation of the appendix to Spinoza's *Ethica*. After *La Vie et l'esprit de Spinosa* had been published by Marchand's friend Charles Levier in 1719,[77] the second section, *L'Esprit*, was reissued by Michael Böhm in 1721 under the new title: *Traité des trois imposteurs*. After being thus retitled, the French text would become inextricably entangled in that broader and longer lived Latin textual tradition which coupled Jesus with Moses and Muhammad.[78]

This textual tradition receives an extended treatment—by far the longest of any in Marchand's posthumously published two-volume *Dictionnaire historique*.[79] Under the rubric 'Imposteribus', Marchand tells about an imaginary book, one that everyone talks about but that no one has seen. In the thirteenth century, a Paris

[75] Silvia Berti, '"La Vie et l'esprit de Spinosa" (1719) et la prima traduzione francese dell'"Ethica"', *Rivista storica italiana*, 98 (1986), 5–47: p. 6. I owe thanks to Margaret Jacob for bringing this article to my attention. The above paragraph is entirely based on Dr Berti's findings.

[76] Spinoza's biographer, or rather hagiographer, Jean Maximilien Lucas, was yet another citizen of Cosmopolis. He belonged to the guild of 'libraires' in the Hague, issued a pamphlet series attacking Louis XIV, and was associated with an Amsterdam bookshop run by the publisher Rieuwertz which was a gathering place for 'independent thinkers', according to Paul Vernière, *Spinoza et la pensée française avant la révolution* (2 vols. Paris, 1954), i. 24.

[77] According to Berti, '"La Vie"', 22, a letter from Fritsch to Marchand written in 1740 asserts that Levier (she spells it LeVier) with Thomas Johnson printed the *Vie et l'esprit* 'at my request'. She also refers (pp. 27–8) to an earlier letter between the same correspondents which indicates that Rousset de Missy collaborated with Levier in doctoring *L'Esprit* for publication.

[78] On this tradition see the references to *Theophrastus Redidivus* (1659) in Berti, '"La Vie"', 30 n. 90.

[79] Prosper Marchand, 'Imposteribus', *Dictionnaire historique*, i. 312–29.

theologian attributed it to Emperor Frederick II. Thereafter, we are told, it has been attributed to Boccaccio, Aretino, Machiavelli, Servetus, Rabelais, Bruno, etc. Each author that is mentioned is discussed at some length, his books listed, and the reasons for regarding him as subversive are adduced. The article adds up to a remarkably detailed history of free thought. It poses the problem of disbelief in a provocative form—one which has continued to preoccupy scholars down to the present time.

The extent of Marchand's collaboration in the doctoring and distribution of such provocative texts as the *Traité* is difficult to determine. But in one case we have ample evidence of the important role he played as a literary collaborator. The author he helped in this instance was Jean-Baptiste de Boyer, Marquis d'Argens (1703–71). D'Argens has been described by Jean Sgard as one of the first of the 'journalistes-philosophes'. He was singled out by Daniel Mornet, together with Montesquieu and Voltaire, as one of the leading lights of the early Enlightenment.[80] The Marquis started out as a Regency libertine who frequented the Paris salons and engaged in diplomatic and military pursuits. While serving in the entourage of the French ambassador to Turkey he spent time in Constantinople. As a cavalry officer, he was crippled by a fall from a horse in a battle in 1734 and this brought his military career to an end. After six years as a man of letters residing in the Netherlands, he entered the service of the dowager Duchess of Württemberg and two years later, in 1742, having won favour from Frederick II, he took up residence in Potsdam. This move provoked Marchand's disapproval.[81] The latter was consistently hostile to despotism however enlightened. Unlike Marchand also, d'Argens remained a nominal Catholic

[80] Jean Sgard, 'd'Argens', in *Dictionnaire des journalistes*, ed. Sgard (Grenoble, 1976), 10–11. Daniel Mornet, *Les Origines intellectuelles de la révolution française* (Paris, 1934), ch. 2, pp. 34–7. A doctoral dissertation on the Marquis, written under Mornet's direction, was published in 1928. It is still the only full-length biography: Elise Johnston, *Le Marquis d'Argens: Sa vie et ses œuvres* (Paris, n.d.).

[81] See Berkvens-Stevelinck, *L'Histoire du livre*; Sgard, 'd'Argens', 10–11; Steve Larkin, 'Correspondance entre Prosper Marchand et le Marquis d'Argens', *Studies on Voltaire*, 222 (1984), 44–5. Although all these authorities agree that Marchand disapproved of the Prussian king, Larkin disagrees with Berkvens-Stevelinck and Sgard that d'Argens's determination to move to Berlin precipitated a rupture between the two men and argues that the initial break was over d'Argens forming an alliance with the publisher Pierre Paupie despite Marchand's objections. (Johnston apparently was unaware of the Marchand correspondence and has no light to cast on the relations between the two men.)

while making no bones about his incredulity. He liked to tell about his reaction to a bad storm at sea when travelling between Rome and Leghorn. The Catholic sailors knelt to pray, the Protestant passengers sang hymns, but he, d'Argens, simply went on reading his book, which, not coincidentally, was a work by Pierre Bayle, and amazed all aboard by his serenity.[82]

During most of d'Argens's stay in the Netherlands, his closest collaborator and most trusted advisor was Prosper Marchand. 'You are the true father of my writings', wrote d'Argens to Marchand. Elsewhere the Marquis addressed his friend as 'brother' and as 'tutelary God'.[83] These expressions of gratitude were for Marchand's help with an immensely popular serial work: *Lettres juives ou correspondence philosophique, historique et critique d'un juif voyageur en differens états de L'Europe*, published in the Hague by Pierre Paupie in 1736. This six-volume work was an immediate success and launched the Marquis on his successful career as a man of letters.[84] The Amsterdam publishers fought over the rights to his subsequent work and at their request the Marquis composed two sequels: *Lettres cabbalistiques* and the *Lettres chinoises*.[85] A new edition of *The Jewish Letters* was issued in 1738. It was reprinted ten times before 1777. As author of this *succès de scandale*, d'Argens became *persona non grata* in France and the French ambassador was instructed to seek him for extradition. D'Argens went into hiding and confided his hiding place to only three people: Voltaire, Abbé Prévost, and Marchand.[86]

The Jewish Letters belongs to the genre made famous by Montesquieu's *Persian Letters* and similarly highlights the foibles and follies of eighteenth-century French society by pretending to see it through the eyes of a foreign observer. Such distancing devices, one might suggest, came naturally to those

---

[82] Johnston, *Le Marquis d'Argens*, 27. The same anecdote is in Rétat, *Dictionnaire de Bayle*, 243. Elsewhere (p. 130) Rétat describes d'Argens as the most capable popularizer of Bayle.

[83] Cited by Berkvens-Stevelinck, *L'Histoire du livre*, 52, 64. See also Larkin, 'Correspondance', 9.

[84] Larkin, 'Correspondance', 26–7, notes that within a year of publication d'Argens knew he could live by his pen. He lists Paupie's payments to the author on p. 30.

[85] All these *Lettres* were published together in a 24-vol. edn. (1768). See Larkin, 'Correspondance', 34–5.

[86] Sgard, 'd'Argens', 10. Larkin, 'Correspondance', 18 ff., describes the many stops (in Utrecht, Maarsen, Maestricht etc.) made by the Marquis while he was on the run.

expatriate writers who had to perceive their former homeland from afar. Of course the need to evade censors also played a role. The first volume opens with a typical disclaimer of authorship; a fictitious translator explains how the letters came into his possession and why they deserve 'translation' even though written by an infidel Jew. Having noted that there had been few objections to the earlier letters of a Turkish spy, the preface-writer feels justified in offering the views of a different infidel. The letters purport to be from one Aaron Monseca, a merchant *en route* to Paris, writing to his friend the rabbi in Constantinople. He writes in a racy vein about the behaviour of adulterous French women whom he contrasts with the virtuous Jewish wives back home (d'Argens's talents as a pornographer are more fully displayed elsewhere) and then goes on to complain about the unnecessary mysteries and complications introduced by French Catholic priests into the worship of divine law. Another letter contains an indignant reference to the way Voltaire was forced in to exile for writing the *Lettres philosophiques* and we are reminded that even the celebrated Descartes had to go north. The French savants (writes the Jewish traveller) are like birds who have had their wings clipped and have been rendered incapable of soaring.[87]

Perhaps this is enough to convey something of the flavour of the work. The decision to use the reasonable Jew as a foil for the superstitious French has been attributed to d'Argens's earlier encounter, while in Constantinople, with a Jewish physician.[88] The description of Holland as a haven for people of diverse faiths, 'nowhere do men of diverse religions coexist more peacefully ... Jews, Nazarenes, Mohammedans treat each other as brothers',[89] may have owed something to Marchand. D'Argens had only been in the Hague for two years before the *Jewish Letters* were published whereas Marchand had lived there for twenty-seven years. His friend Picart had completed (before his death in 1733) a remarkable series of engravings covering reli-

---

[87] *Lettres juives ou correspondance philosophique historique et critique entre un juif voyageur en différens états de l'Europe et ses correspondans en divers endroits* (The Hague: Pierre Paupie, 1738: new augmented edn., 6 vols.), i, preface and *passim*. The comment about Voltaire and clipping the wings of French savants is in the 3rd letter, pp. 22–3.

[88] Johnston, *Le Marquis d'Argens*, 10, notes that the physician's name, Fonseca, probably explains why the protagonist of the *Jewish Letters* is named Monseca.

[89] Cited from *Lettres juives*, no. 101, by Johnston, *Le Marquis d'Argens*, 32.

gious ceremonies throughout the world (Fig. 11).[90] The first volume of this multi-volumed work included a picture of the interior of a Dutch synagogue and detailed views of Jewish vestments and ritual objects (Figs. 12 and 13).[91] The author (and publisher) of this nine-volume pioneering comparative study of the world's religions was Jean Frédéric Bernard (1683?–1744), a fascinating figure in his own right: one of those rare 'libraire-philosophes' who wrote books in addition to publishing and selling them.[92]

Jean Frédéric Bernard was born in Provence of Huguenot parents who left France in 1686. He worked for publishers in Geneva in 1704 and served as an agent for Genevan publishers in Amsterdam in 1709, before being admitted to the Amsterdam guild himself in 1711. He published among other works, a treatise on the history of Swiss quarrels concerning the *Consensus Helveticus* (1726); a three-volume edition of the works of Rabelais, illustrated by Picart; collections of travel books; and a multi-volumed 'history of superstitions ancient and modern'. As author, he completed the *Histoire critique des journaux* by Denis François Camusat after the latter's death in 1732; as publisher, he issued this much cited work in 1734. He also wrote the *Réflexions morales satiriques et comiques* which was issued in four editions (1711, 1713, 1716 and 1733) and which contained a series of 'Persian Letters' that anticipated Montesquieu.[93] An excerpt from the first edition of 1711 is worth citing:

These barbarians view people from other parts of the world with disdain. They treat them almost as savages; especially those who obey the precepts of the Koran. To call a man a Turk, a Moor, an Arab is to designate a scoundrel. We have the same right, dear friend. If we encounter an unjust or vindictive man, a knave or a traitor, we should call him a Christian.[94]

---

[90] J. F. Bernard and B. Picart, *Cérémonies et coutumes religieuses de tous les peuples du monde* (9 vols. Amsterdam: J. F. Bernard, 1723–43). For more discussion of this work see below, Ch. 4, where the publisher-author also figures as the father-in-law of Marc Michel Rey.   [91] Vol. i, facing pp. 122 and 126.

[92] Sgard, *Dictionnaire des journalistes*, 38–9, supplies relevant biography.

[93] J. F. Bernard's *Réflexions morales, satiriques et comiques* which was issued anonymously in 4 edns. (1711, 1713, 1716, 1733) is singled out by G. L. van Roosbroeck, *Persian Letters before Montesquieu* (New York, 1936), as the most important of the many works in this genre which influenced Montesquieu. The relevant sections of the *Réflexions* are reproduced by van Roosebroeck as an appendix.

[94] Cited by van Roosbroeck, *Persian Letters*, 67.

In the third edition of his *Réflexions,* Bernard had speculated about the possibility of a Chinese or a Mexican someday producing their own version of European satires, 'diverting themselves with our manners and ridiculing our fantasies. We supply more than enough for them to call us: the Barbarians of Europe'.[95] This is very much in keeping with the spirit of later series of 'letters' from fictitious exotic observers and may have influenced d'Argens as it had, earlier, influenced Montesquieu.

Such 'influences' are necessarily speculative. The correspondence between Marchand and d'Argens offers more concrete evidence of how the content of the *Jewish Letters* was affected by their collaboration. Marchand vigorously objected to d'Argens's political quiescence. Following Bayle, the Marquis was in favour of the absolute submission of subjects to their king and wrote passages in praise of the Bourbons. Marchand's interventions were aimed at eliminating such praise; in one volume, he managed to slip criticism of Louis XIV's reign into the table of contents.[96] On religious issues, he inserted attacks on Bossuet and objected strenuously to d'Argens's indulgence toward monks and Jesuits.[97] To be sure, he wrote, the Jansenists were probably even crazier than the Jesuits (given their *convulsionnaires*) but they were not as sinister.[98] He also intervened when d'Argens began to write about British churchmen:[99] 'I've modified a letter where you attack the Presbyterians without knowing them and admire the Anglicans without knowing them. I corrected that by showing the latter are the most insolent creatures on earth. You may prefer them because they have bishops but we will work to eliminate such traces of your residual prejudice.'[100] Unlike Jean Le Clerc who sought to curry favour with Anglican bishops, Marchand had a deep quasi-Puritan distaste for hierarchy and

[95] Cited by van Roosbroeck, *Persian Letters*, 83.

[96] Marchand inserted a note observing that Monseca strangely failed to object to Louis XIV's overweening ambition and acts of persecution. Larkin, 'Correspondance', 43.

[97] Mornet, *Origines intellectuelles*, 35, comments on d'Argens's horror of monks, noting that he devoted more than 4 pp. of the 'index méthodique' in the *Jewish Letters* to an enumeration of his griefs. One wonders how much of this anticlerical index was composed by Marchand.   [98] Larkin, 'Correspondance', 37.

[99] Larkin, 'Correspondance', 32, notes that d'Argens relied more and more heavily on Marchand as the *Jewish Letters* began to expand to take in countries outside France with which the Marquis was unfamiliar. Although he needed only a few travel books to work up a chapter, he was caught short on Scotland and begged Marchand to provide some filler material.   [100] Larkin, 'Correspondance', 39.

ceremony. 'Of all Protestants, the best are the Mennonites who approach apostles most closely.'[101]

That Marchand played a major role in seeing the work through the press is clear not only from the correspondence but also from visual evidence supplied by van der Schley's frontispiece to the first volume (Fig. 14). This follows Marchand's own sketch and depicts Don Quixote and Sancho Panza, together with 'Nicolas the Barber', in a library being presented with a copy of *Lettres juives*. Unless clued in by other evidence, it is likely that the reader would miss a joking allusion to three figures Marchand regarded as his enemies: Antoine Augustin Bruzen de la Martinière (1662–1749), who claimed the title of 'geographer to the King of Spain', and his assistant, Des Roches de Parthenay, were jokingly referred to as Don Quichotte and Sancho Panza in Marchand's correspondence with d'Argens.[102] Bruzen had been a friend of Desmaiseaux, had fought with Rousset de Missy, and took exception to passages inserted in the *Lettres juives* characterizing the Spaniards as thieves and assassins and Spain as the land of the Inquisition.[103] Bruzen employed as a copyist and compiler an ex-Jesuit named Yves Joseph de la Motte who wrote under the alias of 'de la Hodde' and was called 'le barbier de Don Quichotte' by d'Argens and Marchand.[104] All three men belonged to a small 'cabale' centred around Jean van Duren, a Catholic publisher in the Hague, who was engaged in a feud with Pierre Paupie and employed La Barre de Beaumarchais to edit a continuation of the *Journal literaire*.[105] The frontispiece showing the first volume of the finished series being presented in the presence of their three enemies caused the collaborators considerable merriment, as their correspondence indicates.[106] Their letters also show how d'Argens, who at one time had admired the geographer, had been completely turned against him by Marchand. The latter's manipulations, behind the scenes, so to speak, are also commemorated in the same frontispiece. A letter written to Marchand in 1739 by

[101] Ibid. Here, as in the case of his intensive Bible-reading noted above, pp. 80–1, one has the impression that Marchand was more genuinely devout than Jacob's treatment suggests.   [102] Larkin, 'Correspondance', 11.

[103] Ibid. 41. Larkin notes that Marchand turned d'Argens against Bruzen after the Marquis had first praised the author of the *Grand Dictionnaire géographique*. See also M. Couperus, 'Bruzen de la Martinière', *Dictionnaire des journalistes*, 216.

[104] Sgard, 'Yves Joseph de la Motte', *Dictionnaire des journalistes*, 220–1.

[105] M. Couperus, Discussion, *L'Étude des périodiques anciens: Colloque d'Utrecht*, 106–7.   [106] Larkin, 'Correspondance', 11, reference to letter no. 19.

Frederick II's chaplain notes: 'I recognized your face next to the inscription: *Alter Emendat* and imagine this was done deliberately by the engraver' (Fig. 15).[107]

Indeed it was done deliberately. The engraver, however, was only following Marchand's instructions. The latter was unusually meticulous about determining every visual detail. Doubtless his intense concern with iconography and illustration owed much to his years of friendship with Picart. His visual memory was quite remarkable. Some of the most intriguing items in the archives are his instructions for illustrations. For example, he writes to van der Schley about a vignette to be divided into two portions; one, to represent ancient times; the other, modern times.

On the left, show inhabitants in delapidated and torn, old clothes working in a rural setting using crude tools. Show canoes rather than boats; streams rather than rivers. On the right, depict similar scenes in an entirely different manner and with the same éclat that my friend Picart displayed in the third volume of the *Works of Fontenelle* where the topic was the renewal of arts and letters during the last three centuries.[108]

The reference to a specific picture to be copied is also typical. 'For your portrayal of Chalcas, you should use the old Greek physician in Lebrun's *Méléagre mourant* or Picart's *Homère* and for Apollo, copy the Rubens in the Luxembourg Gallery but make it more animated.'[109]

Finally, when he was determined to leave nothing to chance, Marchand himself made crude sketches to accompany his instructions. The sketches are so crude, indeed, that they are difficult to decipher even when juxtaposed with finished engravings. Take for example the sketch reproduced in Fig. 16. Without guidance, one is unlikely to recognize it as the visual instruction for Fig. 6. The chief clue, characteristically enough,

[107] Relevant correspondence and sketches are contained in MARCH. 28, fos. 243–7, *Catalogue*, 65. This portrait was first discussed by Berkvens-Stevelinck, 'Prosper Marchand: Trait d'union', 66.

[108] MARCH. 28, fo. 55. This item is listed in *Catalogue*, 59, as a letter to van der Schley concerning a vignette for an unidentified work to be published by Neaulme. The instructions note that the vignette is intended for a chapter covering manners, customs, and voyages.

[109] Cited by Berkvens-Stevelinck, *La Vie*, 162. It seems likely that Marchand frequently consulted his copy of Picart's posthumously published *Imposteurs innocentes ou receuil d'estampes* (Amsterdam, 1734) which contained copies of works by Le Brun, Rubens, and the rest.

is provided by the Hebrew lettering which is carefully done. With this glimpse of how Marchand's hidden hand may be detected behind the seemingly impersonal engraving, we seem to have come full circle and at an appropriate end for this chapter.

Before concluding, however, one more observation is in order. This discussion has stressed Marchand's encounters with two different eighteenth-century sub-cultures: as a privileged *libraire* on the Rue Saint-Jacques and as an *émigré* in the Netherlands. But when one considers the full trajectory of his long career, one is struck by the amount of time that he spent pouring over old books and visiting other centuries than his own, the sixteenth century, in particular. He insisted on travelling with his own library; he always had a much larger imaginary library in his mind. This points to yet another milieu, one that is not designated on any map of Europe and that tends to be neglected both by old-fashioned sociologists of literature and currently fashionable cultural historians of *mentalités*. It was above all in the world of books that Prosper Marchand felt most at home.

4

The Cosmopolitan Enlightenment

THE multifarious activities of Prosper Marchand, occurring as they did outside the boundaries of his native land, are worth keeping in mind when attempting to contextualize the French Enlightenment. Most treatments of the philosophes draw heavily on studies of writers and their publics within eighteenth-century France. Very few, if any, consider that French literary life also flourished outside the Bourbon realm. I say French literary life—perhaps francophone is a better term to describe those expatriate enclaves which were formed around foreign publishing firms and editorial offices. What applies to writers also applies to readers. Markets for francophone books and journals existed in Poland and Russia, in Stockholm and Berlin, as well as in Paris and the provinces of the Bourbon realm.

The existence of an indeterminate francophone zone as a relatively autonomous field of operations tends to be concealed by conventional treatments of that self-congratulatory cultural movement known as *Les Lumières, Aufklärung,* Enlightenment. I agree with the editors of an essay collection—*The Enlightenment in National Context*—that more attention should be given to the 'geographical, social and political *location* of this cultural movement'.[1] But we will be perpetually frustrated in attempting to pin down its location if our inquiries are circumscribed by the boundaries of nineteenth-century nation-states. This is especially true of the French Enlightenment; too many energetic cultural centres were located beyond the Bourbon realm for the movement to be contained within France.

In this connection the exceptionally well documented career of Prosper Marchand is instructive. His work on the third edition of Pierre Bayle's *Dictionnaire* and on the *Journal literaire,* his instructions to book illustrators, his collaboration on the *Jewish Letters* of the Marquis d'Argens, his posthumously published

---

[1] Roy Porter, Preface, in Porter and M. Teich (eds.), *The Enlightenment in National Context* (Cambridge, 1981), pp. vii–viii.

article on the history of free thought, all surely constituted significant contributions to the French Enlightenment. Yet they did not entail attendance at any Parisian salon and were indeed made only after the former publisher-bookseller had left France for good.

The same point applies to many of the engravings of Bernard Picart and all the publications of Jean Frédéric Bernard. As noted above, these two men collaborated on a multi-volumed survey of religious ceremonies throughout the world. Their lavishly illustrated folio volumes were much too sumptuous to be within the reach of ordinary readers. Nevertheless, they were considered offensive by Catholic authorities and were banned throughout the Austrian Netherlands, much to the indignation of the expatriate journalist Jean Baptiste de la Varenne.[2] This work has recently attracted the attention of Odile Faliu, an art historian. In a pertinent preface to her study of Picart's illustrations, Emmanuel Le Roy Ladurie describes the sense of 'culture shock' which is still conveyed to a late twentieth-century French reader by a frontispiece presenting Muslim, Brahmin, and native American priests on the same plane as the Pope (see Fig. 10).[3] When it comes to locating the two men who produced the collaborative work, however, the otherwise perceptive preface-writer seemed to select an unsuitable frame.

To set the work of 'two Bernards' (as he calls author and illustrator) in a suitable context, he offers a description of conditions in France after the death of the Sun King. It is true that Bernard Picart never completely severed his contacts with his native land. He may have travelled incognito from Amsterdam to Paris; he did design engravings dealing with the Mississippi bubble and John Law.[4] Nevertheless, the work of the 'two Bernards' needs to be set in a different context.

The frontispiece in question was designed in Amsterdam for a Dutch edition of the work. Other illustrations also owed less to

[2] M. Couperus, *Un périodique français en Hollande: 'Le Glaneur historique' (1731–1733)* (The Hague, 1971), 31.

[3] Emmanuel Le Roy Ladurie, Preface to Odile Faliu's *Cérémonies et coutumes religieuses de tous les peuples du monde dessinées par Bernard Picart* (Paris, 1988). It seems likely that the sense of 'culture shock' would be more muted among Protestant readers.

[4] His unfortunately timed frontispiece to the 3rd edn. of Bayle's *Dictionnaire* celebrating Law is noted above. Another engraving which satirized the Mississippi affair is described by Faliu, *Cérémonies*, 16.

Picart's trips to Paris than to his residence in Amsterdam. The portrayal of the interior of a synagogue and the ritual objects employed therein (Figs. 12 and 13), for example, were based on his gaining access to Jewish services after prolonged negotiations with a friendly Portuguese Jew.[5] As for the text of the multi-volumed work, its author, editor, and publisher had lived the life of a French expatriate, first in Geneva then in Amsterdam, since he was 3 years old. As noted above, maintaining an authorial distance from Catholic Bourbon France came quite naturally to this *philosophe-libraire*. The first edition of his earlier 'Persian Letters' had been issued before the Sun King had died. His sensitivity to the varieties of religious experience, his hatred of the Inquisition, and his leaning toward deism, all of which are reflected in the text of the multi-volumed work,[6] owed little or nothing to the changes that transpired within France after Louis XIV's death.

The work of the Marquis d'Argens provides another case in point. This libertine author is assigned considerable prominence in studies of diverse phases of the French Enlightenment. He is placed in the company of Montesquieu and Voltaire, to illustrate early eighteenth-century trends, by Daniel Mornet. He is also used to illustrate late eighteenth-century trends as the author of no less than six titles on Robert Darnton's list of 'forbidden French bestsellers' which circulated on the eve of the Revolution.[7] In addition, his name crops up in Darnton's account of mid-century French literary life, based on files kept, between 1748 and 1753, by an inspector of the book trade.

These files 'constitute a virtual census of the literary population of Paris, from the most famous philosopher to the most obscure hack' and enable us 'to trace a profile of the intellectual at the height of the Enlightenment'.[8] One entry concerns a

---

[5] See Faliu, *Cérémonies*, 31 ff.

[6] J. F. Bernard and B. Picart, *Cérémonies et coutumes religieuses de tous les peuples du monde* (9 vols. Amsterdam: J. F. Bernard, 1723-43). The most relevant passage on deism is in vol. iv. 333 ff. The dreadful practices of the Inquisition are described in vol. ii, sect. 3, bks 1-4. Bk. 4 offers illustrations of tortures and executions. Contributions to the 'Black Legend' made by Elizabethans during the era of the Armada were greatly reinforced by the propagandists of the Huguenot diaspora later on.

[7] D. Mornet, *Les Origines intellectuelles de la révolution française 1715-1787* (Paris, 1933), 34-5; Robert Darnton, 'The Forbidden Bestsellers of Prerevolutionary France', *Bulletin of the American Academy of Arts and Sciences*, 43 (1989), 17-45: p. 31 n.

[8] Darnton, 'A Police Inspector Sorts His Files', *The Great Cat Massacre* (New York, 1984), ch. 4, p. 145.

libelliste named Fougeret de Montbrun who wrote a satire 'against
he government of France and especially against M. Berryer and
M. d'Argens who is a particular target of his resentment'.[9] The
satire was aptly titled: *Le Cosmopolite, citoyen du monde.*
Fougeret's satire was printed in the Hague. It was aimed against
the Marquis d'Argens because the Marquis had its author 'run
out of Prussia where he used to live'. It is true that the Marquis
had frequented the salons of Paris before taking off for the
Netherlands and that he later made several trips back to the
'grand ville' after taking up residence at Frederick II's court.[10]
Nevertheless, any composite portrait of 'the intellectual at the
height of the Enlightenment' will be singularly incomplete if it is
restricted to the literary population of Paris.

Marchand's other collaborative ventures point to the formation
of influential literary coteries beyond French borders. The
weekly meetings of the editorial board of the *Journal literaire*
lacked the cachet of regular attendance at Mme Doublet's salon.
Yet these were meetings where papers were read and the issues
of the day were discussed by a varied group of literati, scientists,
and savants. The purpose of the literary-cum-dining society
formed by the journal's editors is more uncertain. Margaret
Jacob has not proved her case that the board constituted the
nucleus of a subversive movement affiliated with freemasonry.
Nor does she really demonstrate that there was any one concerted
movement to be described as a 'radical' Enlightenment aimed at
propagating pantheism, republicanism, and materialism.[11] But
her account of the coteries that were formed around publishing
houses, private libraries, and editorial offices in the Netherlands
during the first half of the eighteenth century does at least draw
attention to those expatriate enclaves and transnational networks
which others are prone to neglect.

Such neglect is due in part to the regrettable tendency (noted in
Chapter 1) to treat extraterritorial publishing as a purely commercial enterprise devoid of any cultural or intellectual ramifica-

---

[9] Ibid. 177–8.

[10] E. Johnston, *Le Marquis d'Argens: Sa vie et ses œuvres* (Paris, 1928), 78–9. See also
app. A, pp. 196–9, which cites a letter from d'Argens to Bachaumont written around
1749 asking that Mme Doublet be assured of his respect and that best wishes be sent to
all her 'parishioners'.

[11] See discussion of *The Radical Enlightenment* in Ch. 3 above.

tions. There is general agreement that almost all the main works of the French Enlightenment—from Montesquieu's *Lettres persanes* (Amsterdam, 1721) to d'Holbach's *Système de la nature* (Amsterdam, 1770)—were first published outside France. To be sure, false foreign place-names were sometimes used to disguise Parisian publication, as was the case with the first edition of the *Encyclopédie*. But the troubled history of that publication suggests why there was a frequent resort to actual publication abroad. Although this frequent resort is often acknowledged, its implications are rarely spelt out. Intellectual interchange among expatriates finds no place in accounts which reduce the operations of a given firm to the functions performed by any service industry. Manuscripts get sent abroad; bales of books get smuggled in or are tacitly permitted in; special arrangements with postal officials and private couriers are made for the regular delivery of journals —all this elaborate machinery gets described in minute detail but only to be assigned a purely instrumental role.

On this point Peter Gay and Robert Darnton are for once in agreement. When discussing the role of Voltaire's favourite agent Damilaville, who facilitated the penetration of French markets, Gay refers rather contemptuously to those 'hangers-on' who acted as the 'distributors' rather than as the 'producers of ideas'.[12] Darnton similarly segregates the creators of literature from the distributors. Publishers and booksellers are described as men 'who made literature happen even if they did not create it'.[13] They belong among 'the forgotten middlemen of literature': a motley crew of travelling salesmen, colporteurs, confidence men, paper makers, typesetters, and wagon drivers.[14] Elsewhere, in one of his many memorable phrases, he refers to 'a fertile crescent of printing houses which arched around France from Amsterdam to Avignon'.[15] The crescent's fertility is manifested in the production of typographical societies which sprang up 'like mushrooms' during the second half of the eighteenth century. But however fertile in printing shops and colourful characters,

[12] P. Gay, *The Enlightenment: An interpretation* (2 vols. New York, 1966), i. 18–19.

[13] 'Philosophy under the Cloak', in R. Darnton and D. Roche (eds.), *Revolution in Print, The Press in France 1775-1800* (Berkeley, Calif., 1989), 27–50: p. 29.

[14] Darnton, 'The Forgotten Middlemen of Literature', *The Kiss of Lamourette* (New York, 1990), ch. 8.

[15] Darnton, 'Sounding the Literary Market', *Eighteenth Century Studies* (special issue) 17 (Summer 1984), 477–93: p. 489.

the border territories are depicted as barren soil for those who cultivate the history of ideas.

French literary life in general and Enlightenment coteries in particular are thus seen to pivot around distinctively French institutions such as 'le cour et la ville', the salons, and the academies. If some room is made for expatriate literati and their cosmopolitan literary reviews, it is made solely in connection with the generation which experienced the revocation of the Edict of Nantes. Once that generation left the scene, it is assumed that the French Republic of Letters became more and more exclusively Parisian. It was no longer 'peopled and defined by scholars with Protestant, emigré, and academic identities'—as one recent study has put it.[16]

Another earlier work, contained in the two-volume *Livre et société* collection, stressed the contrast between the cosmopolitanism of the Republic of Letters represented by Pierre Bayle's journal of the 1680s and the Parisian focus of the later *Mémoires secrets pour servir à l'histoire de la république des lettres* which had initially emanated from Mme Doublet's salon in hand-copied form and was eventually issued in print from London (beginning in 1777).[17] Tables and graphs are produced to show how the content became more French and more Parisian when the expatriate Huguenot editor of the late seventeenth century gave way to the later Parisian *nouvelliste-à-la-main*. Recent computer studies comparing news reports for the year 1768, however, show that some ten out of twenty-one items carried in the Parisian newsletter were precisely identical with items appearing in 1768 issues of an extraterritorial printed journal, the *Courier du Bas-Rhin*.[18]

This twice-monthly journal had been started in 1762 and was issued from the principality of Cleves by two local publishers who hired a French-speaking Piedmontese exile, Jean Manzon (1740–98), as their editor. An ex-Jesuit novice turned Enlighten-

---

[16] Dena Goodman, 'Enlightenment Salons', *Eighteenth Century Studies* (special issue) 22 (Spring 1989), 329–51: p. 330.

[17] Jean Louis and Maria Flandrin, 'La Circulation du livre dans la société du 18ᵉ siècle', in F. Furet (ed.), *Livre et société dans la France du XVIIIᵉ siècle* (2 vols. Paris, 1970), ii. 38–72: pp. 44–5.

[18] François Moureau, 'Les *Mémoires secrets* de Bauchamont, le *Courier du Bas-Rhin* et les bulletinistes Parisiens', in Jean Varloot and Paula Jensen (eds.), *L'Année 1768 à travers la presse traitée par ordinateur* (Paris, 1981), 58–80.

ment publicist who served as a translator for Marc Michel Rey, Manzon is one of those neglected cultural intermediaries (a forgotten middleman?) who deserves to be better known.[19] He was a close friend and ardent defender of Linguet and published the first summary of the latter's *Mémoires sur la Bastille*. He also fits into the later phases of the 'radical' movement depicted by Margaret Jacob, in so far as he sympathized with the 'materialist' views expressed by d'Holbach and saw his journal temporarily banned from France for publishing extracts from the clandestine *Militaire philosophe*. But, as was the case with Linguet also, Manzon was devoid of sympathy for 'republicanism' and favoured the cause of the 'enlightened despots'. His chief support came from the Prussian king who was the overlord of Cleves, and his journal was sometimes described as the 'oracle of Potsdam'. He also received a regular subsidy from the Polish court and despite Russian pressure upheld the cause of the Polish king.[20]

Subscribers to the *Courier du Bas-Rhin* were receiving a journal that was scarcely less cosmopolitan in its editorial policies and its sponsors than had been the seventeenth-century journals of Bayle and Le Clerc. The very title of the Parisian newsletter was largely borrowed from an earlier cosmopolitan publication: the Marquis d'Argens had issued a multi-volume *Mémoires secrets de la république des lettres* from Amsterdam between 1737 and 1748.

Those who frequented the Paris salons of the later eighteenth century seem to have been no less dependent on extraterritorial publication than had been French readers in the age of Louis XIV. To be sure, Parisian *nouvellistes* and *bulletinistes* were responsible for feeding French items to the expatriate publishers and editors, just as they had always been.[21] (One recalls the items sent by Prosper Marchand to Jacques Bernard concerning the foolish

[19] F. Moureau, 'Jean Manzon (1740-1798)', *Dictionnaire des journalistes*, ed. J. Sgard (Grenoble, 1976), 256-7. How Manzon radicalized an Italian work by Pilato di Tassulo in the course of translating it into French for Rey is described by J. Th. de Booy, 'La Traduction française de *Di una riforma d'Italia* de Pilato di Tassulo', *Studies in Voltaire*, 12 (1960), 29-42, and discussed below.

[20] J. Lojek, 'Gazettes internationales de langue française dans la seconde moitié du XVIIIème siècle', in Pierre Deyon (ed.), *Modèles et moyens de la réflexion politique au XVIIIᵉ siècle* (Lille, 1974), 369-81: pp. 374, 377-8.

[21] Moureau, 'Les *Mémoires secrets*', 66-7, offers interesting data on two of Manzon's Paris correspondents: Aubry de Julie and Jean Baptiste Sainte-Marie Plumex, who came under the surveillance of Sartine and other book-trade officials.

action of the Archbishop of Paris.) But the items which were submitted continued to be screened by extraterritorial publishers and editors. The latter continued to serve as 'gatekeepers' or 'switchboard operators' until the collapse of the *ancien régime*.

If anything, the extraterritorial publishers and editors became more influential in shaping French views of the political landscape as the century wore on; francophone political journals produced abroad proliferated during the later decades of the century. These journals, in Graham Gibbs's words, 'embodied the spirit of cosmopolitanism in an unusually clear compact and influential form'.[22] They were used by courts and cabinets throughout Europe not only to supplement diplomatic reports and other sources of intelligence but also to serve as outlets for trial balloons and carefully placed 'leaks'.[23] They served as a main source of foreign news for readers of English newspapers; the provincial papers copied London ones and London papers drew heavily on the francophone press.[24] They also furnished domestic news to readers in France.

In his account of how French readers learned about the political struggle between Crown and parlements during the 1750s over 'the refusal of sacraments', Carroll Joynes brings out the leading role played by a 'foreign press'. He also points out that the cosmopolitan journals took the lead in assuming the existence of a 'public' as a political participant that needed to be informed.[25] In so far as Parisian political consciousness was heightened by receiving news of assassination attempts on Louis XV, or learning about the remonstrances of French parlements to royal edicts,[26] it was indebted not only to local *nouvellistes-à-la-main* but also to

[22] G. C. Gibbs, 'The Role of the Dutch Republic as the Intellectual Entrepôt of Europe', *Bijdragen en Mededelingen Betreffende de Geschiedenis der Nederlanden*, 86 (1971), 323–49: p. 339.

[23] G. C. Gibbs, 'Some Intellectual and Political Influences of the Huguenot Émigrés', *Bijdragen en Mededelingen Betreffende de Geschiedenis der Nederlanden*, 90 (1975), 255–87: p. 286.

[24] Jeremy Black, 'The British Press and Europe in the Early 18th Century', in Michael Harris and Lee J. Allen (eds.), *The Press in English Society from the 17th to the 19th Centuries* (Cranbury, NJ, 1986), 64–80: p. 64.

[25] C. Joynes, 'The *Gazette de Leyde*: The Opposition Press and French Politics 1750–1757', in J. Popkin and J. Censer (eds.), *Press and Politics in Pre-Revolutionary France* (Berkeley, Calif., 1987), ch. 4.

[26] P. Rétat (ed.), *L'Attentat de Damiens: Discours sur l'événement au XVIIe siècle* (Lyons, 1979), *passim*.

dynasties of extraterritorial publishers and editors such as the Tronchins of Amsterdam and the Luzacs of Leiden.

Jeremy Popkin's recent monograph on the Luzacs' cosmopolitan journal of record, *Nouvelles extraordinaires de divers endroits* (or as it was commonly called: the *Gazette de Leyde*), brings out the way this journal consistently supplied French readers with the most detailed and 'reliable' account of current events within France during the second half of the eighteenth century.[27] At the beginning of the century, foreign journals had also supplied English readers in the same way: 'We can read more of our own affairs in the Dutch papers than in any of our own', remarked Daniel Defoe.[28] But papers made in Britain served the British public ever more effectively as the century wore on.[29] The same was not true for French readers.

This striking difference between the British case and the French one is sufficiently important to be worth more comment. The continued reliance of French readers on books and journals produced abroad used to be emphasized by historians of the eighteenth-century press.[30] It was a topic of concern to eighteenth-century officials, such as Malesherbes.[31] But recent attempts to bring out the continuity of pre-revolutionary developments with revolutionary ones have led to discounting this peculiar phenomenon and to blurring distinctions between foreign and domestic output. A review article thus cites with approval Jeremy Popkin's assertion that 'French language periodicals published outside France, were in no sense clandestine or subversive' and 'were a *de facto* part of the French political system before 1789'.[32]

---

[27] J. Popkin, *News and Politics in the Age of Revolution: Jean Luzac's Gazette de Leyde* (Ithaca, NY, 1989).

[28] Cited by Gibbs, 'Intellectual and Political Influences', 286.

[29] Despite conditions which encourage the flourishing of a British press, London was not a propitious location for cosmopolitan journalism because of the delay imposed by Channel crossings. Dutch and German publishers could get their newspapers distributed on the continent two days in advance of their British competitors. Lojek, 'Gazettes internationales', 372.

[30] Louis Eugene Hatin, *Les Gazettes de Hollande et la presse clandestine aux XVIIᵉ et XVIIIᵉ siècles* (Paris, 1865); Pierre André Sayous, *Le Dix-Huitième Siècle à l'étranger* (Paris, 1861).

[31] See e.g. contrast between French and British case drawn by Malesherbes as cited by Pierre Grosclaude, *Malesherbes: Témoin et interprète de son temps* (Paris, 1965), 185.

[32] Benjamin Nathans, review article: 'Habermas's Public Sphere', *French Historical Studies*, 16 (Spring 1990), 620–44: p. 628.

It is true that *ancien régime* officials resorted to a variety of *ad hoc* devices to cope with the penetration of French markets by foreign publications which bypassed preliminary censorship. They created the ambiguous category of 'tacit' permissions for the entry of books; they set up a foreign news agency in Paris which granted access to certain journals.[33] Such devices, however, represented efforts by the Bourbon authorities to make the best of a bad bargain. To say that the gazettes were 'in no sense subversive' seems to fly in the face of the often expressed views of French officials from Colbert through Malesherbes and beyond. 'The Gazettes of Amsterdam and of Utrecht circulate everywhere. They light a fire in this kingdom and continually convey to foreigners views of our troubles that cannot help but prove disadvantageous to the state.'[34] Such officials never found a satisfactory solution to the problem. They never doubted that there was a problem nor that the reliance of French readers on the output of foreign presses had an insidious effect.[35] Popkin himself observes that the foreign papers 'gave a very different image of how French politics worked' from that provided in the officially licensed papers.[36] That the *de facto* situation had to be endured, even though it was in fundamental conflict with royal absolutist policies, was by no means the only contradiction that confronted *ancien régime* officials. For historians who are concerned with pre-revolutionary politics and public opinion, however, this particular contradiction seems too significant to be downplayed.

[33] To be admitted via the Bureau des gazettes étrangères was a typical *ancien régime* privilege, requiring the oiling of palms and pulling of strings. Some officials were lenient; others, strict. Journals which were turned down might still be brought into the kingdom by clandestine means. *Ancien régime* institutions were too unsystematic to be accurately described as 'the French political system'.

[34] Malesherbes, cited by Grosclaude, *Malesherbes*, 73. For a full account of Malesherbes's views see Raymond Birn, 'Malesherbes and the call for a free press', Darnton and Roche (eds.), *Revolution in Print*, 50-69.

[35] That Malesherbes 'saw no real solution to the problem' is noted by J. Popkin, 'The *Gazette de Leyde* and French Politics under Louis XVI', in Popkin and Censer (eds.), *Press and Politics*, 83. Also Hatin, *Les Gazettes de Hollande*, 46.

[36] J. Popkin, 'The Pre-Revolutionary Origins of Political Journalism', in K. Baker (ed.), *The French Revolution and the Making of Modern Political Culture*, i. *The Political Culture of the Old Regime* (New York, 1987), 203-25: p. 209. See also similar comment about 'the independent international gazettes that were not subject to prior censorship' in Popkin, 'International Gazettes and the Politics of Europe in the Revolutionary Period', *Journalism Quarterly*, 62 (1985), 482-8: p. 482.

The *Gazette de Leyde* not only preserved its position as the journal of record that the best informed Frenchmen had to read. It combined relatively accurate reporting with commitment to anti-absolutist views. It consistently upheld the benefits of constitutional 'mixed' governments and supported the cause of the dissident *parlementaires* who opposed the policies followed by the ministers of the King. It also served as a powerful advocate of the cause of the Poles against the Russians, the American revolutionaries against the English, and the Dutch 'patriots' against the Stadtholder. It took the lead in framing the debate over the need for political change and helped to shape the common vocabulary employed by the diverse scattered movements discussed by R. R. Palmer under the rubric of the 'age of the democratic revolution'.[37]

Two generations of Luzacs guided the destinies of the paper; the first had acquired it from an earlier Huguenot dynasty and had intermarried with a Dutch family so that Dutch was literally the younger Luzacs' mother tongue. The latter were assimilated into Leiden society, served on town councils, and were active in local affairs. In these respects, they differed from their unassimilated contemporaries such as Marc Michel Rey. Nevertheless their ties to an ancestral Huguenot tradition remained strong. Thus Jean Luzac, who steered the paper after 1775, retained his membership in Leiden's Walloon congregation and remained attached to Latin learning. After obtaining a law degree with a Latin dissertation on Cicero, he combined a professorship at the university with editing the paper. He ended his life as a full-time classical scholar. His brother, Étienne, who served as the paper's printer and publisher also obtained a law degree at Leiden. The fraternal pattern of allocating printing and publishing to one brother, and editing to the other, had been set by the Luzacs' father and uncle.[38] As in earlier centuries, being a master printer was still compatible with pursuing an academic career.

The versatility of members of the Luzac clan is especially well demonstrated by the career of Élie Luzac—a cousin of the brothers often confused with them and probably the most celebrated member of the dynasty. He published LaMettrie's *L'Homme machine* (1748); was reproached for this act by the Leiden consistory; and then wrote a treatise refuting LaMettrie,

---

[37] Popkin, '*Gazette de Leyde*', 256.   [38] For biographical data, see ibid. 11-23.

entitled *L'Homme plus que machine,* which, of course, helped to keep the controversy alive.[39] Writing to a colleague (the co-editor of the *Bibliothèque impartiale*) who objected to his publishing LaMettrie's godless book, Luzac defended his action: 'just as a wine merchant has no reason to refuse to a drunkard what the latter can always purchase elsewhere, so too a printer is under no obligation to refuse a manuscript which will in any case get published elsewhere'.[40] Should we regard Élie Luzac as a cynical, unprincipled opportunist whose only concern was his margin of profit?[41] He was at the same time the author of an eloquent plea for toleration and a defender of the free press.[42] 'It is impossible', wrote Jacques Marx about this publisher 'to disassociate the attitude of the *philosophe* from that of the *libraire*'.[43]

It was Élie Luzac who took the lead in the so-called 'Socratic war' that broke out in 1767 over the censoring of Marmontel's *Bélisaire* and who led the fight against a proposal to set up a Dutch board of censors.[44] During the struggle that saw Bourbon France supporting the 'patriots' against the House of Orange, he broke with his cousins and authored a pamphlet supporting the Stadtholder's cause. Interestingly enough, this venture in pamphleteering provoked reproaches from other Orangist politicians who complained that he used too many Latin expressions and lacked skill in using colloquial Dutch.[45] During the 1750s, he served as co-founder and co-editor (with Samuel Formey, secretary of the Berlin Academy) of a cosmopolitan review journal with a title that emphasized journalistic neutrality: the *Bibliothèque impartiale.* This was the journal, mentioned before, that issued

[39] Aram Vartanian, *LaMettrie's 'L'Homme Machine': A Study in the Origins of an Idea* (Princeton, NJ, 1960).

[40] Cited by Jacques Marx, 'Élie Luzac et la pensée eclairée', *Documentatieblad #11/12 Werkgroep 18e Eeuw: Frans-Nederlandse Betrekkingen* (Symposium Maison Descartes, Amsterdam, 4–5 Sept. 1970; Nijmegen, 1971), 74–105: p. 76.

[41] Marx, 'Élie Luzac', cites an adverse view of the greedy publisher given by Yves Dubosq, *Le Livre français et son commerce en Hollande de 1750 à 1780* (Paris, 1925). But Dubosq conflated Élie and Jean and Étienne Luzac in an untrustworthy account.

[42] Luzac's *Essai sur la liberté de produire ses sentiments* ('Au Pays Libre, pour le Bien Public', 1747) is discussed by Vartanian, *LaMettrie's L'Homme Machine*, 6–7; Marx, 'Élie Luzac', 80–1.   [43] Marx, 'Élie Luzac', 92.

[44] K.-R. Gallas, 'La Condemnation de l'Emile en Hollande', *Annales de la Société J. J. Rousseau,* 17 (1926), 53–72: p. 72.

[45] Leonard Leeb, *The Ideological Origins of the Batavian Revolution* (The Hague, 1973), 69, 73.

its first number on 1 January 1750 because readers were most likely to be caught when winter cold kept them indoors. Before launching their new venture, Luzac and Formey made a special arrangement to divide markets. They agreed to let all British news be handled by the *Journal britannique* published in the Hague and edited in London by the Huguenot physician-journalist Matthieu Maty (later head of the British Museum).[46] The *Bibliothèque impartiale* would confine itself to covering the continent, a large enough assignment in itself.

Given the proliferation of francophone cosmopolitan journals, and, in view of the continued involvement of extraterritorial publishers in the pamphlet wars and literary reviews of the day, it seems misguided to depict the Republic of Letters as an increasingly Parisian phenomenon after the mid-eighteenth century. Nor does there seem to be any sound basis for peopling it with savants in the age of Bayle and *mondains* in the age of Voltaire. Jean Luzac's Latin learning shows that the career of the savant and that of the journalist remained compatible throughout the eighteenth century. In the late seventeenth century, as we have seen, extraterritorial publishers were already urging editors to reach out to the public at large.[47]

In this regard a disservice was rendered many years ago by Daniel Mornet who casually lumped together the *Journal des savants* and the *Nouvelles de la république des lettres* as journals designed only for *érudits* and of interest only to them. Editors such as Bayle and Basnage de Beauval, Mornet asserted, 'were entirely unconcerned about reaching any "gens du monde" or curious bourgeois'.[48] Elsewhere Mornet cited the *Journal encyclopédique* of 1758: 'We are no longer in an era where journals are made only for savants. Now everyone reads and wants to read about everything.'[49] But Pierre Bayle had already noted in the 1680s that his publisher would be displeased by a journal 'made only for savants'. The biographer of Jean Le Clerc singled out, as a special feature of the interval between 1680 and 1700, a new concern with the tastes of 'l'honnête homme' which, in her view, was linked to the proliferation of cosmopolitan

[46] Uta Janssens, *Matthieu Maty and the Journal brittanique 1750–1755* (Amsterdam, 1975), 56–7. See also J. Marx, 'La *Bibliothèque impartiale*', in M. Couperus (ed.), *L'Étude des périodiques anciens: Colloque d'Utrecht* (Paris, 1972), 89–108.

[47] See Ch. 2 above, pp. 47, 53.   [48] Mornet, *Origines intellectuelles*, 59.
[49] Ibid. 160.

journals.[50] Even while claiming to belong to a new era, the *Journal encyclopédique* was echoing remarks made by Pierre Bayle himself.

To be sure, the Pierre Bayle who served as Voltaire's master was not the same figure who had been known to seventeenth-century Huguenots. His texts had been altered in the course of being edited; his life and his death had been reshaped by myth-making. Nevertheless, even in the seventeenth century, Bayle's appeal was scarcely limited to Protestants and *érudits*. His special gifts as a man of letters had been appreciated by literary arbiters of the 'Grande Siècle', by Boileau and La Fontaine among others. Copies of his journal, bound as books, continued to be à-la-mode and to appeal to *mondains* and *curieux* in the ensuing century.[51] A letter of 1733 written by Mathieu Marais to Bouhier, the President of the Paris Parlement, recommended Desfontaines's *Nouvelliste du Parnasse* as being delightfully reminiscent of Bayle's *Nouvelles*.[52]

This is not to deny that there were many significant differences between the expatriate preachers and teachers who turned pub-licists during the 1680s and those later literati who flocked to Paris in the hope that their poetry, plays, and other writings would win acceptance in Parisian salons, election to royal acad-emies, and favour at the court of Versailles. It is merely to say that significant affinities between the two groups also need consideration. For later literati were not poised only between Paris and Versailles. Cosmopolis had not lost its attractions. Foreign francophone firms continued to provide opportunities for literary careerists, as well as publication outlets for heterodox philosophers and all manner of exiles and refugees. The leading figures of the French Enlightenment may have been lionized by wealthy and powerful Parisians; some became wealthy and powerful themselves. Yet they owed much of their initial celeb-rity to publicity furnished from abroad. The hope of obtaining the glittering prizes that were available within the Bourbon realm did not preclude involvement in a cosmopolitan cultural

---

[50] Annie Barnes, *Jean Le Clerc et la république des lettres* (Paris, 1938), 11-13.

[51] Rétat, *Dictionnaire de Bayle*, 56, 61-63 n., 68-73.

[52] Paul Benhamou, 'The Review in Desfontaines's *Nouvelliste du Parnasse*', in L. E. Brown and P. Craddock (eds.), *Studies in Eighteenth-Century Culture* (East Lansing, Mich., 1989), 367-83: p. 378.

movement which was sustained by forces outside Bourbon control.

Voltaire participated in Mme Doublet's salon, grew rich from his investments, saw his friends take over the French Academy, and accepted the office of 'Secrétaire du Roi'. But even before his years of exile in England (1726-9) he had made two trips to Holland, and would make three more later on.[53] He also resided as a guest of Frederick the Great at the Prussian court. He searched along French borders buying up property here and there with the idea of establishing several residences. After he left Berlin in 1753, he wrote about a landowner's offer to sell him some property: 'I continue to press forward with my plan to have lands in France, Switzerland, Geneva and even Savoy. They say that one cannot serve two masters. I want to serve four in order to have none at all and to enjoy the most beautiful of all estates namely that of being free.'[54]

Voltaire was writing about territories, landlords, and overlords. But his remarks, which were occasioned in part by his recent quarrel with Frederick and by d'Alembert's troubles with the Genevan authorities, were also pertinent to the French writer's estate. The notion that serving many masters was a way to be free of dependence upon any one, was deeply embedded in early modern print culture. It harks back to the strategy Erasmus had employed in the sixteenth century. Provided by his printer with about a hundred complimentary copies of his work, the wily author penned a special dedication in separate copies and arranged to have each one sent off to different potential patrons. By winning pensions and favours from many lords and ladies, he freed himself from dependence on any single one. He thus showed how patronage in the age of the hand press might lead, not to subservience, but to emancipation. Voltaire and Rousseau followed similar procedures. They put their numerous complimentary copies to good use by sending them off to kings, princes, and potential foreign patrons, as well as to the top functionaries of the French book trade.[55] 'Few people have made themselves

[53] Jeroom Vercruysse, 'Voltaire et la Hollande', *Studies in Voltaire*, 46 (1966).

[54] Cited by Sainte-Beuve from Voltaire's correspondence with d'Alembert, 'Voltaire et le Président de Brosses' (8 Nov. 1852), *Causeries du lundi* (15 vols. Paris, n.d.), vii. 105-26: p. 110.

[55] On Erasmus, see Eisenstein, *Printing Press*, i, 401. On Voltaire's practices, see Bernard Gagnebien (ed.), *Lettres inédites de Voltaire à son imprimeur* (Geneva, 1952),

so dependent in order to become independent', remarked Goethe about Voltaire.[56] David Hume joked about d'Alembert's position as an 'independent' philosopher who received five different pensions, one of which came from the Prussian king.[57]

Voltaire was often sarcastic about foreign publishers who made their fortunes at the expense of French authors. But he was fully aware that the free exercise of his pen and his capacity to plead cases before the 'tribunal of the public' hinged on the operations of presses located outside the Bourbon realm.[58] In 1733 he complained about the way Dutch publishers were making millions by exploiting the intelligence of the French. Ten years later, however, he wrote from the Hague, 'I prefer the abuse of liberty to print one's thoughts here to the slavery in which they wish to put the human mind among us'.[59] Despite recent accounts suggesting that the philosophes grew fat and contented as they conquered the establishment and won places in the French Academy, Voltaire's ambivalence about the advantages of Paris as against those of Cosmopolis gave no signs of diminishing in his later years. In 1765, he dreamt of establishing a colony of philosophes in the vicinity of Cleves, modelled on Tycho Brahe's sixteenth-century Uraniborg.[60] He remained as ambivalent about the Swiss as he had been about the Dutch after his departure from Berlin.[61]

Following his break with Frederick, in 1754, he formed an alliance with a Swiss publishing firm. The Cramers of Geneva like the Luzacs of Leiden (and like the sixteenth-century Amerbach-Froben firm of Basel) served a cosmopolitan reading public as printers, publishers, booksellers, and editors, while being fully

introduction, pp. xxxiiii–xxv. A letter from Rousseau to his printer requesting 60 complimentary copies (half on fine paper) is in J. Bosscha (ed.), *Lettres inédites de Jean-Jacques Rousseau à Marc Michel Rey* (Paris, 1858), 38.

[56] Cited by P. Gay, *Voltaire's Politics* (Princeton, NJ, 1959), 81.

[57] Cited by Thomas Schlereth, *The Cosmopolitan Ideal in Enlightenment Thought* (South Bend, Ind., 1977), 12.

[58] Eric Walter, 'L'Affaire La Barre et le concept de l'opinion publique', P. Rétat (ed.), *Le Journalisme d'Ancien Régime* (Lyons, 1982), 361–92.

[59] Rémy Saisselin, *The Literary Enterprise in Eighteenth Century France* (Detroit, 1979), 73, cites both passages from letters of June 1733 and Aug. 1743.

[60] Schlereth, *Cosmopolitan Ideal*, 15.

[61] Graham Gargett, 'Voltaire and Protestantism', *Studies in Voltaire*, 188 (1980). Although chiefly concerned with Voltaire's dealings with the Swiss, ch. 4 supplements Vercruysse's study of Voltaire in Holland.

assimilated into the political and social structures of the town in which they lived. (One brother was a local magistrate member of the Council of 200; the other was an officer in the local militia.)[62] They were descended from French and Swiss publishing dynasties on both sides of their family. A maternal ancestor belonged to the sixteenth-century Lyonnaise printing dynasty of de Tournes.[63] As was the case with sixteenth-century firms, the Cramers extended wide networks from their Genevan office. They exploited local banking connections and kept in touch with their agents not only in Paris but also in Stockholm, Turin, Genoa, and Marseilles. To finance their operations in Southern Europe, they used Protestant connections which extended into such unlikely locations as Naples and Cadiz.[64] In keeping with the tradition of the most celebrated early printers, the Cramers combined their business with the cultivation of literature and the arts. They were atypical, however, in setting aside a diversified publication policy in order to specialize in the works of a single author, as they did for two decades after 1755. The decision to focus exclusively on Voltaire proved to be profitable but did require the adoption of a new strategy of relying almost exclusively on profits made from first editions. After the Cramers had first issued a given work, pirated copies invariably flooded the market.[65]

Specializing in Voltaireana also meant conservative local authorities had to be appeased. Despite at least one seizure, the Genevan authorities were generally mollified by the repeated assurance that potentially poisonous products were aimed at foreign markets alone. (One is uneasily reminded of present-day American exports of tobacco and other products.)[66] Further-

---

[62] Giles Barber, 'The Cramers of Geneva and Their Trade in Europe between 1755 and 1766', *Studies on Voltaire*, 30 (1964), 377–413. Voltaire's publisher Gabriel Cramer should not be confused with a cousin also named Gabriel, who was a professor of philosophy at the Genevan Academy and a distinguished mathematician with whom d'Alembert corresponded.

[63] The de Tournes themselves also had established a firm in Geneva. On Philibert and Gabriel Cramer and their family; see Barber, 'Cramers', and also Gagnebien (ed.), *Lettres de Voltaire*, pp. x–xi.   [64] Barber, 'Cramers', 383.

[65] Barber, 'Cramers', 396.

[66] In Neuchâtel, also, when Voltaire's *Questions sur l'Encyclopédie* was reissued in augmented form by the STN, it received authorization 'on the condition that the work was destined only for foreign markets'. Charly Guyot, *Le Rayonnement de l'Encyclopédie en Suisse française* (Neuchâtel, 1955), 122.

more, the Cramers did not handle Voltaire's most ferocious attacks on priestcraft. For publication of his most scandalous work, Voltaire turned to an Amsterdam publisher, a Genevan expatriate named Marc Michel Rey whom he publicly denounced while secretly using his services.[67]

This brings us to the most fascinating figure among Enlightenment publishers. Rey was the very embodiment of the cosmopolitan *libraire-philosophe*.[68] The services he performed for Jean-Jacques Rousseau and Baron d'Holbach were even more significant than those he rendered Voltaire. He acted as Mirabeau's one-time employer; employed the encyclopaedist, the Abbé Claude Yvon, as his corrector;[69] and was paid by Jean-Paul Marat to publish Marat's early work, *De l'homme*. 'A world separated Voltaire with his 200,000 livres rent and J.-J. Rousseau copying music to earn his living.'[70] A common reliance on the services supplied by Rey, however, did provide a link between these two disparate worlds.

Of course Rousseau's circumstances made him more dependent. His fluctuation between gratitude and hostility was especially pronounced. He agreed to act as godfather of one of Rey's daughters, gratefully accepted Rey's offer to provide Thérèse Levasseur with a yearly pension, wrote letters describing his publisher as honest and generous, and repeatedly asked fondly about Rey's wife.[71] But the relationship was punctuated by quarrels and the entry in the *Confessions* about the only publisher the author always had reason to praise was coupled with a nasty

[67] J. Vercruysse, 'Voltaire and Marc Michel Rey', *Studies in Voltaire*, 58 (1967), 1707–63: pp. 1722–3, 1731.

[68] In 1974, Max Fajn, 'Marc-Michel Rey: Boekhandelaar op de Bloemmark (Amsterdam)', *Proceedings of the American Philosophical Society*, 118 (June 1974), 260–8, noted (p. 260) that a full-scale biography of Rey was being undertaken by J. Th. de Booy and Jeroom Vercruysse but it has not yet materialized.

[69] Bosscha (ed.), *Lettres de Rousseau*, 10.

[70] Jacques Proust, *Diderot et l'Encyclopédie* (Paris, 1982), 19. This statement occurs in a relevant discussion of the social position of the encyclopaedists. Proust does not note that at least two of the figures he discusses, Abbé Yvon and Alexandre Deleyre, worked for Rey when they were in Amsterdam.

[71] Bosscha (ed.), *Lettres de Rousseau*, 129, letter 79 (6 Jan. 1762): 'I'm truly touched by your goodness toward Mme Levasseur and thank you with all my heart in her name and mine.' A letter of 1759 noting that Jean Jacques found Rey 'exact, attentive and honest in all his dealings' is cited by Albert Schinz, 'Jean-Jacques Rousseau et le libraire-imprimeur Marc-Michel Rey', *Annales de la Société de J.-J. Rousseau*, 10 (1914–15), 1–134: p. 15.

footnote about later uncovering Rey's frauds.[72] Given his volatile temperament, however, Jean-Jacques Rousseau got along with Rey surprisingly well. One might argue, indeed, that he was less abusive and less inclined to subject the publisher to negative stereotyping than were some of the other philosophes. In keeping with themes mentioned in an earlier chapter, Rey was accused by others of having 'become completely imbued with the spirit of Dutch commercialism'. Voltaire called him 'a swindler' and Diderot 'referred to him as a Jew, an Arab'.[73] Yet Rousseau was not alone in being ambivalent. Rey received praise as well as condemnation from Voltaire. 'Without you we would have preached in a desert' was Diderot's tribute to Rey.[74]

Unlike the Cramers of Geneva and the Luzacs of Leiden, Rey did not assimilate into local society but rather, as had earlier expatriates, confined his acquaintanceship to French-speaking circles. Given the cosmopolitan character of francophone society in Amsterdam, this still entailed belonging to a large and varied social circle; the Reys were known for entertaining on a large scale and in grand style. The publisher's sociability had an anti-clerical, secular tinge. Although formally admitted as a member of the Amsterdam Walloon congregation, Rey seems to have remained aloof from local church affairs. He married a member of his congregation and his wife saw to it that their children were baptized, reared, and buried within the faith. She also worried about the marriage of a daughter to the son of a Catholic. But Rey himself did not seem to mind being attacked by the local Walloon consistory for publishing offensive material. When he died, in 1780, he was buried, in an elaborate funeral ceremony, outside the church courtyard, thereby provoking long-lasting speculation about the nature of his beliefs.[75]

---

[72] J.-J. Rousseau, *The Confessions*, tr. J. M. Cohen (Penguin Books; Harmondsworth, 1954), 518-19. The dispute over versions of the *Nouvelle Héloïse*, which led to the accusation of fraud, is covered in letters contained in Bosscha (ed.), *Lettres de Rousseau*, 136-9, and discussed by Schinz, 'Rousseau et Rey', 126-30.

[73] Fajn, 'Rey', 262, offers relevant citations. Voltaire's negative assessment cited by Fajn should be balanced against his praise of the publisher cited by J. Vercruysse, 'Marc Michel Rey, libraire des lumières', in Martin and Chartier, *Histoire*, ii. 322-3.

[74] Cited by J. Th. de Booy and R. Mortier, 'Lettres inédites de F. H. Jacobi', *Studies on Voltaire*, 45 (1966), 12.

[75] K.-R. Gallas, 'Autour de Marc-Michel Rey et de Rousseau', *Annales de la Société J.-J. Rousseau*, 17 (1926), 73-82: p. 76. Fajn, 'Rey', 262-3.

He was born in 1720 in Geneva of French Huguenot parents.[76] From 1737 to 1744 he served as an apprentice to Marc Michel Bousquet, a Genevan bookseller for whom his father had worked as a packer.[77] He moved to Amsterdam in 1744 where he bought the rights of a citizen of Amsterdam, was admitted into the guild of booksellers, printers, and binders and joined the local Walloon Church. Two years after setting up business, Rey married Elisabeth Bernard, daughter of Jean Frédéric Bernard, who had died in the year that Rey had arrived in Amsterdam. His dead father-in-law was the author, editor, publisher, and bookseller who has figured in previous discussion as a collaborator with Picart on the multi-volumed survey of world religions. Taken together, the careers of Jean Frédéric Bernard and his son-in-law span the three generations of the French Enlightenment—from Montesquieu to d'Holbach.

With this marriage, Rey acquired his father-in-law's stock and a wife experienced in the book business.[78] Business prospered and the Reys were able to hire servants to help take care of their growing family, thus enabling Mme Rey to work alongside her husband. Bad health plagued the family. Three children died in infancy; three others died before they reached the age of 30.[79] There was one son, Isaac, who outlived his father (with whom he had had stormy relations) and who carried on the business for a time.[80] One daughter, Marguerite Jeanne (known as 'Grittié'), married Charles August Weissenbruch in 1771, thus affiliating the Reys with Pierre Rousseau (Weissenbruch's brother-in-law) and the Société Typographique of Bouillon.[81] Weissenbruch

[76] His parents, Isaac Rey and Marguerite Duseigneur Rey, were both from Truchesne in Dauphiné. They were married in Geneva in Nov. 1715. Fajn, 'Rey', 260.

[77] Although Fajn, 'Rey', 261, asserts that Rey 'worked in Lausanne for his godfather Bousquet from 1736 to 1744', it was pointed out by Schinz, 'Rousseau et Rey', 3, that authorities have been misled by Rey's referring in his later life to once having worked for 'Bousquet de Lausanne'. Bousquet moved from Geneva to Lausanne and became known as a bookseller of Lausanne only after 1754, by which time Rey was well established in Amsterdam. Schinz's point, which seems well taken, is reiterated in a pertinent article by Isabella H. van Eeghen, 'Daniel Elsevier and Marc-Michel Rey', *Quaerendo*, 12 (1982), 183–99: p. 193.   [78] Gallas, 'Autour de Rey', 73.

[79] Fajn, 'Rey', 261–3, gives some details on the family, albeit in a somewhat confusing narrative.

[80] Van Eeghen, 'Elsevier and Rey', 194, notes that Isaac faced hard times after his father's death.

[81] Fajn, 'Rey', 262, notes that Isaac Rey in 1769, during a quarrel with his father, took refuge with Pierre Rousseau in Bouillon and cites a letter of Oct. 1769 from P. Rousseau

himself became an important figure in later francophone publishing circles as a masonic Grand Master and head of a Brussels firm which bears his name to this day.[82]

Rey's affiliations with his son-in-law point to the Napoleonic era and may be of interest to historians of nineteenth-century publishing. Rey's emergence as the most important *libraire-philosophe* of the later French Enlightenment is of more concern to us here. His marriage to the daughter of Bernard Picart's collaborator was not the only connection which linked the Genevan expatriate to Prosper Marchand's world. The two men corresponded during Marchand's last years.[83] A longer-lasting link was supplied by Jean Nicolas Sébastien Allamand, the successor to 'sGravesande as professor of mathematics at the University of Leiden.[84] Allamand, who served as the executor of Marchand's estate and who had completed Marchand's posthumously published *Dictionnaire*, became Rey's chief editorial advisor.[85] Marchand's *Dictionnaire* had publicized the *Traité des trois imposteurs* as a text that everyone talked about but no one read. In collaboration with d'Holbach, Rey put an end to that situation. His edition of the *Traité* was first issued in 1768; before his death three more would appear (in 1775, 1776, and 1777).[86]

As his firm prospered, Rey extended a trade network which reached even beyond that of the Cramers since it reached into Russia as well as into the Dutch colonies overseas. Despite these colonial dealings, Rey never did become fluent in Dutch. He grew rich serving French writers, booksellers, and readers; 75 per cent of his sales were made in France.[87] This concentra-

trying to mollify the angry father. There were thus family connections between the two firms even before 'Grittié's' marriage. (Although Fajn dates the latter as taking place on 5 July 1774, he describes two letters of Mme Rey objecting to her daughter's marrying into a Catholic family as being written in Apr. and June of 1771 'at the time of Marguerite's marriage'. It seems likely that 1771 is the correct date.)

[82] On Pierre Rousseau and his brother-in-law, see discussion below, Ch. 5.

[83] C. Berkvens-Stevelinck, *Prosper Marchand: La Vie et l'œuvre* (Leiden, 1987), 219 n. 180.

[84] J. N. S. Allamand was born in Lausanne in 1713, the son of the regent of the local college. He moved to Leiden in 1738 to study with 'sGravesande and became the executor of the latter's literary estate as well as his successor as professor of mathematics.

[85] J. Vercruysse, 'Marc-Michel Rey et le livre philosophique', *Literatur Geschichte als geschichtlicher Auftrag: In Memoriam Werner Kraus* (Berlin, 1978), 149–57: p. 149.

[86] P. Rétat, Preface, *Traité des trois imposteurs: Manuscrit clandestin du début du XVIIIᵉ siècle* (Lyons, 1973), 7.   [87] Fajn, 'Rey', 265.

tion on French markets helped to protect him from interference from the Dutch authorities. On several occasions in the 1760s, however, Rey was subject to the combined pressure exerted by Paris parlements, Genevan authorities, and Dutch pastors. Yet he managed somehow to ride out the storms. The publication history of *Emile, Contrat social,* and *Letters écrites de la montagne* provide cases in point.

Much as the Cramers had served Voltaire so did Rey serve Jean-Jacques Rousseau. Friendship between the two Genevans began with their first meeting in 1754. Thereafter arrangements were made with a Parisian Farmer-General to serve as a go-between; proofs were sent to Paris and returned to Amsterdam as Rey published one after another of Rousseau's early works.[88] In 1759, Rousseau wrote that he found Rey to be attentive and honest. Two years later he noted that, despite the nasty things that were said about Rey in Paris, he was the only publisher Rousseau could trust completely.[89] This collaboration was interrupted when Rousseau turned over responsibility for printing *Emile* to his patroness of the moment, Mme de Luxemberg. But the interruption did not last long. The condemnation of *Emile* led to difficulties with the other publishers and the persecuted author turned back to Rey. When the latter was ordered by the Dutch authorities on 22 June 1762 to see that no copies of *Emile* were put up for sale, he simply ignored the order.[90] He treated the banned *Contrat social* in the same way.[91] Three years after publishing both works, Rey brought out the *Lettres écrites de la montagne* which had first been sent to Avignon where no publisher could be found who dared touch it.[92]

Rousseau's anxiety over the publishing of this polemical work was reflected in his letter of 9 June 1764 to Rey. In view of the quantity of notes and citations, he wrote, extra care should be taken to get all the numbers and quotation marks in the right

---

[88] Bosscha (ed.), *Lettres de Rousseau*, 2. See also, J. P. Belin, *Le Mouvement philosophique de 1748 à 1789* (Paris, 1913), 79.

[89] Schinz, 'Rousseau et Rey', 111-13.   [90] Gallas, 'La Condemnation', 58.

[91] R. A. Leigh, 'Rousseau, His Publishers and the *Contrat Social*', *Bulletin of the John Rylands University Library*, 66 (Spring 1984), 204-27, points out that although the *Contrat Social* was 'never officially condemned' it was 'rigorously suppressed' by French official action (p. 219). On p. 211 Leigh comments on Rey's 'touching naiveté' and 'doglike devotion' to Jean-Jacques and describes him as being a Genevan married to a woman whose family came from Geneva—which scarcely does justice to Rey's father-in-law.

[92] Bosscha (ed.), *Lettres de Rousseau*, 212.

places. The printer, the foreman (*prote*), and the proof-reader (*correcteur*) should be alerted to take extra pains.

My honour, my peace of mind, my security hinge on having my instructions followed precisely. One error could spoil everything. I cannot stop trembling about possible errors until the last correct sheet arrives here. Also it is absolutely necessary that everything be finished by November at the very latest. We are so distant from each other (Rousseau constantly evaded Rey's invitation that he come stay with his publisher in Amsterdam) I must leave the final proof-reading to you. I beg you to get your wife to go over the final corrections with you and to compare them with the manuscript.[93]

Rousseau trusted Rey to handle his finances and to deal with the voluminous fan mail that was sent to the author care of his publisher.[94] Indeed Rey served his best-selling author much as a literary agent might serve an author today (except of course that he did not work on commission and kept the lion's share of profits). He also acted as Rousseau's publicity agent.

The publisher kept the persecution of *Emile*'s author in the public eye with another of his enterprises—one that is often overlooked, namely, his venture into journalism. In an essay produced for the pioneering collaborative *Livre et société* volumes, two French authorities noted, in passing, that both the *Journal des sçavans* and the *Mémoires de Trévoux* were counterfeited in Holland and that 'an ingenious editor even had the idea of uniting them both in one publication in 1758; an ephemeral periodical published in Amsterdam. He tried to ensure sales by adopting the pretentious title: *Supplément aux journaux des savants et de Trévoux.*'[95] This 'ingenious editor' was none other than our friend Marc Michel Rey who was thus carrying on a Dutch practice which had been initiated by the last of the Elseviers.[96] Rey's updated Amsterdam edition of the *Journal des sçavans* was first published in combination with the Jesuit-sponsored *Mémoires de Trévoux* and was later supplemented by extracts from diverse foreign journals containing reports of current events.[97]

[93] Letter 114, 9 June 1764, Bosscha (ed.), *Lettres de Rousseau*, 213–15.

[94] Schinz, 'Rousseau et Rey', 100.

[95] Jean Erhard and Jacques Roger, 'Deux périodiques français du 18ᵉ siècle', *Livre et société*, i. 33–61: p. 36.   [96] See Ch. 2, above.

[97] H. J. Reesink, *L'Angleterre et la littérature anglaise dans les plus anciens périodiques français* (Paris, 1931), 81 n. 4. Dubosq, *Le Livre français*, 118; Couperus, *L'Étude des périodiques*, 177; Schinz, 'Rousseau et Rey', 27.

These periodicals were issued over the course of several decades, spanning the interval 1754–82. They were neither as ephemeral nor as inconsequential as the above citation makes them appear.[98] They proved useful as vehicles for prolonging concern over the case of *Emile*. In February 1766, a supplement carried notice of 'the unjust persecution of the virtuous M. Rousseau because of his *Emile*'. This was followed in April by a section containing 'extracts from the best journals in Europe'. It consisted of material purporting to be excerpted from the *Monthly Review* protesting the persecution of Rousseau. One especially violent letter attacking pastors as well as priests and upholding natural religion against diabolical priestcraft led to the condemnation of the letter-writer, Vincenzio Gaudio. He was sentenced to thirty years' imprisonment, *in absentia*.[99]

The violently anticlerical tone of the articles published by Rey are compatible with his other activities during the 1760s. Thus he ignored the warning issued by his editorial advisor, Allamand, to hold off publishing a French translation of Pilati di Tassulo's *Di una riforma d'Italia*. The original version of the work had been warmly received by Grimm and Voltaire and favourably reviewed in the *Journal encyclopédique*. Allamand was in favour of having it published in translation. He had indeed initially urged Rey to get a translation made and to plan on a large edition as he expected the work to sell many copies. But he objected strenuously to the notes and interpolations made by the translator selected by Rey. Rey had chosen Manzon for the task and the anticlerical ex-Jesuit Piedmontese editor of the *Courier du Bas-Rhin* had transformed a work which dealt specifically with Italy into a generalized indictment of priestcraft throughout Europe. Rey was warned by Allamand that since the publisher was already 'under suspicion for the Gaudio affair' it would be asking for trouble to publish such an inflammatory translation. But Rey, as usual, turned a deaf ear to the warning.[100]

[98] According to Reesink, *L'Angleterre*, 81, 78 vols. of the *Sçavans* combined with the *Mémoires de Trévoux* were issued between 1754 and 1763 and 71 vols. of the *Sçavans* combined with extracts from other journals appeared between 1764 and 1782. (An issue of 1769 carried a French tr. of an article by Beccaria done by Manzon, the editor of the *Courier du Bas-Rhin*. Moureau, 'Manzon', *Dictionnaire des journalistes*, 156-7.)

[99] Gallas, 'Autour de Rey', 76. Vincenzio Gaudio is described by Fajn, 'Rey', 264, as a 'former professor of law at the university of Naples'. According to Gallas, after the sentence was pronounced, Gaudio 'disappears from the record'.

[100] De Booy, 'La Traduction française', 29-42.

The next decade of the 1770s saw no slackening of subversive activity. On the contrary, Rey became the chief publisher of the most celebrated clandestine texts of the later Enlightenment. In view of his activities in the 1760s and the services he rendered to the Baron d'Holbach during the next decade, he provides a striking exception to the general rule (first set forth by Dubosq and reiterated by Popkin) that Dutch publishers lost ground to 'more dynamic firms' elsewhere after 1760.

> The Dutch publishing industry had maintained its international dominance for a while even after the decline of the country's general economic standing by putting out the works of major writers . . . such as Voltaire, Montesquieu and Rousseau but even this business fell off after 1760 as more dynamic firms elsewhere, like the Société Typographique of Neuchâtel, captured the trade.[101]

It was not until 1769, however, that the STN was founded. As for the decade of the 1770s, it is still difficult to imagine a more 'dynamic firm' engaged in French Enlightenment publications than the one that was run by Rey in Amsterdam.[102]

Perhaps the energy expended by the Amsterdam publisher tends to be discounted because his dealings with French authors became less visible during the 1770s, at the very time that the voluminous archives of Neuchâtel began to fill up. Rey's posthumous catalogue lists not a single prohibited work.[103] Rey's archives, indeed, are completely devoid of any records pertaining to his dealings with the most prolific author he ever served. There is no trace of correspondence between Rey and d'Holbach or between the publisher and any of d'Holbach's agents. Nor is there even a fragment of any document written in d'Holbach's hand. Yet we can be certain, writes an authority, that it was indeed Rey 'who before distributing this manna from heaven to the faithful had seen that it was well kneaded and baked (as Grimm put) in his own oven'.[104]

---

[101] Popkin, *'Gazette de Leyde'*, 28. Dubosq is cited in support of this statement.

[102] Although he lived in the region of Neuchâtel, Pierre Alexandre Dupeyrou directed a steady stream of letters and book orders to Rey in Amsterdam. He would buy up 50-100 copies from Rey and then send some to Voltaire in Ferney and convey others to Fauche in Neuchâtel to distribute. Charly Guyot, *Un ami et défenseur de Rousseau: Pierre Alexandre Dupeyrou* (Neuchâtel, n.d.), 148. This scarcely suggests that Neuchâtel was the location of the more 'dynamic' firm.

[103] Vercruysse, 'Rey et le livre philosophique', 149-50.

[104] J. T. de Booy, 'L'Abbé Coger dit Coge Pecus, lecteur de Voltaire et de d'Holbach', *Studies on Voltaire*, 18 (1961), 183-96: p. 187.

Grimm's metaphor brought to mind a memorable passage from J. M. Thompson: 'The Enlightenment had always fallen like manna from heaven. It had never grown out of European soil.'[105] Rey's firm was located on European soil: first on the Kalverstraat, then the Pype Marcht, and by the 1760s on the Singel near the Amsterdam flower market.[106] His address was widely known as the place where food for thought was prepared and served and was used by those who sent in book orders from distant regions throughout the continent. He was the recipient of a steady stream of correspondence from certain agents in Paris who cultivated book-trade officials. These agents made it possible for would-be purchasers in Paris to bypass local book-sellers in order to procure forbidden books.[107]

An example of the mundane means by which the 'manna from heaven' was obtained is offered by Rey's correspondence with Abbé Coger, a professor of rhetoric at the Collège Mazarin in Paris.[108] The Abbé's letters to Rey in 1770–1 requested some forty books of which well over twenty are now known to have been written by or edited by d'Holbach.[109] The *Traité des trois imposteurs*, *Christianisme dévoilé*, *Les Prêtres démasqués* figured among the titles that were requested. A later letter complained that a copy of *Système de la nature* was in bad condition; a misfortune which was mitigated by the fact that the Abbé had ordered and had received three copies. In the course of assuring the publisher that special precautions were being taken to avoid trouble with French officials, the Abbé wrote that he had secured the services of M. de Sartine, the lieutenant of the police and inspector of the book trade.[110]

The complicity of French book-trade officials in the clandestine trade—the many copies that were creamed off and the black-market profits received—although noted in passing in scattered studies, is worth more focused study. In 1764, the rising pub-

[105] J. M. Thompson, *The French Revolution* (Oxford, 1945), 271.

[106] Fajn, 'Rey', 261, gives these addresses and notes that living in the centre of the city near the canals probably contributed to the poor health of the Rey family.

[107] Dubosq, *Le Livre français*, 32–5, 61 n.; 120 ff. singles out two such agents, Voyard de Chenau and Jacques DeLoches, for discussion.

[108] The following account is based on de Booy, 'L'Abbé Coger'.

[109] Alan Kors, *D'Holbach's Coterie: An Enlightenment in Paris* (Princeton, NJ, 1976), 238 n. 58, notes that Coger worked in tandem with the *syndic* of the Sorbonne, Riballier, in obtaining the forbidden books directly from Rey.

[110] De Booy, 'L'Abbé Coger', 192–6.

lisher Charles Joseph Pancoucke requested that Jean-Jacques Rousseau send him a copy of the banned *Lettres sur la montagne* addressed to M. de Sartine who was at the time the chief inspector of the book trade.[111] Rey's correspondence also reveals how Sartine's successor, Jean Charles Pierre Lenoir, was bought off by superb copies of Helvetius's works.[112] The complicity of the French court also deserves more attention. Valets and other residents at Versailles, whose belongings could be whisked past inspection, made the royal court a major depot. Within France, diverse social sectors helped to activate the so-called 'literary underground' by distributing the products Rey and others supplied.[113]

A somewhat different sort of correspondence shows Rey acting as mentor and advisor to a provincial German youth. F. H. Jacobi was the younger son of a Düsseldorf merchant who felt misplaced handling his father's business. As one of Jean-Jacques Rousseau's many admirers, he kept after Rey to send on every scrap of gossip about the persecuted author whom he idolized from afar.[114] Jacobi's correspondence with Rey in the 1760s seems to prefigure the later correspondence uncovered by Robert Darnton between Jean Ranson, the 27-year-old son of a French Protestant merchant of La Rochelle, and Ranson's former teacher turned STN publisher, Frédéric Samuel Ostervald.[115] There are intriguing similarities in the reactions of these two 'fans' of Rousseau, one German, the other French, but both the sons of provincial Protestant merchants.[116] Correspondence of this kind made it possible for foreign publishers, such as Rey and Ostervald, to keep in touch with the markets they served and also to

[111] Suzanne Tucoo-Chala, *Charles-Joseph Pancoucke et la librairie française 1736-1798* (Paris, 1977), 104. On pp. 392-3 it is noted that the publisher used bribes to win protection from both Sartine and his successor, Lenoir.

[112] J. Vercruysse, 'Les Livres clandestins de Bouillon', *Studies in Voltaire*, 193 (1980), 1840-52: p. 1845. Lenoir's occasional complicity should not be taken to imply 'an extensive alliance with the literary underground', according to R. Darnton, *The Literary Underground* (Cambridge, Mass., 1982), 114.

[113] The pre-eminent role played by 'grands seigneurs' was made clear years ago by Mornet, *Origines intellectuelles*, ch. 4. Mornet in turn drew on J. P. Belin, *Le Commerce des livres prohibés à Paris de 1750 à 1789* (Paris, 1913). See esp. 62-7.

[114] De Booy and Mortier, 'Lettres de Jacobi'.

[115] Darnton, 'Readers Respond to Rousseau', *The Great Cat Massacre* (New York, 1984), ch. 6.

[116] Daniel Roche, 'Négoce et culture', *Les Républicains des lettres* (Paris, 1988), 287, notes that a quarter of Rousseau's correspondents came from merchant families.

help shape the nature of demand. In Jacobi's case, close and quasi-personal bonds were forged by means of the continuous exchange. The client developed sufficient confidence in the publisher-bookseller to ask him to serve as his emissary when trying to deal with the demands of the mother of an illegitimate child he had fathered. He became acquainted with contemporary English literature by reading it in the French versions he ordered from Rey and ultimately became himself a German author of some distinction. Between 1763 and 1771, as one authority put it, Rey served as Jacobi's 'window on the world'.[117]

Rey's correspondence throws light on many aspects of eighteenth-century literary life. But on his dealings with d'Holbach there are no records at all. This points to the dangers of relying too heavily on publishers' archives for information about the clandestine book trade. In this instance the 'flight of manuscripts' abroad was such a secret operation that it lent itself to the dictum 'out of sight out of mind'. The manuscripts were given by d'Holbach to Naigeon who passed them on to his brother in Sedan via the private mail of a friendly tax-farmer, who was also inspector general of the customs bureau. In Sedan, the brother would copy the texts and destroy the originals, sending the new manuscripts in a package covered with two layers of wax-sealed cloth to a Mme Loncin in Liège. This woman, who was in regular correspondence with Rey, sent the parcel on to the Amsterdam publisher.[118] D'Holbach's resort to secret procedures was not an occasional phenomenon. He was enormously prolific, the author or co-author of some fifty books and some 400 articles, all published in the strictest anonymity.[119] The silent fall-out from this 'golden rain' which enriched Rey's Amsterdam firm stands in paradoxical contrast to the noisy conviviality and expansive hospitality which characterized the regular gatherings on Thursdays and Sundays held for thirty-five years in d'Holbach's sumptuously furnished Paris house on the Rue Royale.

In his finely detailed study of the *coterie holbachique*, Alan Kors points to d'Holbach's cosmopolitan background. He suggests

---

[117] R. Birn, 'Marc Michel Rey's Enlightenment', paper given at Symposium, 'Le Magasin de l'univers', held in Wassenaar (The Netherlands), 4–7 July 1990.

[118] Kors, *D'Holbach's Coterie*, 83; Vercruysse, 'Rey', in Martin and Chartier, *Histoire*, ii. 322–3.   [119] Kors, *D'Holbach's Coterie*, 13.

that the special style which characterized the Rue Royal gatherings owed less to Parisian mores than to the Baron's recollection of fraternizing with other students at the University of Leiden in the 1740s. The special attraction exerted by d'Holbach's salon, Kors notes, probably owed much to the rich Baron's lavish hospitality. But equally prized was the chance to indulge in completely uninhibited conversation. Unlike other salons, where certain unwritten rules governing polite behaviour had to be observed, d'Holbach placed no restraints on what could be said. Diderot, for one, felt free as nowhere else to engage in verbal pyrotechnics that witnesses found unforgettable. Yet, for all the noise made by the 'bombs raining in the house of our lord',[120] an absolute silence was maintained even within the walls of his own house about the authorship of every one of the Baron's notorious works. The Abbé Morellet stated in his memoirs that although others may have also been in on the secret he never did know for sure. Within this otherwise gregarious and gossipy circle of friends, this was one topic that was never discussed.[121]

There was, then, a veritable black hole of silence at the centre of the most celebrated assemblage of literary luminaries of the French Enlightenment in Paris. This extraordinary contradiction between the publicity assigned to the books and the silence surrounding their authorship raises questions concerning recent theories about the functions performed by Paris salons. Dena Goodman, for example, suggests that the Paris salon was the main institutional base from which the philosophes could assert and establish an independent position. In contrast to the earlier cosmopolitan Republic of Letters, peopled with Protestants, savants, and *émigrés*, her argument goes, the later Paris-centred Republic of Letters was embodied in the salon which served 'as a central clearing house for news, information and ideas' and as 'a communications center into and out of which discourse . . . flowed'.[122] In making this point, Goodman draws on the seminal work of Jürgen Habermas who singled out the French salon, along with the English coffee-house, as providing a specially privileged quasi-public space where free critical inquiry could occur. 'There was scarcely a great writer of the eighteenth

---

[120] Diderot's comment to Sophie Volland is cited by Kors, *D'Holbach's Coterie*, 83–4.
[121] André Morellet, *Mémoires inédits de l'Abbé Morellet* (2nd edn. 2 vols. Paris, 1822; Slatkine repr.), i. 138–9.   [122] Goodman, 'Enlightenment Salons', 330.

century,' Habermas wrote, 'who would not have first submitted his essential ideas for discussion . . . in the salons. The salon held the monopoly of first publication; a new work, even a musical one, had to legitimate itself first in this forum.'[123]

A 'central clearing house', 'a communications center', 'a monopoly of first publication', a legitimating 'forum'—such terms seem to me to be less appropriate to regular gatherings in the great houses of Paris than to the far-flung operations of those extraterritorial publishers upon whom Voltaire and Rousseau and d'Holbach relied.

[123] Jürgen Habermas, *The Structural Transformation of the Public Sphere*, tr. T. Burger (Cambridge, Mass., 1989), 34.

5

Grub Street Abroad

THE previous chapter stressed the importance of the continued existence of francophone firms outside the Bourbon realm, not only for the exiled Huguenots, but also for those later philosophes who were lionized in Paris salons and conquered the French Academy. Granted that there were significant differences between the two groups, both relied on the initiative of the relatively independent entrepreneurs who hired translators and editors, issued books and journals, and extended far-flung distribution networks from regions outside France.

Now I am going to turn to those more numerous and more obscure publicists and literati who failed to gain admittance to Parisian salons and French academies. Following the influential essays of Robert Darnton, it has become customary to locate these unprivileged writers in 'the Grub Streets of Paris where countless unappreciated successors to Newton and Voltaire cursed the establishment'.[1] As one might expect, such anti-establishment Parisian publicists were prominently featured in conferences held during the recent bicentennial of the French Revolution. Much was made of their anticipation of French revolutionary practices; little was said about their relationship to long enduring cosmopolitan traditions and institutions.

Treatments of Simon Nicholas Henri Linguet provide a case in point. Linguet has been astutely analysed as the most important forerunner of the revolutionary press by Jeremy Popkin. By 'crafting a public persona resembling Rousseau's', 'depicting himself as a persecuted innocent', and conflating his political enemies with his personal ones, Linguet pointed the way to

---

[1] R. Darnton, *Mesmerism and the End of the Enlightenment in Paris* (Cambridge, Mass., 1968), 165. This theme, first developed in the author's unpubl. Oxford D.Phil. thesis, 'Trends in Radical Propaganda on the Eve of the French Revolution' (Nuffield College, 1964) was reiterated and elaborated in the essays which have been collected in *The Literary Underground of the Old Regime* (Cambridge, Mass., 1982), chs. 1-5.

Marat.[2] To contemporary observers without foreknowledge, however, Linguet's brand of journalism was more likely to evoke a scandal-mongering, gazetteering tradition that went back to sixteenth-century Venice. 'The métier of Aretino has always been dangerous', commented Grimm when Linguet was thrown into the Bastille.[3] More remarkable (at least it came as a surprise to me), after Linguet had been disbarred and left law for the roving life of a freelance journalist, he himself invoked the names of Pierre Bayle and Jean Le Clerc as the writers he intended to emulate.[4]

One should not place too much weight on the mere invoking of names, to be sure. But neither should one take too lightly the sense of belonging within a tradition, especially when manifested by the publicist whose 'tirades reverberated up and down Grub street' and who served as 'the most effective sniper and influential outsider of pre-revolutionary France'.[5] Linguet was an outsider in a literal as well as metaphorical sense. In this respect he was not alone. After losing his job as editor of the *Journal du Bruxelles*, and moving to London to prepare the first issues of his *Annales*, he took his stockpile of *libelles* and portable press with him.[6] But many of his contemporaries found their way to more substantial extraterritorial firms.

Linguet's one-time employer, Charles Joseph Pancoucke, the so-called 'Atlas of the book trade', press baron before the fact (he owned some seventeen journals), made energetic efforts to shake off the hold of the extraterritorial publishers. During the 1770s he bought up foreign journals and took other measures in order to achieve his aim of creating a 'grand national press' modelled on the British example. But in the end he had to admit defeat and come to terms with the enduring system by forming alliances with francophone firms in Geneva, Liège, Bouillon, Neuchâtel,

---

[2] J. Popkin, 'The Pre-Revolutionary Origins of Political Journalism', in Keith Baker (ed.), *The French Revolution and the Creation of Modern Political Culture*, i. *The Political Culture of the Old Regime* (Oxford, 1987), 203–25: pp. 215–17.

[3] Cited by Louis Trénard, 'La Presse française des origines à 1788', in C. Bellanger et al. (eds.), *Histoire générale de la presse française* (4 vols. Paris, 1974), i. 25–402: p. 280.

[4] Myriam Yardeni, 'Journalisme et histoire à l'époque de Bayle', *History and Theory*, 12 (1973), 208–29: p. 224.   [5] Darnton, *Literary Underground*, 24.

[6] Darline Gay Levy, *The Ideas and Careers of Simon-Nicholas-Henri Linguet* (Urbana, Ill., 1980), 178. After his embastillement in 1782, Linguet again went to Brussels and then embarked for England (p. 207). See also his letter to the STN (probably to Ostervald) written on the eve of his departure in 1776 cited by Levy, pp. 21–2 n. 15.

and the like.[7] Not until the collapse of the *ancien régime*, and the reshaping of the map of Europe during the revolutionary and Napoleonic wars, did French reliance on extraterritorial publishing come to an end.

Later on, something will be said about the fate of the cosmopolitan Republic of Letters after 1789. But first I want to supplement previous treatment of major figures, such as Voltaire, Rousseau, d'Holbach, with a look at the activities of some lesser lights and later epigoni. In so doing I will argue in favour of taking a more nuanced approach than that offered by the sharply bifurcated scheme which sets a 'high' Enlightenment, represented by satisfied mandarins who fattened themselves on pensions, against a literary low life endured by hordes of resentful poor hacks who found no room at the top.

First presented some twenty years ago,[8] this scheme has been reasserted in so many recent accounts and is now etched on so many minds that it seems worth taking a brief detour to examine its components. It hinges on the binary pair, high and low, and uses the first term in an idiosyncratic fashion—not merely (sociologically) to designate upward mobility and acceptance by 'high' society; but also (chronologically) to apply to the last phases of the Enlightenment as a cultural movement. Usually the term 'high' is reserved for the zenith of a movement.[9] In this instance the term 'heroic' designates the central decades of the 1750s and 1760s;[10] 'high' is reserved for the twilight years after the deaths of Voltaire and Rousseau: 'With the death of the Old Bolsheviks the movement passed into the hands of nonentities and lost its fire.' Although it goes unnoted, this aspect of the scheme entails a fairly drastic revision of previous treatments of the Enlightenment as a cultural movement. For it is generally held that, far from losing fire, the movement was radicalized as the century wore on, culminating in the atheism and materialism which were expressed in d'Holbach's works. After all, the Baron lived until

[7] Suzanne Tucoo-Chala, *Charles-Joseph Pancoucke et la librairie française 1736–1798* (Paris, 1977), 194, 351 ff.

[8] Darnton's 1971 *Past and Present* essay on the 'unusual gulf' between high and low which was 'opened up during the last 25 years of the Ancien Regime' now appears as ch. 1 of the *Literary Underground* (p. 16).

[9] The years 1748–53 are thus equated with 'the height of the Enlightenment' by Darnton himself in *The Great Cat Massacre* (New York, 1984), ch. 4, p. 145.

[10] Darnton, *Literary Underground*, 13.

1789; his writings loomed large among the pre-revolutionary bestsellers of the 1780s. As Peter Gay pointed out, there was a paradoxical coupling of growing acceptance by salon and academy with a growing espousal of radical views.[11] But this paradox finds no place in the bifurcated scheme. Acceptance by the *haute monde* leads ineluctably to enervation. Radical energy comes only from below.

The selective portrayal of fashionable nonentities and contented mediocrities who represent the high Enlightenment seems to have been drawn mainly to set off by contrast the other side—the down side—of the binary scheme. Radical energy was generated among frustrated and resentful young men from the provinces who flocked to Paris with high hopes of achieving literary fame only to end up in garrets and gutters as Grub Street hacks and police spies. Corrupted and humiliated, driven into an underworld, living off the scraps thrown to them, they seethed with hatred of the system of privileges and developed a Jacobinical determination to wipe out the aristocracy of the mind.

This description of literary low life is richly documented. It offers a seemingly plausible explanation for the verbal violence of revolutionary pamphlets and journals: 'it was from visceral hatred, not from the refined abstractions of the contented cultural elite, that the extreme Jacobin revolution found its authentic voice'.[12] But this view treats a given revolutionary text, such as Hébert's *Père Duchesne*, as if it was entirely 'transparent', as if it simply mirrored the 'gut reaction' of its author; yet it was, in part at least, a stylized exercise which mimicked the (inauthentic?) voice of a popular stage character. The view also fails to account for the many texts expressing a violent hatred of aristocracy and privilege that came not from 'Grub Street hacks' but from publicists such as Volney or Sieyès.[13] Finally, it is based on the unproven and perhaps unprovable assumption that 'social and economic conditions opened up an unusual gulf . . . during the last twenty-five years of the Old Regime'. 'While the mandarins

---

[11] P. Gay, *The Enlightenment: An Interpretation* (New York, 1966), i. 18-19.

[12] Darnton, *Literary Underground*, 40.

[13] The verbal violence of Sieyès's 'Qu'est-ce que le Tiers État?' has given rise to much comment. See e.g. Bronislaw Baczko, 'Le Contrat social des français; Sieyès et Rousseau', in Baker (ed.), *Political Culture*, 493-513: p. 499. On Volney's *Sentinelle du peuple* (Oct. and Nov. 1788), see E. L. Eisenstein, 'Le Publiciste comme démagogue', in P. Rétat (ed.), *La Révolution du journal 1788-1794* (Paris, 1989), 189-95.

fattened themselves on pensions, most authors sank into a sort of literary proletariat.'[14]

Given the difficulty of categorizing 'authors', no conclusive verdict can be rendered concerning what 'most authors' did.[15] It does seem clear, however, that many writers who never got pensions still escaped sinking into the Parisian lower depths. They followed the route taken by Linguet and became 'outsiders', at least for a time. In this regard, it is probably a mistake to take at face value the observations of contemporary observers on the dismal fate of those would-be poets and playwrights who presumably descended on Paris in droves.[16] The topos of intellectual overproduction is too deeply rooted in European print culture, too many similar observations have been made about diverse locales in other eras, for any such comments to be given much weight.[17]

Was not an equally dismal view offered by contemporary observers of the late eighteenth-century London scene? *'Canaille*, forlorn grubs and gazeteers, . . . tradesmen thrice bankrupt, . . . hungry pettifoggers, . . . felons returned from transportation. These are the people who proclaim themselves free born Englishmen and . . . insist upon having a spoke in the wheel of government.'[18] The citation from Smollet reminds us that 'Grub Street' had a more definite location in London than in Paris. The term does not really apply to conditions in eighteenth-century France,

---

[14] Darnton, *Literary Underground*, 16.

[15] Darnton's recent attempt to support this thesis with new statistics, 'The Facts of Literary Life', in Baker (ed.), *Political Culture*, 261-91, has been criticized by Benjamin Nathans, 'Habermas's "Public Sphere"', *French Historical Studies*, 16 (1990), 620-45: pp. 630-1. Nathans points out that Jean Sgard has come up with findings that point to the opposite trend of decreased 'proletarianization'.

[16] Relevant passages from Rivarol, Mercier, and Mallet du Pan are cited in *Literary Underground*, 17; *Mesmerism*, 165; 'Facts of Literary Life', 279. In the 19th cent., Eugène Hatin described the 'lava flow' of literati in pre-revolutionary Paris, citing Mallet du Pan on the hordes of would-be writers who invaded the city, begged in the streets, and published pamphlets. *Histoire politique et littéraire de la presse en France* (8 vols. Paris, 1859-60), iv. 7. The most celebrated 19th-cent. formulation is Hippolyte Taine's reference to garrets which contained 'doctors without patients, lawyers without clients' and served as a breeding ground for future Jacobins. H. Taine, *Les Origines de la France contemporaine* (14th edn. 4 vols. Paris, 1890), ii. 10.

[17] For general treatment of the theme of 'frustrated intellectuals' see Roger Chartier, *Cultural History*, tr. L. G. Cochrane (Ithaca, NY, 1988), ch. 6.

[18] Tobias Smollet, *Briton*, 15 (Sept. 1762). Cited by Robert Rea, *The English Press in Politics 1760-1774* (Lincoln, Nebr., 1963), 3.

according to Franco Venturi.[19] It is clearly difficult to translate into French.[20] The French translator of the *Literary Underground* also ran into difficulties and felt the need to substitute a different title. He chose 'Bohème littéraire'.[21] This entails a temporal rather than a spatial dislocation, transporting us to the age of the steam press and the Paris of Balzac and Murger.

The existence of an actual 'Grub Street' in pre-revolutionary Paris is especially problematic because there was no French equivalent of the lively domestic British press. As for the hybrid term 'Grub Street hack', wherever and whenever we locate the phenomenon, we will probably need to make room for the difference between the genuine hack-writer and the would-be *philosophe* playwright or poet. For assiduous practitioners, hack-writing was remunerative. 'He left the Jesuits naked as a worm and now enjoys a 10 to 12000 livres income', wrote Pidansat de Mairobert about the Abbé de la Porte, 'Did he then obtain some benefice? Not at all. He set up a book manufacturing company and uses five or six printers at a time. He writes journals, dictionaries, travel accounts, almanacs. He abridges long works and augments short ones. He has a marvelous talent for writing the same thing in 5 or 6 different ways.'[22] Book historians have reason to be grateful to this industrious hack. With aid from collaborators, he compiled the first volumes in the series *La France littéraire*, which provide data on *ancien régime* authors.[23] De la Porte was too industrious to be regarded as

[19] F. Venturi, *The End of the Old Regime in Europe 1776–1789*, tr. Burr Litchfield (2 vols. Princeton, NJ, 1991), i. 427 n. 7.

[20] A French citation of the celebrated essay on Brissot refers to the 'Grub style [*sic*] of Politics': Marie-France Silver, 'Mirabeau', *Dictionnaire des journalistes*, ed. J. Sgard (Grenoble, 1976), 280. When referring to Darnton's down-and-out literati, the French seem to prefer the phrase 'les Rousseau du ruisseau' (i.e. 'Gutter Rousseaus').

[21] R. Darnton, *Bohème littéraire et révolution: Le Monde des livres au XVIIIᵉ siècle* (Paris, 1983). On the coinage and usage of term in the 19th cent. see Pierre Labracherie, *La Vie quotidienne de la bohème littéraire au XIXᵉ siècle* (Paris, 1967), where the author points to the development of an 'intellectual proletariat' during Louis-Philippe's reign (p. 11). Applying the term to earlier phenomena is, however, not uncommon. See e.g. reference to an 18th-cent. 'bohème' largely composed of ecclesiastics by Pierre Barrière, *La Vie intellectuelle en France du XVIᵉ siècle à l'époque contemporaine* (Paris, 1961), 289.

[22] Rémy Saisselin, *The Literary Enterprise in Eighteenth-Century France* (Detroit, 1979), 78, cites this passage from Pidansat de Mairobert's *Espion anglais* (29 Feb. 1776).

[23] See e.g. *La France littéraire pour l'année MDCCLVII par M. l'abbé de la Porte* (Paris: Duchesne, 1758). An account of the successive vols. issued under this title is given by Darnton. He bases his statistical analysis on the data they contain: 'Facts of Literary Life', 263.

typical but he does disclose a respectable, quasi-professional aspect that needs to be considered before it can be concluded that 'the hack was a particularly dangerous species'.[24] The compilation of pocket dictionaries, almanacs, medical reference works, and other guidebooks was probably not the best way to become a culture-hero—although the existence of 'Dictionary Johnson' and Diderot of the *Encyclopédie* suggest otherwise. Still some room needs to be made for the many writers who were situated between glittering celebrity and abysmal failure.

Old-fashioned literary history, it is argued, was focused too narrowly on great writers and great books. The great men 'have squeezed out the middlemen'. To supply these missing intermediaries, we are told about publishers, papermakers, journeymen printers, salesmen, and others 'who operated everywhere . . . sorting out supply and demand, filtering the flow of literature before it took the form of books loaded on wagons'.[25] Elsewhere, we are offered a case-study of a neglected middleman who did more than produce, package, and transport books. He is presented as one of those 'literary agents, popularizers, polemicists, journalists and ideological "carriers"' who were recruited by the philosophes to propagandize on their behalf.[26] He turns out to be one Abbé Le Senne, 'a pamphleteer on the run', a smuggler, pedlar, and petty criminal who sinks into obscurity after surfacing briefly in the papers of the STN. Although his later activities cannot be traced, his experience 'shows where the rage of the enragés came from: it was a deep visceral hatred of a regime whose corruption had spread into their own inner beings'.[27] But this presentation is open to the objection that less marginal intermediaries are still being squeezed out so that the gulf between high and low seems wider than perhaps it was.

It may be partly because Paris is viewed as 'the nerve center of the publishing industry'[28] that opportunities extended to French literati by extraterritorial firms are downplayed. Yet even La

[24] Darnton, 'Facts of Literary Life', 268. Saisselin, *Literary Enterprise*, 79–82, stresses the need to distinguish between the quasi-professional writer and the semi-adventurer or 'grub street' type.

[25] R. Darnton, 'The Forgotten Middlemen of Literature', *Kiss of Lamourette* (New York, 1990), ch. 8, esp. pp. 136, 145.

[26] Darnton, *Literary Underground*, ch. 3, p. 112.

[27] Ibid. 118. The description does not fit the careers of the real *enragés*.

[28] R. Darnton, *The Business of Enlightenment* (Cambridge, Mass., 1979), 84.

Senne, one of the most desperate of Darnton's many desperate characters, knew enough to look to a foreign publishing house for rescue. 'He offered to come to Neuchâtel on foot, to correct copy and read proof, and to accept any wages he could get.'[29] When we look outside the Bourbon realm, as previous discussion suggests, we will find literary agents, popularizers, polemicists, journalists, and other cultural intermediaries who propagated the Enlightenment without starving or turning to crime. In other words, the *ancien régime typographique* provided French writers with a different and more cosmopolitan career trajectory than would the Paris of Balzac's *Illusions perdues*.

A version of *La France littéraire* was issued from Berlin in 1757 by a Huguenot pastor turned publicist named Jean Henri Samuel Formey (1711–97).[30] It included coverage of French writing done outside France by persons such as Formey himself. Formey was an industrious compiler. He was also an accomplished popularizer who did much to make the philosophy of Christian Wolff accessible to the reader at large. His advice on 'how to form a library with few but well chosen books' went through many editions. Following the pattern set by Fontenelle, he also produced a collection of *Éloges* or biographical tributes to academicians and savants. He joined forces with Élie Luzac of Leiden to bring out the *Bibliothèque impartiale* and served as secretary of the Prussian Academy of Sciences in Berlin.[31] He was certainly a popularizer and might be described as a 'hack'. But he does not belong on Grub Street—however such a locale may be defined.

'The study of careers old fashioned . . . as it seems may provide a needed corrective to the more abstract study of ideas and ideologies.'[32] Let us look at one well-documented case-study.[33]

---

[29] Darnton, *Literary Underground*, 115.

[30] J. H. S. Formey, *La France littéraire ou dictionnaire des auteurs françois vivans corrigé et augmenté par M. Formey* (Berlin, 1757).

[31] Uta Janssens-Knorsch, 'Against Voltaire: An Unfavorable View . . . among French Expatriates in Berlin', *Studies on Voltaire*, 267 (1989), 119–26: p. 120. Formey is best known for *La Belle Wolfienne* (1742), a popularization à la Fontenelle of the philosophy of Christian Wolff. His *Éloges des académiciens de Berlin et d'autres savants* (1757) is noted by Jacques Marx, 'La Bibliothèque Impartiale', in M. Couperus (ed.), *L'Étude des périodiques anciens: Colloque d'Utrecht* (Paris, 1972), 89–108: p. 96. The Library of Congress has the 5th edn. of his *Conseils pour former une bibliothèque peu nombreuse mais choisie* (Amsterdam: J. H. Schneider, 1764).

[32] Darnton, *Literary Underground*, 69–70.

[33] Unless otherwise indicated, the following account is based on the excellent monograph by Raymond Birn, 'Pierre Rousseau and the Philosophes of Bouillon',

A young man from the provinces, the son of a Toulouse school-master, found himself in Paris in the middle of the eighteenth century in the typical posture of a lawyer without clients. Having abandoned the study of surgery for that of law, he then abandoned law for literature and turned to writing plays. Although one *opéra comique*, written with a collaborator, was performed by the Comédie-Française,[34] the would-be playwright had little success. In the summer of 1755 he got a job editing an advertising sheet, *Affiches de Paris*, which led, in turn, to a post as Paris news agent and book dealer for the Elector Palatine. With an annual pension from his German patron secured, a good marriage was made with the daughter of a German official. Pierre Rousseau then decided to capitalize on the excitement generated by the publication of the *Encyclopédie* by turning out a journal devoted to extracts, articles, and anecdotes about the volumes that were still appearing. He first considered and then dismissed the idea of setting up operations in Mannheim, under the protection of his patron. He thought the locale would be unsuitable because Calvinist sentiment was too strong and the French language too little known.[35]

The French-speaking ecclesiastical principality of Liège, where the prime minister favoured the philosophes and the Catholic prince-bishop was an absentee overlord, seemed to furnish the environment he sought. He made arrangements with a local printer, dedicated his first issue of the *Journal encyclo-pédique* to the absentee ruler, and threw himself into his self-appointed task of keeping the *Encyclopédie* in the public eye during an interval when the Diderot's enterprise appeared to be

Studies on Voltaire, 29 (1964). After finishing the lecture upon which this chapter is based, I found that Pierre Rousseau's career had been singled out as paradigmatic many years ago by Febvre and Martin, *L'Apparition du livre* (Paris, 1958), 238–40. There the 'journalist-publishers' of the 18th cent. are likened to the author-printers of the 16th.

34 Gustave Charlier and Roland Mortier, *Le Journal encyclopédique (1756–1793): Notes, documents, extraits* (Paris, 1952), 9.

35 Birn, 'Pierre Rousseau', 40–1. Although Pierre Rousseau may not have known it, Mannheim actually had a sizeable French-speaking contingent with some French authors in residence and francophone journals intermittently produced. French was one of the three official languages adopted by the local Academy of Sciences. The elector's court had its own 'comédie française'. A francophone publishing firm, established in 1742 by Charles Fontaine, continued in operation until the end of the century. Jürgen Voss, 'La Librairie Fontaine à Mannheim et la présence du livre français', in F. Barbier et al. (eds.), *Livre et révolution* (Mélanges de la Bibliothèque de la Sorbonne, 9); Paris, 1988), 221–32.

coming to a standstill in Paris.[36] I say 'self-appointed' for there is nothing to suggest that Pierre Rousseau was recruited by the philosophes to do their bidding and much to indicate he was a true enthusiast acting on his own initiative.[37] Although ostensibly produced by a 'société de gens de lettres', the *Journal encyclopédique* was at the outset essentially a one-man production. This was by no means the only such fictive presentation of a 'society'; print culture encouraged this kind of deception. (The 'Athenian Society' concocted by John Dunton was perhaps the first to have pointed the way.)

Within a year of his move to Liège, Pierre Rousseau had acquired his own press. Aided by the exiled encyclopaedist Abbé Claude Yvon, the former playwright set type, did bookkeeping, wrote articles, reproduced extracts, and began to form liaisons with other francophone publishers including Yvon's sometime employer, the formidable Amsterdam publisher, Marc Michel Rey. His first letters to Rey were written in the abject tone of one who solicited the aid of a noble patron. A useful working partnership developed in a short time; he took care to advertise Rey's books, and to review them favourably. He helped Rey smuggle his editions of Jean-Jacques Rousseau's works into German and Habsburg lands.[38] Legal entry of his own journal into France was blocked at first by Malesherbes who was in charge of the French book trade. In view of his well-known sympathy for the encyclopaedists' cause, Malesherbes's reaction to Pierre Rousseau's initial attempt to penetrate French markets was surprisingly harsh and also remarkably chauvinistic in tone. In a letter from the minister (16 April 1759) the editor-publisher was told that, since he had abandoned his native land, he ought to abandon all hope of having his work sold in France. He chose to become a citizen of Liège, let him be content to have his journal sold there. It was absurd for a man who had sought refuge from the laws of France to request help from the government of

[36] R. Birn, 'The French Language Press and the *Encyclopédie*', *Studies on Voltaire*, 55 (1967), 263-86: pp. 282-3.

[37] Jacques Wagner, 'Pierre Rousseau à Liège (1756-1759)', in Daniel Droixhe et al. (eds.), *Livres et lumières au pays de Liège (1730-1830)* (Liège, 1980), 15-31.

[38] Some 74 letters from Pierre Rousseau's correspondence with Rey have been preserved. See J. Vercruysse, 'Les Livres clandestins de Bouillon', *Studies on Voltaire*, 193 (1980), 1840-52.

France.[39] But as was so often the case under the *ancien régime*, an abrupt change in ministerial policy occurred;[40] permission was granted for the journal to go on sale in Paris at the Bureau des Gazettes Étrangères.

While manœuvring to get his journal admitted to France, the expatriate publisher lost his own place of residence in Liège. The canons of the local cathedral chapter gained the upper hand in the bishopric and acted upon an unfavourable report by the theologians of Louvain. They accused Pierre Rousseau of confusing liberty with licence and spreading a subtle encyclopaedic poison from their city. A warrant for arrest was issued and the publisher-editor fled with his presses in time-honoured style— floating down the Meuse on a raft. After an abortive attempt to settle in Brussels, where the Austrians (who needed the help of Liège in their war against Prussia) were dissuaded from harbouring the refugee, an ideal sanctuary was found in the tiny principality of Bouillon. Here local rivalries worked in the publisher's favour. Charles Godefroy de la Tour, the Prince of Bouillon, was at odds with the rulers of Liège. Economic considerations, typical of old Europe in the age of the hand press, also came into play. The Prince welcomed the establishment of a new industry within his realm which meant employment for local labour and a favourable balance of trade. When Louis XV issued orders to clamp down on subversive publication, the Prince pretended to obey; but, reluctant to inhibit the most beneficial industrial development of his reign, he allowed the operations to go on.[41] There was considerable opposition from local church authorities and for a time sacraments were refused to any printing worker employed by the publisher. Court intervention overcame this additional obstacle.

By 1765, five years after his move to Bouillon, Pierre Rousseau was employing about twenty workers and turning out three additional journals along with the *Journal encyclopédique*. In 1768 he founded his own Société Typographique. (He thus reversed

---

[39] Malesherbes, letter of 16 Apr. 1759, cited by Pierre Grosclaude, *Malesherbes: Témoin et interprète de son temps 1721-1794* (Paris, n.d.), 71-2. In keeping with previous remarks concerning the tendency to blur distinctions between journal and book, Malesherbes refers to Rousseau's journal as 'votre Livre'.

[40] Jack Censer informs me that he has found documents in the French Ministry of Foreign Affairs indicating that Choiseul was responsible for changing the policy pursued by Malesherbes at the time.   [41] Birn, 'Pierre Rousseau', 95.

the usual procedure, of having the journal serve as a spin-off from the book business, by beginning with journals and going on to books.) During the late (or high?) Enlightenment, he had achieved financial security and social respectability equal to that of the Amsterdam publisher he had courted in earlier years.[42] In 1771, family ties with Rey were established by the marriage of Pierre Rousseau's brother-in-law and business associate, Charles de Weissenbruch, to Marguerite Jeanne Rey. Weissenbruch (1740–1822) proved adept at handling the clandestine book trade, using his position as masonic Grand Master to facilitate getting parcels past officials and transforming the Société Typographique de Bouillon into a central letter-box for correspondence with the Lodge of the Grand Orient in Paris.[43] Pierre Rousseau died in 1785. Three years later, the firm was renamed 'Imprimerie Weissenbruch'; in 1795 it was moved from Bouillon to Brussels where it continues to this day.

The interlocking by marriage of the family firms of eighteenth-century expatriates (Jean Frédéric Bernard, Marc Michel Rey, Pierre Rousseau, Charles de Weissenbruch) recalls the practices of earlier eras. Pierre Rousseau's establishment in Bouillon in the 1770s and 1780s evokes descriptions of the extended households of sixteenth-century master-printers such as the Estiennes. An entry in Bauchamont's *Mémoires secrets* described the singular fate of M. Pierre Rousseau of Toulouse who had risen from the position of a mediocre and disdained Paris author to become a highly esteemed and very prosperous manufacturer: 'the head of a little republic of more than sixty people whom he lodges, feeds, and pays; within which everyone works including his wife and children'.[44] The 'little world of the book' thus survived under

[42] R. Birn, 'Le Livre prohibé aux frontières: Bouillon', in H. J. Martin and R. Chartier (eds.), *Histoire de l'édition française*, ii. *Le Livre triomphant 1660–1830* (Paris, 1984), 334–42: p. 341 discusses the fluctuations in the firm's fortunes during the 1770s and 1780s. The best years were 1775–9; thereafter P. Rousseau went into semi-retirement and bad investments by an associate led to trouble. After a low point in 1783, Weissenbruch pulled the STB out of debt.

[43] J. Vercruysse, 'Les Livres clandestins', 1842. Birn, 'Le Livre prohibé', 341, notes that Weissenbruch helped to arrange for hiding one of Mirabeau's works under the floor of the carriage of Mirabeau's mistress. See also description of letter from P. Rousseau to a Reims book dealer about Weissenbruch's contacts in Charleville making it possible to evade officials in Sedan: 'once you have received the books, you can poison the entire realm'. Cited in J. P. Belin, *Le Commerce des livres prohibés à Paris de 1750 à 1789* (Paris, 1913), 48–9.

[44] Cited from *Mémoires secrets* (London, 1783), xix. 103–4, by Birn, 'Le Livre prohibé', 337.

foreign protection until the very end of the *ancien régime typographique*.

As manager of an extraterritorial typographical society, Pierre Rousseau was clearly engaged in the 'business of Enlightenment'. But it seems perverse to insist that the founder, publisher, and editor of a journal which was aimed at keeping the public updated on news of the *Encyclopédie* was interested only in making money.[45] When presented as just another 'hack writer who made a fortune defending the philosophes'[46] Pierre Rousseau appears in the guise of a middleman who has been deservedly forgotten.

When viewed from a different angle, the expatriate publisher is less likely to be summarily dismissed. Jacques Wagner, for example, has argued that Pierre Rousseau exhibited considerable originality in his conception of his mission as journal editor and in his appreciation of the 'communicative energy' of the periodical press. Even while defending Diderot's project and diffusing its message, he took issue with Diderot's scornful view of journalism. Periodical publication in his view could serve to propel and accelerate that process of data collection which had been envisaged by Francis Bacon. Whereas there were limits to the number of new lands and new oceans to be discovered, reporting on an expanding knowledge industry set the journalist on a voyage without limits; one which led beyond the pillars of Hercules into the infinite and the unknown. 'The Louvain theologians who succeeded in dislodging Pierre Rousseau from Liège and prevented him from establishing himself in Brussels perfectly understood the thrust of his enterprise.'[47]

As did other extraterritorial firms, the Société Typographique de Bouillon provided hospitality and employment to literary adventurers on the run. Jean Louis Carra, a disreputable young man from the provinces, worked for a while in Bouillon for Rousseau's firm before moving on to work for the Cramers in Geneva, travelling to Italy, Greece, and Turkey, and acting as a tutor of the children of a Moldavian prince in St Petersburg.[48] After a decade of travels abroad in the 1770s, Carra returned to Paris to win the favour of Loménie de Brienne who found him a post as librarian to the director of the book trade, Jean Charles

[45] See above, Ch 1 n 96.　　[46] Darnton, *Literary Underground*, 74.
[47] J. Wagner, 'Le Rôle du *Journal encyclopédique* dans la diffusion de la culture', *Studies in Voltaire*, 4 (1980), 1805-12; see also Wagner, 'Pierre Rousseau à Liège', 15-31.
[48] Jean Sgard, 'Jean Louis Carra (1742-1793)', *Dictionnaire des journalistes*, 67-71.

Pierre Lenoir. As the official who got Brissot to serve as a 'police spy', Lenoir plays an important role in Darnton's pioneering study of 'the Grub Street style of politics'.[49] He also crops up in the affairs of Pierre Rousseau's firm, agreeing to look the other way when Bouillon engaged in clandestine trade, in exchange for de luxe volumes of Helvetius.[50] After Carra and Lenoir had a falling out, Carra directed a vituperative pamphlet campaign against his former employer. Carra's pamphleteering was exceptionally vicious; his finding employment in foreign firms and foreign households as well as in the library of a Parisian official was unexceptional for one of his kind.

In a wry comment on the corruption of book-trade officials, Brissot noted how inspectors of the book trade profited from seizing forbidden books and then selling their large collections to wealthy businessmen. The financier, having thus acquired a library, found he needed a librarian. So a new job was created to supply a living for some poor author and everyone benefited from the system in the end.[51] Service in great households as tutors, secretaries, and librarians provided young men from the provinces with an alternative to leading a miserable existence in garrets and gutters. Filling the difficult split role, half confidential clerk, half domestic servant, probably fuelled resentment of privilege.[52] Masters rarely appear in a worthy, dignified guise to their servants—as is shown most divertingly by Beaumarchais's play. Figaro, one recalls, combined the *métier* of the gazetteer with observing aristocratic behaviour at close quarters.[53] Figaro's creator knew about gazetteering at first hand. During the 1770s, Beaumarchais served the French foreign minister as a secret agent, travelling abroad to pay off blackmailing pamphleteers who threatened to make trouble for the French government.

---

[49] 'The Grub Street Style of Politics: Jacques Pierre Brissot, Police Spy' was the title of the essay which first appeared in the *Journal of Modern History*, 40 (1968), 301-27. Citations come from *Literary Underground*, ch. 2, where it is retitled: 'A Spy in Grub Street'.   [50] See above, Ch. 4. n. 112.

[51] Jacques Pierre Brissot, *Mémoires (1754-1793)*, ed. C. Perroud (2 vols. Paris, n.d.), i. 106. Brissot specifically refers to d'Hémery (the book-trade inspector who is depicted by Darnton as sorting his files) as among those who sold confiscated books for profit.

[52] See pertinent essay by Daniel Roche, 'Le Précepteur, éducateur privilégié et intermédiaire culturel' (1985), *Républicains des lettres*, ch. 14.

[53] Jacqueline Sabattier, *Figaro et son maître: Maîtres et domestiques à Paris au XVIIIᵉ siècle* (Paris, 1984), ch. 11. The older works by F. Funck-Brentano, *Figaro et ses devanciers* (Paris, 1909) and *Les Nouvellistes* (Paris, 1905), are also still pertinent.

Later, after searching for a location in which to produce his edition of Voltaire's works, he found in Kehl yet another of those tiny quasi-independent principalities which sustained cosmopolitan francophone publication.[54]

The inadequacy of the 'Grub Street' thesis, set forth by eighteenth-century critics such as Rivarol, was noted by a nineteenth-century historian. On the eve of the revolution, what do we find? asked Granier de Cassagnac. We find a regime which employed Billaud de Varennes and pensioned Chamfort. Fauchet had a benefice; Fouché a professorship. Marat was serving as a physician in the retinue of the Comte d'Artois. Brissot was employed at the chancellery of Monsieur.[55] These last points need qualifying. Marat had ceased his services to d'Artois in 1783. Although Brissot had been employed as a secretary to the Chancellor of the Duc d'Orléans, he was actually travelling in America in 1788. Nevertheless the comment is worth pondering.

Furthermore, as Carra's journeys remind us, and Brissot's adventures show, secretaries and tutors had frequent opportunities to travel abroad. While serving as a secretary to the Marquis Ducrest, Brissot went to Holland in 1786.[56] Marat's younger brother David, who accompanied Brissot on a pilgrimage to Ferney, later taught French in Russia (to Pushkin among others).[57] Gilbert Romme, the future martyr of Prairial, was hired as a tutor of the son of a Russian prince; he spent 1779–86 in Russia before taking his charge on a European tour and parted from his pupil only after getting caught up in revolutionary

[54] For details see Louis Léonard de Loménie, *Beaumarchais et son temps* (2 vols. Paris, 1856); Paul Robiquet, *Thévenau de Morande* (Paris, 1882), 48 ff; Gunnar and Mavis von Proschwitz, 'Beaumarchais et le *Courier de l'Europe*: Documents inédits ou peu connus', *Studies on Voltaire*, 273 and 274 (1990). Giles Barber, 'The Financial History of the Kehl Voltaire', *The Age of Enlightenment: Studies Presented to Theodore Besterman* (Edinburgh, 1967), 152-71. Despite Beaumarchais's prominence as a *libelliste* in the 'Goezman affair', his imprisonment in 1785, and his role as go-between with Thévenau de Morande, Darnton places him among the contented mandarins and mediocrities: 'most of his energy went into speculation and ultimately into building the biggest townhouse in Paris ... the arriviste's dream'. *Literary Underground*, 15.

[55] M. A. Granier de Cassagnac, *Histoire des causes de la révolution française* (2 vols. Paris, 1850), i. 71-4.

[56] Norman Hampson, *Will and Circumstance: Montesquieu, Rousseau and the French Revolution* (Norman, Okla., 1983), 98.

[57] Brissot, *Mémoires*, i. 280; Charly Guyot, *De Rousseau à Mirabeau: Pèlerins de Môtiers et prophètes de 89* (Neuchâtel, 1936), 131.

politics.[58] Alexandre Deleyre, the future Montagnard, arrived in Paris aged 24 without a sou. He first worked for d'Holbach and Diderot, contributing articles to the *Encyclopédie* and the *Journal encyclopédique*, before finding several lucrative posts abroad, serving as secretary in the French Embassy in Vienna and as librarian to the Duke of Parma.[59]

In view of the many voyages made by the figures singled out as representing a pre-revolutionary literary 'proletariat', it is difficult to see why we should envisage their being 'trapped in a situation that had no exit'.[60] There were intervals of being 'down and out in Paris'.[61] But there were also many chances to be up and around abroad. After all, there was a real Grub Street across the Channel and a 'fertile crescent' offering job opportunities just beyond the borders of France. Brissot met Linguet in London, Mercier in Neuchâtel, Sieyès in Rotterdam.[62] When Mirabeau was released from the prison of Vincennes in 1780, he refused to go into the custody of his father in Provence and headed instead for the extraterritorial publisher Samuel Fauche of Neuchâtel. Previously he had spent time in Amsterdam acting as an assistant to Marc Michel Rey.[63]

The initiation of future revolutionaries into the discourse which was common to the so-called 'Atlantic' or 'Democratic' revolutions was not limited to their getting a glimpse of journals such as the *Gazette de Leyde*. His observation of the Wilkite agitation in London during his eleven-year stay in Great Britain inspired Marat to adopt the pen name of Junius in the 1790s.[64] Brissot and Mirabeau, the two journalists who first challenged *ancien*

---

[58] Alessandro Galante Garrone, *Gilbert Romme, storia di un rivoluzionario* (Turin, 1959), chs. 3, 4, 5. Romme's considerable influence on his charge, the future Count Paul Stroganov, is brought out by Galante Garrone.

[59] Marie-Rose de Labriolle, 'Alexandre Deleyre', *Dictionnaire des journalistes*, 114.

[60] Darnton, *Literary Underground*, 21.

[61] The Orwellian phrase is used on p. 17.

[62] Brissot's encounter with Sieyès in July 1787, while the Abbé was travelling in the entourage of Lubersac, is noted by Paul Bastid, *Sieyès et sa pensée* (2nd edn. Paris, 1970), 51.

[63] J. Bénétruy, *L'Atelier de Mirabeau: Quatre proscrits genevois dans la tourmente révolutionnaire* (Geneva, 1962), 40. Herman de la Fontaine Verwey, 'The Netherlands Book', in W. G. Hellinga (ed.), *Copy and Print in the Netherlands* (Amsterdam, 1962), 3–70: p. 47.

[64] Gérard Walter, *Marat* (Geneva, 1977), 13, 22–23. See also E. L. Eisenstein, 'The tribune of the people: a new species of demagogue', *Studies on Voltaire*, 287 (1991), 145–59.

régime controls and demanded a free press in 1789, had previously followed similar itineraries. Both made stops in Switzerland during the Genevan revolution and they frequented the same circles while residing in London.[65]

In 1784, Mirabeau arrived in London with a letter of introduction from Benjamin Franklin to Richard Price urging publication of Mirabeau's treatise attacking hereditary aristocracy. The manuscript was taken to Joseph Johnson, the London printer, publisher, and bookseller who served a large circle of dissenters and radical Whigs. It was quickly published in French and an English version (coupled with Price's 'Observations on the American Revolution') soon followed.[66] While the English translation was being made, its author attended parliament and heard debates between Pitt, Burke, and Fox.[67] During that same stay in London, 1784-5, Mirabeau also drew a comparison between the way English statesmen engaged in journalism and their French counterparts disdained to do so.[68] A few years later Mirabeau himself would emerge as a journalist-deputy, a hybrid species that would eventually come to seem more characteristic of French than of Anglo-American political culture.[69]

Brissot, who played a similar hybrid role in the French Revolution, owed his first job as a journalist to his having mastered the English language (a most useful tool for any eighteenth-century French writer in need of employment, as Jean Le Clerc, Abbé Prévost, Diderot, Suard, and others showed). In 1778, when he left Paris for Boulogne-sur-mer to work on the *Courier de*

---

[65] The important role played in Mirabeau's career by the exiles from the Genevan revolution and his stormy relationship with the Swiss financier Clavière who helped Brissot are discussed by Bénétruy. See also Guyot, *De Rousseau à Mirabeau* and Derek Jarrett, *The Begetters of Revolution* (London, 1973).

[66] G. Tyson, *Joseph Johnson* (Iowa City, Ia., 1979), 86-7.

[67] Guy Chaussinand-Nogaret, *Mirabeau* (Paris, 1982), 88 ff. This seems to contradict Brissot's statement in his *Mémoires*, ii. 38, that Mirabeau 'had no knowledge of English nor of England' and thus had to get Brissot's help in launching his *Analyse des papiers anglais* in Nov. 1787. Brissot also claims he wrote the attack on Mallet du Pan which was signed with Mirabeau's name and appeared in the *Analyse*.

[68] See letter from London to Montmorin, 25 Nov. 1785, cited by Chaussinand-Nogaret, *Mirabeau*, 88, where Mirabeau seems to be echoing Voltaire's celebrated comparison: 'In France, Mr Addison would have gotten into trouble . . . In England, he has been a Secretary of State.' Voltaire, letter 23, *Letters on England* (*Lettres philosophiques*), tr. and ed. L. Tancock (Harmondsworth, 1980), 111.

[69] How a convergence of politics as a vocation with journalism as a profession occurred during the French Revolution is discussed in my 'tribune of the people'.

l'Europe, he made only a brief visit to London.[70] Four years later, however, he acquired a closer acquaintance with the English political scene. While in London during the early 1780s he ran into the sort of trouble one might expect of a denizen of 'Grub Street'. He complained in his memoirs of having been cheated by expatriate blackmailers; he endured a brief imprisonment for debt. But he also encountered a circle of eminent dissenters, political reformers, and philosophical radicals: Jeremy Bentham, Joseph Priestley, Richard Price, Catherine Macaulay, David Williams.[71] This was the same circle that Mirabeau's London publisher, Joseph Johnson, served. It contained the foreigners who would be accorded honorary French citizenship by the National Convention after Louis XVI's fall.

It would be a mistake to discount such encounters when considering Brissot's later activities as a revolutionary journalist and Girondin politician. The epigraph which would be repeated on every issue of his revolutionary journal, *Patriote française*, 'a free press is the eternally vigilant sentinel of the people', was taken from an address given by Dr John Jebb (1736–86). During Brissot's London stay, Jebb had been engaged in organizing the Society for Constitutional Information, circulating petitions and setting up committees of correspondence aimed at dissolving George III's 'unrepresentative' House of Commons and at creating a National Assembly.[72] A decade later, after the French had succeeded in dissolving an 'unrepresentative' Estates General and creating their own National Assembly, the name of Dr John Jebb would become familiar to all French readers of Brissot's journal.

The year immediately preceding 1789 found Brissot travelling in North America. He visited Washington in Mount Vernon, thanks to a letter of introduction from Lafayette. (To stroll along the banks of the Potomac is surely far from being trapped in the gutters of Paris.) He tried without success to persuade George

[70] On this journal see Ch. 2 above, p. 50. When the British became offended by its pro-American position and took measures to prevent its importation into France, a special office was set up in Boulogne-sur-mer to evade the embargo and Brissot was hired to work there. E. Hatin, *Les Gazettes de Hollande et la presse clandestine* (Paris, 1865), 41; Brissot, *Mémoires*, i. 39–40.

[71] Brissot, *Mémoires*, i. 347–9, 363, 366, 372. See also Eloise Ellery, *Brissot de Warville* (1st edn. 1915; Franklin repr. New York, 1970), 24–5. David V. Erdman, *Commerce des Lumières: John Oswald and the British in Paris* (Columbia, Mo., 1986).

[72] Albert Goodwin, *The Friends of Liberty* (Cambridge, Mass., 1979), 60–2, 114.

Washington to free his slaves and join the movement for emancipation.[73] During his American journey, Brissot was especially
impressed by the remarkable success of Tom Paine's *Common
Sense*. He was persuaded that Paine's work would have remained
without much effect had it been left in its original pamphlet
form. The idea that its success was due to its being repeatedly
reprinted in newspapers underlines his often cited remark:
'without newspapers the American Revolution would never have
succeeded'.[74]

As these remarks may suggest, Brissot's encounters with
English and American publicists and politicians were no less
significant (and perhaps more so) in shaping his particular 'style'
of revolutionary politics than were his contacts with blackmailing
pamphleteers. Indeed, it is by no means clear how the shady side
of his pre-revolutionary career affected his later activities. On
this question, Darnton's 1968 essay, 'The Grub Street Style of
Politics: Jacques Pierre Brissot, Police Spy',[75] stops short of
providing a clear answer. The essay points out that one should
not take Brissot at his word when he denied being drafted into
service as a paid informer by the chief book-trade official of the
ancien régime. Its purpose, however, is not merely to underscore
flaws in Brissot's idealized self-portrait, 'but rather to understand
the making of a revolutionary'.[76] Towards this end, it offers a
touching portrait of an earnest young idealist traumatically
corrupted and 'deflowered' by vicious officials. The reader is
asked to believe that Brissot seethed with hatred ever after: 'How
he must have reviled the men who . . . dishonored him by making
him their agent.'[77] This is purely speculative and not altogether
plausible.[78] The assumption that Brissot felt dishonoured fails to
allow for Brissot's considerable capacity for self-deception. It
also blurs the difference between *ancien régime* and revolutionary
attitudes. Doubtless after 1789 it was only prudent to deny complicity with *ancien régime* authorities; before 1789, agreeing to
serve as an agent of a royal official was not necessarily an

---

73 Ellery, *Brissot*, 79–80.
74 Brissot, *Mémoires*, ii. 179–80. The often cited remark appears in the prospectus of
the *Patriote française* (16 Mar. 1789). E. Hatin, *Bibliographie historique et critique de la
presse périodique française* (Paris, 1866), 142.   75 See n. 49 above.
76 *Literary Underground*, 41.   77 Ibid. 68.
78 Hampson, *Will and Circumstance*, 95, also expresses scepticism about Darnton's
analysis.

occasion for shame. In 1781, three years before his supposedly traumatic agreement with Lenoir, Brissot had written to the STN that he had inside information from a book-trade official and his letter was written 'not without a touch of pride'.[79] Whatever the case, it remains unclear how his dealings with book-trade officials (whether shameful or not) affected the future Girondin's particular 'style' of revolutionary politics.[80]

In 1784, the same year he was presumably scarred for life by dealings with 'the police', Brissot found a new patron in the Genevan financier Clavière. His first encounter with Clavière had occurred two years previously, when being neither trapped in Paris nor down and out in London but while travelling in Switzerland to visit his publisher in Neuchâtel.[81] There he luxuriated in the hospitable environment provided by his host, Samuel Frédéric Ostervald and by Ostervald's widowed daughter, the cultivated Mme Bertrand, who served as a head-mistress of a girl's school in Mannheim. His lyrical description of the STN (noted in passing above) elaborated on the 'free air' of the remote sanctuary in the mountains. 'The Inquisition of the ministry of Versailles thought it was closing all pathways to the Enlightenment by blocking the frontiers, but the goddess of liberty changed location and carried her shops to a place which was encircled by mountains and could not be penetrated by the Inquisition.'[82] Incidentally, Louis Sébastien Mercier, who was in Neuchâtel correcting proofs at the time, fell on Brissot the moment he arrived, asking for the latest news from Paris. Mercier was bored to tears by his stay in the country and could not wait to get back to the excitement of city life.[83]

'Once he had fallen into Grub Street,' we are told, 'the provincial youth who had dreamt of storming Parnassus never extricated himself.' After Grub Street had left its mark on Brissot and his companions, 'they could not penetrate into polite society

[79] *Literary Underground*, 65.

[80] This point still holds good, despite the recent debate between Darnton and Frederick A. de Luna over whether Brissot was or was not a 'police spy'. 'Forum: Interpreting Brissot', *French Historical Studies*, 17 (1991), 159–205.

[81] According to Guyot, Brissot first met Clavière at the Neuchâtel home of Jean Jacques Rousseau's patron, Alexandre Dupeyrou in July 1782. Charly Guyot, *Un ami et défenseur de Rousseau: Pierre Alexandre Dupeyrou* (Neuchâtel, n.d.), 151. He was in Geneva observing the revolution there on 12–17 June. (Bénétruy, *L'Atelier de Mirabeau*, 36.)

[82] Brissot, *Mémoires*, i. 284 (ch. 11, pp. 244–302, is devoted to Switzerland).

[83] Ibid. 286–7.

where the plums were passed around so they cursed *the closed world of culture*.[84] But there was nothing closed about Brissot's cultural world.[85] When attention is focused only on the blocked mobility of the literary careerist and his career is reduced to consorting with blackmailers and spying for the police, we are in danger of overlooking what seems most remarkable about Brissot's world-view. That is, we are likely to pass over the grandiosity of his ambition and the extraordinary expansiveness of his plans. In the 1780s, he set out to organize all the savants and reformers of Europe by means of a London-based Lyceum.[86]

Like the encyclopedists he would popularize knowledge. He would unite men of letters of all quarters of the globe in a single body so that, to quote his own language, a Laplander transplanted to Paris or Madrid would be as much at home as though he were a Frenchman or Spaniard since he would realize that he belongs to all countries.[87]

'Seen from the perspective of Grub Street,' the argument goes, 'the republic of letters was a lie'.[88] Seen from the wide-angled cosmopolitan perspective of the French journalist who crossed the Channel, the Alps, and the Atlantic Ocean, the Republic of Letters was an expansive phenomenon which encompassed all the peoples of the world. Even within France in the 1780s, writers such as Brissot, far from sinking into a proletariat, were welcomed by the *haute monde*. Radicalism from above led to the formation of new associations and 'clubs à l'anglaise'. Doors were opened to the well-travelled *hotelier*'s son from Chartres. Brissot belonged to the same Mesmerist coterie as did those who 'enjoyed very exalted positions in the Ancien Regime'.[89] In helping to found the Gallo-American Society and the Society of Friends of the Blacks, he was joined by Lafayette and other

84 *Literary Underground*, 20. Italics mine.

85 In fact, Brissot did not entirely fail to win prizes and recognition. His essays in favour of a more humane penal code won him prizes offered by the Academy of Châlons-sur-Marne and a later essay gained him membership of that provincial Academy. Ellery, *Brissot*, 19. One ought to distinguish between Brissot's position and that of an entirely unprivileged outsider, such as François Noël Babeuf, who never did manage to become a member of a provincial academy.

86 Ellery, *Brissot*, 20. Brissot's plan for his London-based *lycée* included a corresponding society, a journal, and regular meetings. His trip to Switzerland was based partly on his hope of raising money for this programme. In the end he fell back on his mother-in-law's help. The *lycée* proved to be short-lived.

87 Ellery, *Brissot*, 52. The translated quotation is from Brissot's *Journal du lycée*.

88 *Literary Underground*, 23.   89 Darnton, *Mesmerism*, 104.

French grandees. His membership in such organizations leads at least one authority to place him among 'the notables of the progressive bourgeoisie'.[90] When one surveys developments during the 1780s, one is impressed less by the exclusion of obscure writers from privileged circles than by their inclusion in societies where nobles and commoners worked together for political change. Expanding social horizons accompanied the expansive new visions of 'a parliament of man and a federation of the world'.

When the events of 1789 paved the way for freedom of the press, the francophone Republic of Letters could reclaim its central city at long last. The so-called 'explosion of print' was accompanied by an implosion: an ingathering of editors, publishers, typographers, pressmen. In a dramatic rupture with the past, more than 100 new presses were set up in crowded city streets. Roughly 140 new periodicals appeared during the first year.[91] Over the course of the Revolution the number of printers active at any given moment in Paris nearly quadrupled; the number of bookseller-publishers nearly tripled.[92]

The fate of Jean Luzac's *Gazette de Leyde*, as recounted by Popkin, is instructive. After the Declaration of the Rights of Man, French journals began to enjoy a clear constitutional protection that the extraterritorial papers had never possessed. Publications in Paris were now free to give direct reports about events that reached readers in Paris on the same day as their occurrence and that arrived in the provinces long before the Dutch paper did. Although readers in the Netherlands and Northern Europe continued to rely on the journal as a dependable source of news about France, the emergence of an unfettered press in France meant that the paper largely lost its relevance for readers there. Extraterritoriality no longer served as an indication of relative independence but, quite the reverse, a foreign place of publication began to imply possible complicity in counter-revolution.[93]

---

[90] Leo Gershoy, *Bernard Barère: A Reluctant Terrorist* (Princeton, NJ, 1962), 54.

[91] J. Popkin, *Revolutionary News: The Press in France 1789-1799* (Durham, 1990), 33. On the 'spectacular expansion' see also Jack Censer, *Prelude to Power: The Parisian Radical Press 1789-1791* (Baltimore, 1976), 8.

[92] Carla Hesse, 'Economic upheavals in Publishing', R. Darnton and D. Roche (eds.), *Revolution in Print* (Berkeley, Calif., 1989), 69-98: p. 92.

[93] J. Popkin, *News and Politics in the Age of Revolution: Jean Luzac's Gazette de Leyde* (Ithaca, NY, 1989), 201-15.

Within a short time, the Leiden *Gazette* had lost its best Paris correspondent, Pascal Boyer, to the boom in local business. In collaboration with Luzac's one-time editor, Antoine Marie Cerisier, Boyer launched his own Paris paper: the *Gazette universelle.* As a hard-working *bulletiniste,* Boyer had also served as the Paris reporter for Manzon's *Courier du Bas-Rhin* so that his defection entailed a double loss for the extraterritorial press.[94] More important than the loss of personnel was the disadvantage of pitting a biweekly or thrice-weekly foreign paper against a daily Paris one. 'Boyer and Cerisier took direct aim at their former employer's publication': in their prospectus for the *Gazette universale* they pointed out that it would 'always be ahead of the foreign papers, particularly that of Leyden . . . and it will not cost extra although it will appear every day'.[95] The extraterritorial gazettes would never again recover the commanding position they had once enjoyed.

Boyer and Cerisier were only two of the many French writers who had worked for foreign firms until 1789 enabled them to go into business for themselves. This same pattern was followed by Jacques Pierre Brissot upon his return from America. Indeed Brissot pioneered in calling for an unfettered press and in taking advantage of the end of the *ancien régime typographique.* After he missed, by only four votes, getting elected to the Estates General he put his years of apprenticeship to good use by turning out the *Patriote française,* one of the first and one of the most successful revolutionary newspapers. This venture gave him sufficient name recognition to win a post in the new municipal government of Paris and then get elected to the Legislative Assembly in 1791. By the spring of 1792 he had achieved the position of a 'party' leader. As head of the 'Brissotin' ministry, he led France into its fateful declaration of war against Austria and Prussia. The experiences which had shaped his views of the world are thus not inconsequential and need to be considered with some care.

In his *L'Ancien Régime et la révolution,* Alexis de Tocqueville devoted a celebrated section to the 'abstract literary politics' which filled the vacuum left by the destruction of the intermediate powers and the moribund condition of the Estates General. Writers who were 'quite out of touch with practical politics', who 'lacked the experience which might have tempered their

---

94 Ibid. 72-4. 95 Ibid. 203.

zeal', who 'had no acquaintance with the realities of public life which was terra incognita to them', became 'the leaders of public opinion', took charge of 'the political education' of the entire country, and ultimately organized 'a vast movement to demolish the entire social and political structure of the nation'.[96]

Given their pre-revolutionary careers, however, French literati such as Brissot may not have been quite as out of touch with practical politics or the 'realities of public life' as Tocqueville's remarks suggest. Norman Hampson has recently observed that 'Brissot combined radical objectives with quite a shrewd sense of political realities, born of his considerable knowledge of the working of parliamentary institutions in Britain and the United States'.[97] Although Brissot and others like him were acquainted with Genevan politicians, English radicals, and American rebels, however, they did lack experience with dynastic politics as practised in the courts and cabinets of old Europe. They were also under the misapprehension that the cosmopolitan Republic of Letters encompassed the entire world.

'The French Jacobins of 1792, among whom a few individuals like Robespierre were the exception, turned to the idea of world revolution because they felt so insecure at home.'[98] Perhaps this idea was also attractive because of pre-revolutionary experiences abroad. 'Brissot argued before war was declared, that it would be short and easy because people everywhere would rise up and sympathize with the French.'[99] Robespierre was a provincial lawyer and not a well-travelled journalist. That he had never crossed the Alps, the Channel, or the Atlantic may help to explain why his views on foreign affairs were so much less grandiose and universalistic. 'It was a fixed idea of Brissot and his followers that their revolutionary principles were of universal application. They imagined that, when French troops crossed the Rhine, they would be received with acclamation by the

---

[96] A. de Tocqueville, *L'Ancien Régime et la révolution* (*Œuvres complètes*, ii), ed. J. P. Mayer (Paris, 1952), bk. 3, ch. 1, pp. 193-202. Tr. taken from *The Old Regime and the French Revolution*, tr. S. Gilbert (New York, 1955), part 3, pp. 138-50.

[97] Hampson, *Will and Circumstance*, 105. There is a passage in his *Mémoires*, i. 321-2, where Brissot notes the ignorance exhibited by *ancien régime* officials about English parliamentary politics, which supports this view.

[98] Robert R. Palmer, *The Age of the Democratic Revolution* (2 vols. Princeton, NJ, 1964), ii. 54.   [99] Ibid.

oppressed subjects of the princes of western Germany.'[100] Nor did Brissot's grand design stop at the Rhine. France could not rest, he said in November 1792, until 'all Europe was in flames'. He hoped to drive the Bourbons out of Spain and envisaged the liberation of Spanish America as well.[101] He was never disabused of his belief that the cosmopolitan francophone press spoke for all mankind.[102]

In August 1791, shortly before he was elected as a deputy, he complained in his journal that his friend, Nicholas de Bonneville (the guiding spirit behind the *Cercle social* and Tom Paine's closest friend) was too absorbed in the local activities of a single Paris club where only those who stood within earshot could be reached. 'The great tribune of humanity has been found', he wrote, 'it is the press. If only we could convince all men to speak the same language, the press would soon spread the French revolution everywhere'.[103] This was written at a time when the French language had not yet conquered local dialects or patois in hundreds of towns and several large provinces within France. But, as noted above, a deafness to local dialects came naturally to inhabitants of the francophone Republic of Letters.

The relatively abstract conception of the unity of all mankind assumed a more practical and concrete form among eighteenth-century literati who had seen Germans and Italians vying with each other to explain how French had become the universal language. When the Abbé Grégoire in January 1794 proposed a decree to convert all inscriptions on public monuments into French, he observed that French had become the language of the family of man. No other language was so well known over the entire globe, he said. The exile of the Protestants by despots had contributed to its diffusion. Now the *émigrés*, by continuing to spread the use of French, were serving as the unwitting instruments of the liberty they were trying to stifle.[104] Grégoire's conviction that French was destined to become a universal language and that its spread signified adherence to the revolu-

---

100 J. M. Thompson, *The French Revolution* (Oxford, 1945), 279–80.

101 Palmer, *Democratic Revolution*, ii. 60.

102 On Brissot's 'cosmopolitanism' see Ellery, *Brissot*, 417.

103 Gary Kates, *The Cercle Social, the Girondins and the French Revolution* (Princeton, NJ, 1985), 177.

104 See citations from Grégoire's Report to National Convention (11 Jan. 1794) in Bernard Plongeron, *L'Abbé Grégoire (1750–1831)* (Paris, 1989), 46.

tionary cause survived long after the First Republic. It continued to animate some members of the radical Russian intelligentsia in Dostoevsky's time: '"No, that's not taken from the French," Liputin cried with positive fury. "That is taken from the universal language of humanity, not simply from the French, from the language of the universal social republic and the harmony of mankind!"'[105] Yet the spread of French had been due not only to the Huguenot diaspora, but also to the influence exerted by the Bourbon kings over foreign courts. Royalists and reactionaries among the *émigrés* gave the lie to Grégoire's wishful thinking; even while perpetuating the spread of French abroad, their writings exuded hostility to the revolutionary cause. Nor did literati belonging to other European nations continue to equate the use of French with the cause of liberation—quite the contrary.

The mistaken notion that the spread of French prepared the way for enlisting support for the revolutionary cause from among Prussians, Austrians, Russians, and Spaniards (and Laplanders as well) was by no means the only miscalculation to which well-travelled literati were prone. There was also the belief that a free press would usher in a new era of rational politics and put an end to the dangerous enthusiasms kindled by rabble-rousing preachers and orators. This view was articulated most clearly in the numerous publications issued by the *Cercle Social*, which was distinctive among the revolutionary clubs in owning a publishing house and in developing an ingenious plan to link newspaper subscription to club membership.[106] Unlike the Paris club with a limited reach of which Brissot complained, the *Cercle*'s numerous publications gave it a national following. Among club members, perhaps the most celebrated was Condorcet, one of several late Enlightenment figures who was neither mediocre nor lacking in radical energy. In 1791, Condorcet declared that printing had made it possible for people in a large territory to enjoy the freedom once restricted to citizens of small city-states.[107] He described how it brought into existence a new independent public tribunal, thereby anticipating recent

---

[105] Fyodor Dostoevsky, *The Possessed*, tr. by Constance Garnett (New York, 1936), ch. 2, part 3, pp. 50-1.   [106] Kates, *The* Cercle Social, 178.

[107] Condorcet, 'Des Conventions nationales' (1791) cited by Kates, *The* Cercle Social, 180.

accounts of the emergence of a public sphere. In his celebrated 'Sketch of the Progress of the Human Race', he inaugurated a new era with the invention and argued with considerable eloquence that printing had weakened the hold of human passions while strengthening the power of reason.[108]

In this respect Condorcet, Brissot, and their friends seem to have been strangely blind to the rabble-rousing potential of printed agitation and propaganda. Recent accounts have made much of the destabilizing effects of the pre-revolutionary barrage of anti-Bourbon scandal sheets 'which blasted away so effectively that they made the whole regime seem rotten'.[109] *Ancien régime* writers themselves had held printing responsible for the outpouring of subversive *libelles*.[110] Yet the emotive power of the press seems to have been left out of accounts by members of the *Cercle Social*. Perhaps they believed that scandal sheets would disappear together with *nouvellistes-à-la-main* and the entire 'Gothic' structure of the *ancien régime*. During the *ancien régime*, after all, Parisian gutter journalism had been associated in large part with hand-copied newsletters, in contrast to the more responsible and more distant reportage of the extraterritorial gazettes. Perhaps also they regarded the pamphleteering 'barrage' which presumably destabilized the monarchy as a necessary prelude to the construction of a more rational order where printing could be employed in a more appropriate manner. In the case of weights and measures, for example, the use of the new medium proved successful. The spread of French would eventually be arrested; the substitution of the revolutionary calendar for the Gregorian one was relatively short-lived. But with the adoption of the metric system, the revolutionary legislators did manage to replace many different and irrational local systems by a single rational universal one. In any event, it seemed self-evident to members of the *Cercle Social* that the invention of printing was

---

[108] Condorcet, *Esquisse d'un tableau historique des progrès de l'esprit humain*, ed. M. and F. Hincker (Paris, 1966), 178. See also Keith Baker, *Condorcet* (Chicago, 1975; paperback edn. 1982), 298.

[109] Darnton, 'The Forbidden Bestsellers of Prerevolutionary France', *Bulletin of the American Academy of Arts and Sciences*, 43 (1989), 17–45: p. 33.

[110] M. Fousooint, 'Sur les avantages et les inconvénients de l'imprimerie', *Mercure de France* (Oct. 1750), 71–87. p. 83, cited by H. J. Lüsebrink, 'Hommage à l'écriture et éloge à l'imprimerie', in Barbier et al. (eds.), *Livre et révolution*, 133–45: p. 139 n. 19).

providentially designed to put an end to charismatic demagoguery and bring about the triumph of rationality in human affairs.

Drawing on earlier articles and essays devoted to praise of printing themes,[111] members of the *Cercle* elaborated on the mythology which had developed around the invention of printing and the figure of the publisher. Gutenberg's discovery was viewed 'as the most important event in the history of mankind'; it spelt the end for political systems based on secrecy and arbitrary power. Echoing the title of Prosper Marchand's engraving, a *conventionnel* who served with Condorcet on the Committee of Public Instruction played a variation on Condorcet's periodization scheme. 'It was necessary to have religions before the invention', claimed Joseph Lequinio, but printing, 'the most beautiful gift from the heavens', had freed man from bondage to conflicting confessional creeds. The *ancien régime* had been 'the Age of the Church'; the new would be 'the Age of the Publisher'.[112]

The glorification of the invention went together with that of the inventor. Homages to Gutenberg reached a climax in the address which was pronounced in the newly formed National Convention on 9 September 1792. In the name of all printers, it requested that the remains of the inventor be placed in the Pantheon. A paraphrased excerpt runs as follows:

If God invented the sun, man invented the printing press. The divinely created sun dissipates physical darkness, the man-made sun vanquishes spiritual darkness. Let us celebrate an inventor who was the first true revolutionary, without whom we would be mute and isolated on earth, without whom we would never have known either a Voltaire or a Rousseau or a Pantheon.[113]

This passionate plea for pantheonizing Gutenberg was delivered by an eccentric German–Dutch baron named Jean-Baptiste Cloots who found his first names too Christian and substituted

---

[111] Lüsebrink offers useful examples of prize essays and dictionary articles on the topic which were produced after 1750.

[112] Kates, *The* Cercle Social, 179–80.

[113] 'Discours prononcé à la barre de l'Assemblée Nationale au nom des imprimeurs par Anacharsis Cloots, orateur du genre humain, le 9 Septembre 1792 l'an IV de la Liberté et le 1er de l'égalité', *Anacharsis Cloots: Écrits révolutionnaires 1790–1794*, ed. Michèle Duval (Paris, 1979), 391–6. The *Cercle Social* article of 4 Oct. 1792 by Boileau (which is cited by Kates, *The* Cercle Social, 180) echoes Cloots's remarks about Voltaire and Rousseau almost word for word.

the more pagan 'Anacharsis'.[114] Although Cloots assigned himself the title of 'orator of the human race', he was, unlike Brissot, no friend of the Blacks. His family was engaged in the Dutch Indies trade and he opposed the freeing of slaves. He was certainly not a Grub Street hack but he was a revolutionary zealot nevertheless. He claimed to have come by his cosmopolitanism naturally, having been born into a Dutch family in the principality of Cleves which owned properties in different parts of Europe. After being educated in Brussels and pursuing a short-lived military career in Berlin, he settled down in Paris while maintaining his far-flung holdings. In his background and convictions he rather resembled Baron d'Holbach. But it can scarcely be said of him, as has been said of the Baron, that his radical philosophy went together with political moderation.[115] A Voltairean and zealous dechristianizer, he demonstrated his emancipation from religious intolerance by presenting the Legislative Assembly with a work in praise of Muhammadism.[116] When the Brissotin ministry declared war against Austria, Cloots offered to help equip a foreign legion; he himself organized and joined a German regiment. He was made an honorary French citizen and (along with Tom Paine) was elected deputy to the National Convention at a moment when cosmopolitanism was in vogue.[117] But this moment passed swiftly. Little more than a year after his plea for pantheonizing Gutenberg, Cloots was denounced as a foreign agitator and expelled from the Convention. In March 1794 he was caught up in the purge of the

---

[114] Thompson, *French Revolution*, 271, asserts that the name was chosen to commemorate Solon's Scythian friend. But Albert Soboul, 'Anacharsis Cloots: L'Orateur du genre humain', *Annales historiques de la révolution française*, 52 (Jan.–Mar. 1980), 29–58, points to the influence of the Abbé J.-J. Barthélemy's popular fictional work, *Voyage du jeune Anacharsis en Grèce dans le milieu du quatrième siècle avant l'ère vulgaire.*

[115] See characterization of d'Holbach by D. Roche, 'Salons, Lumières, engagement politique', *Républicains des lettres*, 252. Soboul does describe Cloots as 'prudent' because he first sided with Lafayette and later with Brissot against Robespierre. But he was also more extreme about dechristianizing than Robespierre and was, ultimately, guillotined along with the Hébertists. [116] Thompson, *French Revolution*, 271–2.

[117] On the eve of elections to the Convention in Aug. 1793 some 17 notable foreigners were singled out as benefactors of the human race, made honorary French citizens, and offered a chance to stand for election. In addiition to Cloots and his Dutch uncle, Cornelius de Pauw, the list included Kosciuszko, Klopstock, Pestalozzi, Washington, Madison, Hamilton, and six Englishmen (including Brissot's friend, David Williams). Only Cloots, Joseph Priestley and Tom Paine were nominated. Priestley went to America; Cloots and Paine accepted the election and sat in the Convention. Thompson, *French Revolution*, 343. Palmer, *Democratic Revolution*, ii 55,

Hébertists, who were accused of being implicated in a foreign plot. Before he was guillotined, he had preached a sermon on atheism to his fellow prisoners.

By 1794, French energies were being focused on the organization of victory by a nation-in-arms. The First Republic succeeded, where the Bourbon monarchy had failed, in taking over the border territories that had housed foreign firms. Under the Directory and then Napoleon, French forces overran all the territories that had sustained extraterritorial publishing for two and a half centuries or more. With each annexation after 1792, the cosmopolitan Republic of Letters lost some ground. The firms which remained in cities such as Liège no longer served francophone Europe but catered to the needs of local administrators and provincials seeking local news.[118] By the end of the era, not only had many firms lost their markets; there were almost no small quasi-independent principalities left. The 'fertile crescent' had been almost entirely absorbed. Under Emperor Napoleon, most of the 350 separate political units of the Holy Roman Empire were eliminated. The expansion of 'la grande nation' also led to the curtailment of the once far-flung operations of Swiss and the Dutch, who were confined to the more restricted orbits assigned to satellite states. The *Courrier d'Avignon* had faded into insignificance with the French annexation of the papal state at the very beginning of the Revolution. The *Gazette de Leyde* which had managed (barely) to survive into the Napoleonic era 'as a shadow of its former self' received its *coup de grâce* after the Republic had given way to the Empire. It was purchased by Napoleon's brother Louis, King of the Netherlands, and turned into 'a servile government organ', sinking quickly 'into complete insignificance'.[119]

Another act of considerable symbolic as well as practical significance for the francophone press occurred during the Napoleonic wars. The Roman printing office of the *Congregatio de Propaganda Fide* (Congregation of the Propagation of the Faith), founded in 1626 to convert infidels and win back Protest-

---

[118] J. Popkin, 'The Book Trades in Western Europe during the Revolutionary Era', *Papers of the Bibliographical Society of America*, 78 (1984), 403–45: p. 440. Popkin describes how the Revolution dealt a mortal blow to the vitality of the extraterritorial francophone press but downplays the significance of this development. He stresses the persistence of óther book-trade patterns into the post-revolutionary era (pp. 444–5).

[119] Popkin, '*Gazette de Leyde*', 246.

ants, was taken over by the French. The punches, matrices, types, and other equipment designed to handle some twenty Asian and African languages became the property of the Imprimerie Nationale. Even before this transfer the term 'propaganda' had begun to resonate with secular significance. It was first linked to efforts to 'internationalize' the Revolution by enlisting support from foreigners in diverse lands.[120] As Tocqueville noted, the French Revolution differed from all previous upheavals in its aspiration to be world-wide. 'This was something quite unprecedented: a political revolution that sought proselytes all the world over and applied itself as ardently to converting foreigners as compatriots. Of all the surprises that the French Revolution launched upon a startled world, this surely was the most astounding.'[121]

Internationalizing the Revolution ironically went together with dismantling the cosmopolitan institutions of old Europe. Alsatians who wished Strasbourg to return to its old status as a free city of the Empire, for example, were viewed as traitors to the Jacobin regime.[122] The first use of the term *propagande* for secular purposes was by a dechristianizing society formed in Strasbourg in 1793. Led by Euloge Schneider, a defrocked German monk, it tried to eradicate the use of the German language (denounced as indicating pro-Austrian sympathies). After having introduced into Alsace 'the horror of nationalistic persecution',[123] Schneider was himself arrested (by Saint-Just) as a 'cosmopolitan charlatan'. As Cloots had also found out, 'the Revolution had become a national enterprise; foreign enthusiasts were not wanted'.[124]

Under Napoleon I, the cosmopolitan institutions of old Europe together with the hundreds of small German states of the Old Reich received their *coup de grâce*. Unlike the last Bourbon kings, the Emperor was adept at manipulating media. As First Consul in the Year VIII he reduced the number of daily papers in Paris

---

[120] Palmer, *Democratic Revolution*, ii. 51–4, stresses the use of the term by frightened conservatives who claimed that a secret international organization modelled on the Catholic Office of *Propaganda Fide* was fomenting trouble in diverse lands. He discounts the existence of any far-flung organization, noting that the only actual society using the name *Propagande* was the short-lived 'ultra-revolutionary organization' in Strasbourg.

[121] Tocqueville, *The Old Regime*, 11.

[122] R. R. Palmer, *Twelve Who Ruled* (Princeton, NJ, 1941), 187.

[123] Ibid. 189.   [124] Ibid. 191.

from seventy-three to thirteen; as Emperor in 1811, he cut them back to four. He also reinstituted preliminary and preventative censorship and subjected printers and publishers outside France to strict controls.[125] Not even a master propagandist, however, could do much to mitigate resentment against foreign armies of occupation.

In the pre-revolutionary era, Dutch patriots in the United Netherlands had given vent to outbursts of francophobia. As noted above, the 1730s saw the publication of a series of francophobic articles; in the 1740s measures were passed to ensure that the children of French expatriates learnt Dutch and attended Dutch schools; later a pamphleteer was chided for failure to make full use of colloquial Dutch and for indulging his fondness for Latin locutions.[126] These episodes foreshadowed a later drama which would be played out on a vast scale. The attack mounted against foreigners and cosmopolites by French Jacobins was not merely imitated in other lands. It was greatly reinforced by reactions against all things French. The francophone Enlightenment and its cosmopolitan ethos came to be depicted as part of a vast conspiracy to subvert loyalties which were rooted in blood and soil, a conspiracy which was aimed at the destruction of mother tongues and fatherlands.

By 1815, when francophobia was in full swing, the world known to the extraterritorial publishers and literati had been altered beyond recognition. Some borders had been redrawn; others had been completely erased. All that remained of the far-flung networks were thousands upon thousands of pieces of fine rag paper stored in scattered libraries and archives—libraries and archives which have now become the property of the governments of separate nation-states. With the disappearance of the quasi-independent small political units that had sustained it, Cosmopolis would appear to posterity as an imaginary realm and the French Enlightenment would seem to be no more firmly grounded than that 'manna which descended from the heavens'. I hope this book has shown that the realm was not nearly as

---

[125] Robert Holtman, *Napoleonic Propaganda* (Baton Rouge, La., 1950), ch. 3. Holtman points out that Napoleon himself never used the term 'propaganda'.

[126] G. C. Gibbs, 'Influences of the Huguenot Emigrés in the United Provinces', *Bijdragen en Mededelingen Betreffende de Geschiedenis der Nederlanden*, 90 (1975), 255-87: pp. 271-2. Leonard Leeb, *The Ideological Origins of the Batavian Revolution* (The Hague, 1973), 69, 73.

insubstantial as it now appears to be. Between the 1680s and 1780s, printers, publishers, and booksellers, by continuing to behave much as they had been behaving for two centuries and more, had provided the heavenly city of the eighteenth-century philosophers with solid foundations on earth.

Index